‘Th

‘A brilliantly original premise which is horrifyingly believable’
Catherine Cooper

‘An original and action-packed thriller, with a perfectly unnerving premise that hooked me from the start’
Philippa East

‘A twisty, action-packed plot makes this intriguing thriller unputdownable’
Roz Watkins

‘Perfectly realised’
Trevor Wood

‘Tense, claustrophobic and oh-so addictive’
Penny Batchelor

‘A compulsive and tightly woven thriller’
Karin Nordin

‘A captivating and distinctive thriller’
Sarah Clarke

‘A complex, clever novel with memorable characters . . . A truly gripping rollercoaster ride’
Vikki Patis

Author photo: Nigel Brown

LOUISE MUMFORD was born and lives in South Wales. From a young age she loved books and dancing, but hated having to go to sleep, convinced that she might miss out on something interesting happening in the world whilst she dozed – much to her mother's frustration! Insomnia has been a part of her life ever since.

She studied English Literature at university and graduated with first class honours. As a teacher she tried to pass on her love of reading to her students (and discovered that the secret to successful teaching is . . . stickers! She is aware that that is, essentially, bribery).

In the summer of 2019 Louise experienced a once-in-a-lifetime moment: she was discovered as a new writer by her publisher at the Primadonna Festival. Everything has been a bit of a whirlwind since then.

Louise lives in Cardiff with her husband and spends her time trying to get down on paper all the marvellous and frightening things that happen in her head.

Also by Louise Mumford

Sleepless
The Safe House

The Hotel

LOUISE MUMFORD

ONE PLACE. MANY STORIES

This novel is entirely a work of fiction. The names, characters and incidents portrayed in it are the work of the author's imagination. Any resemblance to actual persons, living or dead, events or localities is entirely coincidental.

HQ
An imprint of HarperCollins*Publishers* Ltd
1 London Bridge Street
London SE1 9GF

www.harpercollins.co.uk

HarperCollins*Publishers*
Macken House, 39/40 Mayor Street Upper,
Dublin 1 D01 C9W8

This paperback edition 2023

2

First published in Great Britain by
HQ, an imprint of HarperCollins*Publishers* Ltd 2023

A catalogue record for this book is available from the British Library.

ISBN: 9780008589943

This book is produced from independently certified FSC™ paper to ensure responsible forest management.

For more information visit: www.harpercollins.co.uk/green

Printed and bound in the UK using 100% renewable electricity at CPI Group (UK) Ltd

To Jason, always.

To my grandmother who was, without fail, so fiercely supportive and who would have been so proud.

Prologue

Most evenings, before she went to bed, Bex Harrison played the end of the video.

It was the most-watched scene in the film.

Those few minutes of grainy, badly shot action had been paused, picked apart, zoomed in on, mapped out, enlarged and argued about for ten years. Everyone had a theory about what happened that night.

Bex watched as, wide-eyed and out of breath, the young man in the green raincoat ran with the camera jolting in his grip, its lens trained on his face. Leo Finch. The baby of the group, bespectacled, barely eighteen, quick to smile, slow to speak; a fan favourite. He was silent, moving fast, and the audience ran with him, held in his hand.

Her friend since childhood.

Bex paused the video and shuffled closer to the television so she could see the pixels that made up his face. Now he was only a refraction of light played upon countless screens, but she put her hand to his cheek anyway, feeling the tears sting.

By pressing play she brought him to life once more, if only for a few minutes.

For a dizzying second there was a blur as the camera fell out of his grip but when it landed, it faced the steps: narrow slick chunks of rock dug out from the cliff face. In the film they had climbed those steps only a few hours ago and, to Bex, sitting in front of her television, it felt like that, only hours since she had seen him, though she knew it was now far too many years. They had jostled and pretended to push each other over the gaping edge where there was no safety rail to save them, their laughter a jittery sound of excitement mixed with something darker, as black as the rock above and below them.

On the screen Leo ran against a sky where night was draining away but morning was a sick colour, infection red and broiling with cloud. It was hard to tell if he was running towards something . . . or running away from it. He did not cast a look behind him as he took the steps, far too quickly, with too much reckless abandon, his arms out at his sides as if they could balance him. There was a shout then, the sound twisted by the wind battering the cliff, but Bex knew the voice.

It was hers.

Leo stood close to the edge on a wide curve in the rock steps, his back to the camera. Then a foot appeared on the screen: purple leather boot, bright yellow laces, mud on the toecap. That was hers too.

Pause. Bex stopped the video.

She knew what happened next. At least here, in her half-empty house, a glass of wine on the table with the remains of a microwave meal sticky in its plastic tray next to it, she could stop, pause, freeze it there in that moment so the rest never happened.

But that would not be suitable penance.

Play. She had to watch it all the way through to the end.

She saw herself stumble towards the steps, arms stretched out to the young man in the green raincoat with his back to her, facing the sheer drop below. The footage became dark and grainy and on the screen the wind made her long hair writhe and lift as if it wanted to be free of her, of that place. Then her ankle wobbled and she tumbled to her knees. As her head dipped and she fell face-first onto the ground, beyond her Leo seemed to sway and either jump or fall – despite all of those people watching the film over the years no one could work out which, whether he had meant to send himself plummeting from the edge or whether it had been a tragic accident. Hauling herself up, the Bex on the screen staggered and the fuzzy splash of Leo's green raincoat fizzled out like static.

The film ended as it always did – with her, alone.

The step was empty.

Leo had gone.

Chapter 1

Bex Harrison stood on top of her world and considered shooting the man below her.

Not anywhere vital, of course. No, just a kneecap, or a hand or something, though she wasn't convinced that her aim was good enough to not hit an artery by mistake. She sighed. It didn't matter: the gun was fake anyway, bought as a deterrent rather than a weapon. Lowering her binoculars, she wrapped her blanket tighter around her middle and sipped her coffee.

There had been two reasons she had decided to live in this London house all those years ago: the roof and the wall. Built in Georgian times, the place had fancy crenellations at the top like a castle, and a lovely flat roof, perfect for sitting on, hidden from view to spy on the street below.

After all, they had tried to spy on her in that first year after the film came out.

But their spying hadn't been very successful due to that wall. Bex had thought long and hard about it and had decided that the way to get total privacy was to live right in the middle of a big city. She realised that seemed counterintuitive. Countryside, a secluded valley, the top of a big hill – those were the places people thought would guarantee privacy. But people were wrong. Those places were too easily breached, all that space where intruders could hide and then, when they pounced, no one around to hear you scream.

Bex was literally boxed in. First by the massive stone wall that almost entirely circled her house and second by all the other houses around her, each garden, each wall of their own backing onto hers. No sneaky crawl spaces. Lots of people to hear the screaming.

Because, if the events nearly ten years ago had taught Bex anything, it was that the screaming was never far away.

She raised the rifle and took aim. The man below bothered her. His face was as badly creased as his trousers and he wore one of those utility vests with lots of pockets. His camera was slung around his neck as he munched his way through a never-ending supply of snacks that he conjured out of those pockets, like a shabby magician. Photographers had given up waiting outside her house years ago and she was none too pleased to see one come creeping back.

Through the gun's sight she chose the kneecap she would aim for, angling the barrel through the gaps in the stone balustrade.

An overfed pigeon she called Bob eyed her from his perch nearby, seed scattered around him, probably too fat to fly off. She wasn't even sure that was the original Bob, if she was honest, but it didn't matter – she enjoyed their intellectual exchanges over mixed nuts.

'Bang,' she whispered, lowering the gun, blowing away imaginary smoke from the barrel. Even if the weapon had been real, it would have been useless against the kind of things that frightened her.

Of course, she knew why the photographer was there. Ten years, soon. It was an anniversary of sorts. She didn't know what he was thinking though – that she would appear at her gates dressed in gold lamé and wearing a feather headdress ready to do the can-can to mark the occasion?

And it wasn't him she had to worry about really.

Something was being planned, she could smell it in the air mixed in with the traffic fumes. Someone had probably been trying to get in touch with her but that would be tricky as she never looked at her email and rarely answered her phone or her door. More coffee, that was what she needed. Taking her mug with her, she hauled herself up from the chair and trudged down the steps that led through the top floor of her house, a ghost of itself draped in dustsheets. She didn't need those rooms. On the ground floor she walked through a large hallway with chequerboard tiling on which she had set out a chessboard on a little table, two chairs on either side. She stopped and considered the game, then pushed a rook into position. It was a sneaky move. Tomorrow-Her would be angry.

She never played anyone except herself.

As she walked through a doorway the ghost house burst into colour. There was a sleek, modern kitchen somewhere under the mess, she knew because she had had it fitted nine years ago when she had bought the house. Now, however, the room was a cross between a garden centre and a library, except the librarians had gone on strike and the plants were staging a coup.

Bex pushed a pile of magazines from a concrete bench that flanked a dining table built for Vikings and sat on it, moving a plant's questing tendrils from her face. Pouring more coffee from the cafetière into her mug, she raised it and toasted herself, tapping the edge of the mug four times against a plant's leaf. Clean-living, book-reading, plant-tending, record-listening, yoga-bending Bex – that was her. There was a danger in letting herself go, in letting things slip or slide because that was when the darkness got in . . . and she'd seen enough of that.

There was a pile of post on the table in front of her. In the early days of the whole *Ravencliffe* madness she had gathered it together and burnt it in a metal bin in her back garden. Her bills had been paid by direct debit and the house had been bought with a lump sum. There had been nothing she needed to see in those letters. Now she sometimes opened the mail and sometimes didn't: it depended on her mood.

She eyed the envelopes. Perhaps someone *had* been trying to get in contact with her.

But she didn't want to know that either. Whatever people were planning for the ten-year anniversary, she didn't want to have anything to do with it, no matter if they pleaded, begged, threatened.

She would never go back to that place.

Drumming her fingers on the table, she thought about how there was somewhere she had been planning to go tomorrow, however. She had been before, each year – a punishment of sorts. Her own personal purgatory and a place where she had always hoped she would find answers. If anyone would know what was about to happen, then it would be the people there.

She tapped her fingers four times on the tabletop. Then four again. Then again, each time not quite right, not the correct rhythm to make her feel like she could stop. Four was key – a magic number, a spell that kept her safe. By the time she had tapped out that beat of four in a way that stopped her heart fluttering, there was sweat prickling on her brow.

She sighed. It was nearly time to leave the house.

Chapter 2

Hello, fellow Ravens!

RavenCon 10

Join us for an EPIC celebration of all things *Ravencliffe*!

It has been nearly ten years since Bex, Richard, Oscar and Leo set out to film at the Ravencliffe Hotel. Ten years since they rowed that boat over to the steps. Ten years since they climbed them, ten years since, torch in hand, they wandered the corridors of the old hotel and were stalked by the terror that haunts the place. Ten years since Leo disappeared . . .

And what a ten years it has been!

RavenCon 10 is going to be THE place to be on Saturday the 4th of June! If you thought our other conventions were amazing, then this year we are going to BLOW YOUR MINDS. Come and join us with our two floors of dedicated *Ravencliffe* content: stall holders selling memorabilia, graphic novels, souvenirs and T-shirts; there will be panel talks discussing the theories and myths behind the film; a rolling screening of *Ravencliffe* itself; and, to top it all, a special mystery guest who will announce something very exciting indeed, something to truly celebrate ten years of the best found-footage horror film ever made.

YOU DON'T WANT TO MISS OUT!
BOOK YOUR TICKET NOW!

Chapter 3

Looking around the crowded hall, Bex was surrounded by herself.

She had attended every RavenCon since the very first one. It was a bit like going to a grave: an act of remembrance, a needle scratching against scarred skin. Leo had a headstone of his own of course, after he had been officially declared dead, but it was simply a chunk of granite, no body under the turf.

It wasn't a rational thing to do, Bex understood. As a woman who wanted to keep out of the limelight, it seemed reckless to walk into a convention dedicated to all things *Ravencliffe*. But she thought of it like a goldfish trying to hide. It would be easily spotted amongst a bunch of . . . say, eels. But put it amongst other, near-identical goldfish and it instantly blended in. She was that goldfish.

There was another reason, of course. Bex went to RavenCon because here, within its walls, were gathered hundreds of specialists on the film, hundreds of people who had spent almost as many hours as she had combing through the footage for a clue about Leo's disappearance. Here were the experts. Every year she went in the hope she would find out something, some glint of a throwaway comment that would allow her to finally work out what happened to him.

It was the day after she had watched the photographer from the roof of her house, but, much to her relief, he had not appeared that morning and so her train journey had been uneventful. She had angled herself towards the window, her hood pulled up to hide as much of her face as possible. Nobody ever really recognised her on those rare occasions when she went out and for that she was grateful. She wasn't that Bex anymore.

But many people in the large conference hall were doing a much better job than she was of being that Bex. As she walked through the crowds, she tried to decide which one was best out of all of the people dressed as her. There were criteria to consider. The boots first. They were the most important part of the costume, instantly recognisable, an iconic piece of attire. It was easy to find the correct purple leather colourway, but it was the laces that showed the amateur from the committed fan. A fan took the trouble to source the exact shade of yellow with black tips. That same commitment to detail meant finding the authentic (now discontinued) brand of black leather biker jacket and carefully measuring the knee rips in her black jeans.

'You look *just* like her.' The man next to her nodded in approval, dressed as Richard. He had tried, at least: the flecked grey of his woollen coat was a good colour match if you didn't look too hard but his floppy hair was beginning to thin and he lacked the overall swagger. 'If you don't mind a suggestion though – the jacket is wrong.'

Bex stopped herself from laughing. She wore the exact clothes from that night, even down to the blood-stained jumper that she had never washed. The only thing that was fake about her was the hair. Back then she had had long curls in a shiny copper colour that could only be achieved by dye, but now her hair was part bleach and part neglect. Hence the cheap wig.

RavenCon 10. She gazed around her. The first convention had been organised by a small group of fans and held in one room in a two-star London hotel with free tea and coffee provided from urns that looked as if they had survived the Second World War. She could only vaguely remember that event having been grief-blurred and exhausted, over a year since Leo's disappearance, a few months after the film had aired on cinema screens. She had gone hoping that someone there in that room would have had some answers because it had been full of people who all cared about the same thing as her: *Ravencliffe*. The film. The myth. The mystery.

She was a legend in an overheated conference hall.

Everyone knew the story. Four Welsh eighteen-year-olds, two of them armed with handheld cameras, bored in the summer between sixth form and new lives at university, had decided to indulge in a bit of 'dark tourism' – a visit to the rugged coast of West Wales upon which stood the supposedly haunted, definitely creepy Ravencliffe Hotel.

Everyone *thought* they knew the story.

'Nah, mate – you've got it wrong.' Bex walked past two men standing by a stall where you could buy Ravencliffe snowglobes complete with a tiny holographic Leo who, depending on the way you turned the object, flashed in and out of existence. 'Leo couldn't have jumped because his body would have been visible on the rocks below, yeah, and his body was never found—'

'But the tides at that time have shown—'

'Nope. The water didn't reach that bit under the steps, it looked like it was always dry . . .'

She had eavesdropped on so many conversations like this one over the years but she kept listening anyway, just in case. As they spoke a woman in plaits and black lipstick picked up one of those snowglobes and shook it three times. Bex watched the tiny Leo blinking in and out of sight, there one minute, gone the next. When the woman put the globe down, Bex couldn't help but take it and give it an extra shake. Four. Better. Except that wasn't enough. No, she had to shake it again – one, two, three, four – and then again because that last round hadn't felt good either. Her heart pounded but she forced her hand to put the snowglobe down and not draw attention to herself.

Upstairs was where she needed to be.

Others were already taking their seats. Bex slipped into a spot at the back. She could already feel it, a thrill of excitement from the people filing in, not the usual level of fan adoration but something else, something twisted to high vibration. Ten years. A celebration.

'So, who d'you think it'll be?' A woman sat next to her, not even costumed.

The seats faced a stage with a projector screen on it and one lone microphone stand. The event poster had promised a special guest and rumours had swirled downstairs as to who that could be. Richard maybe, the one who had done much of the filming, the self-styled director of the whole thing, but there were, technically, three to choose from. Four teenagers had gone to the hotel that night and three had come back. Of those three, both Bex and Richard led normal lives out of the public eye and everyone had had more than enough of Oscar.

'Richard.' Bex kept her words gruff as if she had a bad throat in case the woman recognised her voice.

'Yeah. I agree. Richard. Has to be. Ten years, after all. Not Bex.'

'No.'

A man dressed like a version of Bex at the end of a raucous hen do sat next to them and butted in. 'Ah, man – Bex could have been a star!'

'Bex *is* a bloody star, you moron!' the woman snapped and raised her eyes. 'She's like, the heart of the group, y'know? After the film became big she could have carved a stellar career for herself. Stellar!'

'I'm not disagreeing.' The man held his hands up in surrender. ''Course, she wasn't an actress . . . what they did was real and there was no script, but Bex had star quality, anyone could see that . . .'

Bex moved away from the pair.

The seats around her filled up and she recognised the musty smell that lingered over their heads like a poorly washed canopy, the scent of costumes stored away all year without being given enough of an airing. Soon enough the lights dimmed, then began to sweep over the audience in a way that was meant to build excitement but made Bex feel slightly seasick. The music began and the RavenCon master of ceremonies bounded on stage to applause, holding out his hands and bowing his head in humility.

'Fellow Ravens!'

She tuned out much of what the man on stage said. It was pretty much the same thing he had said for the past ten years, in fact she was almost sure he wore the same T-shirt every year, though his paunch struggled against it nowadays. What was left of his hair was artfully ruffled into a punk-style mess.

There was a hush before the RavenCon promotional video started. A sweeping shot of the hotel filled the screen and then began a voiceover that was so deep, submarines could have got lost in it:

'It was 1878 and Reginald Henry Morwood decided on Cardigan Bay in West Wales as the perfect spot for his new spa resort; somewhere men and women could enjoy fresh cliff-side air, icy cold hydrotherapy treatments and a few very exciting new-fangled health machines. Not many agreed with his choice. Despite being touted as "The New Brighton" the location was a long way from the fashionable London crowd and his preferred spot high on a clifftop was a forbidding place. From the mainland, the road in was steep and behind his proposed hotel the land fell away into a sheer drop. But Reginald had a plan. He intended to capitalise on the new railway lines being proposed for the area, in particular the Cardigan Extension line to entice rich folk from South Wales or London to this stretch of the coast for their holiday. He argued that they would not be able to resist the magnificent building that would become the jewel in the coastline's crown: his Ravencliffe Hotel.

'The design for the hotel was ambitious in its scale. Though the reception area and some rooms and suites would be on the land at the top of the cliff, the rest of the facilities would cling, limpet-like to the rock face below, accessed by steps and interspersed with pools and terraced gardens.

'Fired by the desire to get the resort up and running as soon as the first train arrived in the proposed new Cardigan station, Reginald used the money he had leveraged on his woollen factory and began to build at such a speed that accidents were bound to happen. The project was dogged by bad luck, near misses and dangerous working conditions. One worker, a carpenter called Peter Manning, plummeted to his death on the rocks below, not that this curbed Reginald's need for speed. He was also not a sympathetic master. There was tension between him as an English owner and his Welsh workforce, not aided by his ban on their speaking Welsh whilst on-site. The build ate through his and his rich wife's money at an alarming speed, but he managed to get most of the hotel finished before disaster struck.

'Nearly two years later in 1880, just as the ornate Italian fountain was set in the drive of the Ravencliffe Hotel, the plans for the railway line to Cardigan stalled. It became clear that it would be years before the track was finished and that progress would be too slow for the hotel to easily entice the London crowd. Reginald did not have the luxury of waiting years: he was already drowning in debt.

'He returned to the deserted hotel with the tattered remains of his dream, knowing that the bank would soon call in their loan, take his factory and effectively leave him bankrupt. Retreating to his office, Reginald had a glass of whisky, put one bullet in the gun he had brought with him and then placed the gun in his mouth and pulled the trigger.

'The hotel fell into disrepair and the steep road became impassable. Stories clung to the place. It was said to be haunted by the carpenter who had fallen to his death, by Reginald himself, stalking the corridors of the hotel, vengeful and ready to take the life of

anyone trespassing on his land. It was said to be cursed. It would have become a forgotten space, perhaps bought by developers somewhere down the line if it hadn't been for Bex, Richard, Leo and Oscar, their boat and the film of what happened that night which is now a cinema sensation.

'Ravencliffe awaits.'

Bex could almost recite the voiceover word for word and some people did, happily shouting out some of the most familiar lines like 'Ravencliffe awaits!' Seeing Leo on screen, his chubby-cheeked sweet face, made tears sting. But when the final shot turned to black an expectant hush fell.

'So, this is a special RavenCon, yes? Ten years. And we have a treat in store for you, a treat that needs a special introduction from a very special person . . .' He let the pause drag and Bex mentally re-worked his words so that 'special' was only mentioned once '. . . So without further ado, let's all give a warm RavenCon welcome to Oscar Haines!'

Bloody Oscar. Bex heard the woman next to her sigh. Oscar bloody Haines. The one who stayed with the boat. No one cared about Oscar, though he walked on as if they did, hand on his chest as if he was about to swear allegiance to a flag, dressed in artfully distressed jeans and too-shiny shoes. There was no treat in seeing Oscar Haines – he was everywhere, selling his own brand of Ravencliffe T-shirts, hawking his memoir which told the reader absolutely nothing about that night – and why would it? He knew sod all. Oscar who had stayed at the jetty; a bit-part player, the footnote, too scared to even climb the steps to the hotel.

'RavenCon 10, nice to see you!' Oscar waved. There was applause. There was even cheering, because, well, a bit of *Ravencliffe*, no matter how small, or annoying, or how shiny its shoes were, was better than nothing. Just. 'Have I got a surprise for YOU!' Oscar continued. If it turned out to be another T-shirt, Bex suspected that some of the crowd would start throwing things.

'Ten years, yeah? Ten years since Bex and Richard and I . . . and

Leo . . .' – Oscar hung his head for a second – 'went to Ravencliffe. And since then, you, the fans, have taken us all to your hearts, you have been with us on this incredible, this *devastating* journey and we wanted to repay that. So, for one night only, people . . . we are going *back*!'

A hushed muttering swirled around Bex, who gripped her seat.

'That's right. Me, Richard and Bex – we are going back to Ravencliffe!' The muttering became a swell of sound threatening to tip over the crowd.

'One night. A ten-year reunion film. Ravencliffe awaits!'

Chapter 4

Ravencliffe did not bloody await. Not for her.

Bex stood and pushed her way along the row of seats, not listening to whatever Oscar said next, intent only on getting free, back to her house behind the wall which would keep everyone out.

Forever.

Behind her tall stone wall, high on the roof an hour later, Bex peered out through her binoculars at the photographers.

There were three of them now. She had had to rush past them to get through her gate.

It was a bit early for alcohol but she sipped from a glass of wine as she sat in her deckchair, hoping the drink would buff the edges off this day that had turned out to be surprisingly sharp. Early June was beginning to lend a summery vibe to the street below: the trees were in their full greenery and the people below had begun to dust off their hot weather wardrobe. Feet that should never see the light of day were basking in the afternoon sun.

Bex realised, as she stared through the binoculars, that they weren't all photographers waiting below. No, the crazies were creeping out from the woodwork once more. She thought she had bored them away, the super fans of the film. They called themselves Ravens and, in the early years, once they found out where in London she had moved after leaving Wales, they had started drawing and writing on the bit of her wall that faced the street: big, looping letters spelling out 'What happened to Leo?' or 'Richard and Bex forever'. Bex had had the wall re-painted in the kind of substance that repels graffiti and tore down the posters and art in the middle of the night when the street was dark and silent. They eventually got the message.

Two photographers. One crazy. There would be more. Word would spread. Even now, on the internet she deliberately avoided, the news was out that there was going to be a *Ravencliffe* reunion show, back at the hotel.

What were they thinking?

Not Echelon, the film company. She knew exactly what they were thinking: money. But Richard and Oscar. What about them? She knew Oscar was on board, but she couldn't believe that Richard had agreed to it. They had been there with her; they knew exactly the horror of that night. Afterwards, Oscar had seen her run to him in her blood-splattered jumper, he had seen the total shock and terror on her face and Richard, well . . . it had been Richard's blood. She might have been the only one to see that figure stalking the grounds, stalking them, but they had all felt the malignancy of that place. It did not want visitors. It ruined lives.

She would not go back.

She sipped four times from the glass, messed it up, did it again and again, little burning gulps until she hit on the four-time combination that soothed her heart rate.

An hour passed and Bex continued to imagine all the various ways she would say no to all the various people who would come asking her. And they would come, no doubt. Oscar's announcement had included her name: *Me, Richard and Bex – we are going back to Ravencliffe!* Okay, so they hadn't been able to get in contact with her but that didn't mean they had the right to sign her up to something she didn't want to do. She wasn't going to sign up for anything, and they couldn't make her.

The light was beginning to fade and those people who had decided to wear sandals in the warmth of the midday sun were now looking as if they regretted it as the night promised only a chill kiss. Bex came in from the cold, glass in hand, walking down the stairs into her kitchen. On the bench were her discarded Bex clothes, the wig tangled in a plant, and in one corner was what looked like a wardrobe, a huge thing in heavy dark oak. She opened its doors to reveal a desk and shelf space, a stool tucked underneath. In every drawer, on every surface, filed on each shelf was all the research she had done over the years – the original photocopies she had made about the hotel when she had been eighteen and planning the trip, and every wild theory and unsubstantiated claim made about the film since. On the back board she had pinned a hand-drawn floorplan of the hotel and had plotted in different colours little footstep tracks to show where each of them had gone that night. On a memory stick in a drawer was all the raw footage they had shot that night, this copy given to her by Oscar who had ended up doing the editing of the original, amateur internet film that began it all.

In that cupboard was everything she knew about Leo's disappearance. And she still hadn't worked it out.

It was time to check her voicemail.

'Hello, love.' Her mum. Slippers. *Wheel of Fortune*. Findus pancakes. 'Just me checking in with you again. I know, I know – you ring us on a Friday, but it worries me, you in that house on your own—'

Message deleted.

'Have you been involved in an accident that wasn't your fault—'

Message deleted.

'Bex . . . hi. It's me again—'

Richard's deep voice. Floppy hair. Stomach flip. No. Message deleted.

'Bex? Bex, did you listen to my last . . . oh I don't know, a thousand messages?' That was her agent. She was surprised she still had an agent. 'Answer your phone, or your door, or check your email. This is ridiculous. Anyway, reunion show, right? You need to tell me what you want to do. They've asked for a meeting—'

Message deleted.

No.

Maybe she should get a bedsheet and spray the word onto it, two huge letters in red: NO. Hang it over the front wall. No to everything. No, no, no, no, no, no, no, no. Never again would she stand at the bottom of those cliff steps, the ones where she had last seen Leo, the hotel looming over her not like a nightmare, because you woke up from those, and this place would never let her.

It would take more alcohol for her to be able to sleep that night without seeing danger in every shadow, so she finished the bottle of wine and played Disney movies into those small hours, aptly named because they made her feel smaller and smaller against the great blackness of night.

The next morning she woke up late, brain as knotty as her uncombed hair, vowing, as she flip-flopped out to the postbox set into her wall, that today she would focus on something else. Yoga, green juice and pints of water. She would force Ravencliffe to the back of her mind.

There was one package waiting for her: a neatly wrapped cube with her address printed on it in careful capital letters. Later she thought back to this moment stood in front of her postbox and she wondered why she chose to open that parcel out of all the ones sent to her. But then, before she knew it, the brown paper was at her feet and the small cardboard box was unwrapped. It only took one look inside for her to know, with a sinking certainty, that the idea of ignoring the hotel would be impossible.

Chapter 5

It was a bit of plastic.

Bex slumped onto her front doorstep, the cardboard box discarded at her feet. Only a bit of plastic. One side of it was orange but if she flipped it over it would show . . . she knew exactly what it would show.

It couldn't be. She knew this bit of plastic. She had watched it being made. A gift, a silly token, a reminder of a fun day at the beach. It had always been kept in the pocket of his jeans – jeans he wore that night. Jeans he disappeared in.

It should have disappeared with him.

She knew what she would see on its underside when she turned it over but the picture still brought a squeeze to her throat. Barry Island. Sunny day, ice-cream smiles, sunglasses and her wearing a Kiss Me Quick hat. Next to her – Leo. For a second there was a screech of seagulls above her and the sugar smell of candyfloss in the air.

Over the years she had had her fair share of crazy post. Early on there had been sacks of it with the postman making special deliveries just for her. She had rarely looked at it; all of those cards and pictures and words . . . tiny hooks that wanted to rip into her, to get her to spill the secrets they thought she had. Fan mail. She did not deserve fans. That had eased off as the years had gone by, though. No doubt, with this ten-year-anniversary business it would all start up again, a circus with her in the middle as the reluctant performing elephant.

This was not crazy post. There were only two of these things and hers was safe with her in her handbag that she never used because she hardly went out. She could see it on the hall table and rummaged in it to check. Yes. Orange for Leo. Purple for Bex. They had had them made together, waiting at the shop counter for the man to finish, sunburn tingling on their necks.

A lighter. The cheap plastic kind, meant to be disposable but this one still had a full chamber of fuel. Leo had been the only one of them to smoke back then, his single vice apart from a weakness for chocolate mice. He had thought it made him look grown-up and sophisticated.

This lighter couldn't be in her hand. Leo had taken cigarettes on that trip, believing he would need them that night and into the next morning, foolishly thinking that for him, there would be another day.

It had never been shown on film. Leo had worn his hideous bright green raincoat the entire time and his jumper had covered the pocket where he kept the lighter. In the end, he hadn't even had time to sneak a cigarette. No fan could have possibly known that this object even existed. Richard and Oscar, though, that was a different story: they would have recognised the thing straight away.

Bex wasn't sure how long she sat there on the step, the bit of plastic in her palm. She thumbed the wheel, hearing it ratchet, not expecting a flame to appear, but it did. She held it too long until heat began to prickle her finger and she at last realised that there might be something else in the box. She grabbed at the cardboard, ripping out the tissue paper until she found the postcard underneath.

A black-and-white shot of Ravencliffe, the kind of thing sold at every RavenCon over the years, red letters printed at the bottom:

Ravencliffe Awaits! Bex turned it over. Handwritten in block capitals on the back were only eleven words but those words were enough to bring the blood pulsing to her temples:

IT'S TIME THE WORLD KNEW WHAT REALLY HAPPENED TO LEO FINCH.

It wasn't something that had been created for promotional purposes, Bex knew. That writing was not print, she could see how the unknown hand had pressed the nib of the Biro onto the card. She cried then, cradling the plastic lighter as if it were a baby animal of some sort, silent tears running down her face, wanting to curl up on the step with the tiny picture of Leo held tight to her heart. She wanted to let time wash over her, carry her away to some point where she would not have to face this. She didn't want to have to think.

But her brain had not got the message.

If this lighter was in her hand now, then that meant that at some point after Leo disappeared from those steps at Ravencliffe someone had found him alive, or dead. She did not want to think again of Leo's lifeless body – she had imagined that far too often over the years. The bluish tinge to his skin, a hundred imagined wounds to his lovely face, his hands stiff and clenched, limbs twisted and broken.

It's time the world knew what really happened to Leo Finch.

No corpse. Without a body to bury, the grave hole filled itself with something even worse – hope. Hope that he was still alive somewhere. All the possible scenarios. Her favourite was that he had fallen into the water but had drifted into a lonely cove, unable to remember who he was due to a head injury, that he had been living a quiet life for ten years in a small town, running a souvenir shop, making plastic tat for tourists.

Eventually, the tears dried up, as tears always did. The reunion show and now this. It felt like events were . . . not nudging her, no, that was too gentle a word. It felt like events were hurtling her towards something she did not want to face.

Gathering the box and its contents to her chest, she closed the door with her foot and went back to her plants and books in the kitchen that was mostly greenhouse. Just like her counting to four, these plants helped protect her too: staving off the death that stalked her with all of their living, breathing, photosynthesising leafy lives.

It no longer worked.

Her head pounded. She moved a seedling tray out of the way and then moved it back, four times. Four times again . . . and again and again and again, hoping she could hit the magic combination that would make all of this feel safe. After far too long, she was satisfied enough that the tray had been moved in the exact way needed and so she laid her head on the table, intending to close her eyes for only a few minutes, to hide away in unconsciousness for a while. A respite.

When she woke, the darkness behind her eyelids had taken over the room.

It was night once more. She had slept through the rest of her day.

Her tongue was a dried dead thing and she needed water and the loo in equal measure, glad to move away from the cardboard box that sat waiting nearby on the table. After washing her hands and her face at the bathroom sink, she moved to the doorway of the kitchen.

It's time the world knew what really happened to Leo Finch.

His lighter had been picked up by someone else, someone who had then packaged it and sent it to her on the ten-year anniversary of the film. Someone who perhaps knew more about his disappearance than she did. In return she should have been doing something more than just having a nap or standing like a statue in her kitchen.

She should be . . . Bex. The Bex from the film. A created creature, with her glossy curls and plucky bravery in the face of adversity, her confident stride in purple boots. But she wasn't her, had never been her in the first place. The sensible thing to do would be to leave: tomorrow, leave the house as it was, take her passport and skip the country, skip the reunion, go to a place where no one knew her and where mysterious boxes filled with heartbreak could never reach her. The sensible thing to do would be to pack a small bag right now.

But she was not a sensible woman – that had been proved far too many times. The lighter and those handwritten words had changed everything. She had to find out, well, lots of things, but first how that object had ended up in a box in her mail. This knowledge was something she needed like those plants around her needed water and light and there was of course one way of discovering it. The reunion show. It could hold all the answers.

That was when the buzzing began.

Chapter 6

At first, Bex simply ignored it.

They would go away.

They always did.

Bex glanced at her watch. Nearly one in the morning. It was probably someone drunk and on their way home, pressing the button for every hidden house they walked past, thinking it funny.

The buzzing continued.

There was a rhythm to it, she noted. Long, long, short. Each long getting longer, each short a stab of sound. There was something about the rhythm that was beginning to buzz its way into Bex's skull as she stood in the doorway, unable to move. Three beats, not four. The lack of that final buzz jarred her. It was just a silly prank, though. It would stop soon.

It did not stop.

Long, long, short. Longer, longer, stab.

It sounded angry and Bex wanted to put her fingers in her ears but even that wouldn't block out the sound. She had never realised that her intercom was so loud. Her gaze was drawn back to the lighter on the kitchen table and the postcard that came with it: *It's time the world knew what really happened to Leo Finch.*

She imagined a hand, dripping with water, the flesh sliding off its bones – ringing her bell. A spectral Leo, risen from a watery grave.

No. She steadied herself against the doorframe as if the room had tilted around her. No.

Long, long, short. Longer, longer . . . *stab.*

Three beats, not four. She desperately needed that fourth buzz. Darting through the kitchen, she ran into the hallway with its black and white tiles and the chess game she had been playing against herself. But the buzzing held her like a web, each crackle a strand that wound even tighter around her. Her feet wouldn't move, flat out refused to take her the last remaining steps to the wall where the intercom was fixed.

A dripping hand with soft bloated flesh.

Longer, longer . . . *stab.*

The buzzing web around her broke and pushed her forward so she stumbled to the monitor, a small screen that showed a black-and-white version of the street outside her gate. Except, it wasn't her street she saw as she peered at it and because the image was so still it took her a few moments to realise what it actually was.

A dark circle within grainy white.

An eye.

It blinked.

Bex recoiled from the screen but the eye did not move. The pupil remained fixed, staring, not at her, because it couldn't see her, but that didn't matter because it felt like it was gazing at her, pinning her to the spot.

Longer, longer . . . *stab.*

The eye blinked again.

Once more Bex thought of a ghostly Leo, come to reclaim his lighter and ask why she had not spent the last ten years searching for him, wanting to be invited in so the flesh could slide from his bones whilst he sat, running with water, on her kitchen bench.

With a hand that should have trembled, she lightly touched the screen, the iris of the eye. Leo had had soft green eyes, like old moss. If he was looking at her, what did he think of this Bex, the Bex she had become? Ratty hair, stained tracksuit bottoms, all the promise of eighteen years old gnawed away like the skin around her fingernails. She pressed her head to the wall and averted her gaze.

When she looked back, the eye had disappeared.

What she saw next made up her mind. Because with the eye gone the street once more was in view, a version of it drained of colour and slightly blurred.

The buzzing fell silent.

The quiet was worse. The quiet was waiting and it didn't have to wait long. Bex had been foolish to think that whatever was at her intercom was Leo, she had been deliberately naïve. It would never be him. If he'd lived, if he had survived that night, then he would have come back to them years ago.

There were other nightmares stalking her.

And there it was. It lurked at the edge of the picture, a blurred, dark shadow of a hooded figure in what looked like a long coat, stooped over as if about to whisper a secret to the nearby lamp-post. The thing was a curl of dead hair trapped under the glass of her screen.

She had been an idiot to think she could escape it. Him. Morwood.

Ten years was time, that stooped figure told her. It was a clearing of the throat, a reminder that it didn't matter where she hid, how high the wall was or how many years had passed. It didn't matter if she packed a bag and ran. It would follow.

The time had come.

High on a cliff, there was a hotel waiting for her. The reunion show was the perfect place to work out who had sent Leo's lighter to her and why, to search all those corners of Ravencliffe for their secrets and finally find out what happened to her best friend. It was time to find the old Bex again and put a stake through the heart of the nightmare that had haunted her ever since she had left that place.

There was no escape. Ravencliffe waited.

Chapter 7

The cold light of day only brought daylight and the cold.

It did not change her mind. There was someone Bex had to see before she set this reunion horror show into gear. Well, there were actually a few people she had to see, her parents probably being the first, but she couldn't stand the idea of trying to explain it to them. They were cuckoo-clock people, snug in their little house, venturing forth at set times along set grooves. She would talk to them later.

At one point she thought she was going to be stuck counting to four behind the gate forever, her hand hovering over the button that would set it sliding across, but she gritted her teeth and slammed her hand against it and waited.

The world revealed itself to her, inch by inch, darkened by the huge sunglasses she wore even though the sky was cloudy. She had thought about dressing the part, go the full Bex costume or maybe ballgown with tiara, give whoever was waiting a real show because that was all they wanted at the end of the day: a show, something to watch on their laptop whilst eating popcorn.

But that would have been disrespectful to the person she was planning to see.

The gate stopped, only open a sliver, wide enough to let her squeeze out. In the end she had gone for a subtle nod, the kind of thing the Ravens would obsess over for days and weeks to come – was it a sign, was it a message?

It was a T-shirt.

Faded black. Half-hidden under her cardigan. Red letters and an outline of a building on a cliff.

She had expected to be ambushed as soon as she stepped on the pavement, to hear shouting and have flashbulbs popping and pens and posters being pushed into her face to sign. What she got were four faces staring at her, one of which was halfway through a sandwich.

'Holy shit.' The sandwich-eating one wiped its mouth.

'Holy shit.' The usual photographer struggled out of his camping chair and grabbed at his camera. 'I didn't actually think you were in there.'

The other two faces just gawped. One had on a *Ravencliffe* T-shirt very similar to hers, possibly even picked up at the same convention, and she nudged her dungaree-clad friend who began to rummage in her rucksack.

'Are you going to . . . y'know, take a picture?' Bex asked. Mr Sandwich Face nodded, stuffed the rest of his pastrami on rye in his mouth and dutifully snapped away.

'You're Bex,' the girl in the *Ravencliffe* T-shirt said, only moving to nudge her friend again. Bex smiled. 'I mean, you know you're Bex! What a stupid thing to— It's not like that's a surprise to you, is it? Oh God, I'm rambling . . . I do that when I'm nervous and well . . . you're Bex . . .'

'Shut up, Monica. Here. Can you sign this please?' Her friend finally found what she had been looking for in her rucksack, a pen and a film poster. 'We're big fans. Can we have a selfie?'

Bex signed the poster and smiled for thc photo, which in the end one of the paparazzi took because Monica's hands shook too badly to keep the shot in focus.

'We can't wait for the reunion show!' Monica pressed the signed poster to her chest.

The four of them even gave her a little wave as she got into her barely used car and Bex found the smile that had begun as a pasted-on thing was actually genuine as she waved back, counted them: one, two, three, four, put the key in the ignition, prayed to the engine gods and heard the vehicle splutter into life.

* * *

Then she went backwards in time.

Caerphilly. Bex's childhood town. Not far from the capital city of Cardiff, it was surrounded by hills where it could be sunny in the valley below whilst the mountaintops held back a dark smudge of brooding cloud. The place had its claims to fame: it produced a well-known cheese, the Sex Pistols once played there and it was home to the largest castle in Wales, guarded by a fearsome mob of geese who were adept at stealing snacks from tourists. Her parents had moved away long ago, into a neat bungalow in a Cardiff suburb with a tiny front lawn and symmetrical hedges. But it wasn't her parents she needed to see.

When she got there, she saw that the house hadn't changed. It was a plain Sixties-built semi with pebble-dashing on the top half and an aluminium porch where the same two plants somehow managed to keep up the good fight despite being broiled in summer and frozen in winter.

Bex stepped into the porch, rang the doorbell and waited.

'Sod off!' A faint gruff voice floated to her through the door.

'Mr Finch? It's Bex!'

'I don't care what your name is. I don't want new windows, I don't give a shit about God or charities and I don't want a new driveway! Sod off!'

'It's Bex!' She raised her voice. 'Leo's Bex!'

There was silence on the other side of the door. Bex waited, and then waited some more and was finally going to turn away when the door opened an inch. A waft of stale garlic escaped as a slice of face eyed her.

'I've a good mind to tell you to sod off too, y'know.'

'I know.'

The door opened some more. 'Well, come in if you're coming.'

In the living room time had stopped. On the mantelpiece a broken carriage clock, its hands forever stilled at a quarter to three, stood next to a photo of a woman in her forties, smiling into the camera as the wind whipped her hair over her face. On the other side of the dead clock was a photo of Leo. The only used piece of furniture in the room was an armchair opposite the television. There was a deep indentation in its seat pad and a tray table was swung across it, holding a pack of cigarettes, a can of beer and two plates with crumbs of pastry on them. The room smelled of microwave meals and old sweat.

'I came to—' Bex tried to speak above the television.

'I bloody know, don't I?' Mr Finch sat heavily into the chair which had a worn patch on the carpet in front of it. 'Shut up until my episode is over.'

Bex did. She thought about sitting down, but one glance at the other available chair covered in old magazines, newspapers and some unidentifiable things in paper bags that seemed to be oozing a bit put her off. As far as she could tell, in the show a woman with big hair and bigger earrings had been sleeping with a weaselly looking man but was unsuccessfully trying to keep it from her husband. The credits rolled over a dramatic close-up as the husband found out the truth and overacted shock and anger.

'If you're expecting a cup of tea, you can make it yourself.'

'I'm not. I just wanted to let you know—'

'That you're all swanning back to that place, yeah? Some stupid reunion show? After what happened to my Leo?' Mr Finch stabbed at the remote control and the television went black.

She didn't have the energy to explain it to him, her reason for going back, so she changed the subject instead. 'How's Soph?'

'Straight As in her exams.' His eyes brightened. 'Having something they call a gap year before university so she's working at this summer camp for the next few months. And before that, she did this thing called interrail where she travelled across Europe with a friend.'

Leo's little sister, Sophie, was permanently stuck at the age of eight in Bex's mind, her blonde hair escaping her plaits, her face flushed from running about, dressed in mini Dr. Martens and a selection of bright leggings. It was hard to imagine her as a young woman, off to start a degree. There was also a photo of her on the mantelpiece, a cap jammed over her blonde hair, sunglasses so big they nearly reached her jaw. Bex hadn't seen her for years.

'That sounds amazing.'

'Yeah, she is . . . I messed it all up a bit with Leo, y'know, when his mum was ill, but with Soph it was always easier – I've got it right with her . . .'

'Well, it's her I've come to speak to you about. You know that account I set up for her—'

'I haven't touched a penny. It's hers.'

'I know.'

'I mean, we used a tiny bit for the rail tickets—'

'Look, I'm not questioning you. The money is yours and Sophie's to spend as you want. This new filming, there will be more. I don't want it. It's yours.'

'No.'

'Wait—'

'I took it last time because . . . Soph deserved a chance, stuck with me. But I won't take any more.'

'Leo would have—'

'Leo would've wanted to be here, that's what he would've wanted! But he's not, is he? Because of that sodding place! It's blood money, is what it is.'

They fell silent. Through the back window, Bex could see the old climbing frame where she and Leo had spent many summer hours hanging upside down from the monkey bars discussing their favourite television shows. The rope ladder was missing. Along with the dead clock, the dead people watched them from the mantelpiece: Leo's mum, cancer carrying her off before her fiftieth birthday, only days after Leo himself had turned eighteen. And Leo? Possibly dead. Probably. Most likely. An empty grave.

'What's got into you?' Mr Finch picked at a thread on the arm of his chair.

'What do you mean?' Bex knew exactly what he meant.

He fixed her with a sharp look. 'You've been a hermit for ten years. What's changed your mind?' Bex watched him pull on the thread. That's what this was, she thought, this was a thread she had to pull; she couldn't stop herself even though she had managed to keep her hands off it for the past ten years. She had to watch it all unravel. Letting the thread drop, Mr Finch glanced towards the mantelpiece. 'Don't go back there. That place. It's a . . . what you called it in the film . . . a bad luck place.'

Pausing, Bex tried to think of a way to explain. 'You ever feel like something's unfinished?'

Mr Finch snorted. 'My whole bloody life, girl, after Leo and his mum went.'

'It's like . . . it's like I'm in a game of hide-and-seek and the seeker's gone quiet, right? So I know they're close, they're coming for me. The game's not over.'

'Run then. Stay away from that hotel.'

Bex sighed. 'Can I go up?'

'Yes. Don't move anything.' Mr Finch stabbed at the remote again and the television flared into life once more. Bex left him illuminated in its cold glow.

Upstairs the house was dim, the landing curtains drawn so only a weak light made it through. She recognised those curtains and the carpet and the bathroom suite she could see through the half-open door. Nothing had changed in ten years, nothing would. That was why she had never had to worry about Mr Finch syphoning away the money meant for Sophie – for someone to do that they would have to have an interest in the future. Mr Finch only thought of the next television show and the next beer. Even before Leo's disappearance the future had been none of his concern.

There was the door. Bex opened it into Leo's bedroom and stood on the threshold. His bed, his posters, his desk, his computer, all were exactly as he had left them, the bed neatly made, the posters stuck up in ordered rows, his books and schoolwork in ring binders and on shelves. No pop stars for him; the prints on his walls were old Hammer Horror movie posters: Dracula suave in his cape, fangs dripping blood, women frightened in diaphanous negligees, the dark outlines of Gothic castles in the background. Glorious technicolour.

'Hey, Leo,' she said, long past feeling silly about talking to the wallpaper.

In her hand she gripped the small plastic lighter. By rights she should have placed it on his desk, next to his pencil case covered in Tipp-Ex graffiti but she continued to keep it in her grasp. It had been sent to her for a reason, even though she didn't yet know what that reason was.

'I'm going back. Finally. I'm sorry it's taken so long. But I promise this time I'll do whatever it takes to find out what happened to you. Pinky swear.' She crooked her little finger and imagined a ghostly finger hooking through hers.

Chapter 8

When Bex buzzed her mother in, she arrived bearing a trolley case, a large box of charity Mills & Boon books and an empty plate.

'You've been giving cookies to the photographers again, haven't you?' Bex stooped over a plant, writing neat letters on a little card.

'They love my chocolate chip! And, Rebecca Harrison, it costs someone nothing to be polite. They're nice folks and your little fans too, the ones in the T-shirts. They've been standing outside for ages, they need a snack.'

'Well, you don't have to make it for them, Mam. It's weird.'

The first time around, before she had the money to buy her London house, Bex had holed herself up at her parents' tiny semi-detached in Caerphilly with its square of front lawn and apple blossom tree and watched the crowd gather. She remembered that her mother had made quite a fan club of her own, bringing out biscuits and flasks of tea for the people waiting outside. Her father had rolled his eyes and muttered when someone stepped on his floral borders.

'You should go and give a little wave.'

'I'm not royalty, Mam.'

Her mother sighed and put her box of books down on top of a seedling tray. Once again, Bex noted, her mother was auditioning for *Woman & Home* cover girl, dressed as she was in freshly pressed beige ankle-length trousers and a cashmere sweater in the most powdery of pinks. Moving the box of books, Bex continued writing on the small cards.

'You've made me a list?' Her mother picked up a piece of paper, printed on both sides.

'Yes. You've got to remember to look after the plants, not just water them but feed them too. They'll need to be moved in and out of the sun and you've got to wipe their leaves.'

'Wipe their leaves?' Bex's mother cast her gaze around the plant-stuffed kitchen. 'That's a lot of leaves to wipe . . .'

'Yes and you'll need to know their names so I'm writing them down on these bits of card which I'll stick to their pots.'

'Their species? Like their Latin name?'

'No, their name – like we have names. This one is Cordelia.' Bex gave the distinctive holly leaf of the nearest plant to her a gentle pat and spiked her finger on its prickled bite.

'They have names,' her mother muttered. 'Of course, of course, they have names. Should I ask them what they want to watch on telly each evening, how their day went, that kind of thing?'

Bex blinked and sucked the blood from her finger before replying. 'Yes. Seriously. If you talk to a plant, it grows better. I don't know how or why, but it does.'

'Well, I guess it'll be a bit like talking to your dad then. I don't get any response from him half the time either.'

For a few minutes, there was only the slight scratching sound of Bex writing plant names. 'Is Dad okay with this? It'll only be a week, tops.'

Removing a cactus from a stool first, Bex's mother perched on top. 'Oh, he's delighted. He'll spend every afternoon in the pub, roll home for one of the dinners I've left in the freezer for him and be asleep in front of the television by nine.' She paused and pushed at a bit of soil on the kitchen worktop with the tip of her finger. 'I still don't know why you had to move all the way out here, away from your family – your friends. To London.'

Bex remained silent. Her mother made the word 'London' sound like 'outer space'. This was a well-worn conversation, its sentences handled so much they were floppy with age and liable to tear. Over the years she had tried to explain it, how she had had to leave Wales completely, put miles and miles between her and that stretch of coastline where the hotel clung. As if the place could lever itself up from its perch and haul itself out of the rock, pipes dangling from it like roots before lurching across the country to find her.

Each time her mother had refused to understand.

And, in the end, the hotel had found her anyway.

A woman called Marsha had explained the filming schedule to Bex yesterday via a video call that Bex's internet connection could not handle and so the woman's face had frozen and then sped up at intervals, her lips never quite connecting with her words. She had had a quiff of frost-coloured hair and bright red glasses and had introduced herself as an executive at Echelon, the film company that had bought the rights years ago. 'Well, we've changed a bit since then,' Marsha had said – at least Bex heard her voice as her mouth struggled to catch up. 'Bit of a management shake-up – clearing out the old guard, y'know? Fresh faces, fresh purpose and a fresh way of doing things. I will personally be on location every single day to oversee filming.' Marsha had told her the shoot would last a week including set-up and orientation and that later the footage would be cut into a one-hour special. Both the cast and crew would stay in trailers around the hotel so valuable time wouldn't be lost waiting for people to turn up. Bex hadn't liked the sound of that, but Marsha had assured her that the hotel would be strictly off-limits between shoots due to health and safety reasons. 'We really don't need anything happening like it did the last time you were there – I can only imagine the lawsuits!'

Not able to keep still for more than five minutes maximum, Bex's mother got up, filled the kettle and inspected two mugs. They did not pass muster so as she spoke she rinsed them out. 'You don't have to do this, y'know.'

'Yeah, I know. Mr Finch told me too.' Bex finished the final card and sellotaped it to a plant pot.

'Well, he's got his faults but he's right on this one. How was he?'

'Drinking too much. Stuck in that house.'

'That started months before . . . Leo, so don't you go blaming yourself for that. The man fell apart after Linda got diagnosed. We all tried to help, the street, y'know – but he made it clear he didn't want any of it. What can you do? Oh!' Rummaging in her handbag, Bex's mother brought out a photograph. 'Look what I found! It was so sweet, how you and Leo were glued to each other, even when you were little. I think this is from that caravan holiday we did when you were ten . . .'

The smell of bleach in the communal washrooms, blasts of sun when it came out that tipped the grass brown and made the sea glitter so hard that it hurt to look at it. She had spent every evening with Leo in the clubhouse's children's disco, whirling each other round and round to the music. This photo showed them with their sweaty heads pressed together, Leo's glasses a little askew, both wearing smiles that couldn't have got any wider.

'He wore that T-shirt nearly every day that summer,' Bex said, staring at the picture.

'Obsessed with green, he was. He had to be prised away from it when it needed a wash.' There was a pause.

'I have to go back, Mum . . . because of him.' Bex propped the photo up against the nearest plant.

'I know.' As they drank their tea in silence, Bex's mother glanced around the kitchen. 'Do you mind if I tidy up a bit whilst you're gone?'

'Yes.'

* * *

Later that evening, sat in her camping chair on the roof, Bex scattered seeds for Bob the pigeon, who perched on the low wall. He twitched his head to look at the seeds, considered moving and then decided against it.

There was nothing else left to do. Her case was waiting by the door; she had finished her game of hallway chess and moved the table out of the way; her plants were labelled and looked after. She had taken what paper she thought she might need from the cupboard, stared at the floorplan of Ravencliffe one last time and then locked the doors.

Ruffling his feathers, Bob looked at her in a way that suggested she was a complete and utter fool. She couldn't disagree with him. Through her binoculars she scanned the street below, the shadows of night already creeping in. No dark, ghostly figure in a greatcoat waiting for her. Morwood. No need. Soon she would be back exactly where he had always wanted her, amongst the rot and ruin and the lingering scent of dead things. In her pocket was the lighter and the note.

It's time the world knew what really happened to Leo Finch.

Chapter 9

Hallowe'en recording of *Live With Jasper St Clare*

(The only appearance of the Ravencliffe Three together on television, just over one year since they filmed at the hotel. Often found by searching for 'car crash TV' on YouTube.)

Jasper does not sit behind a desk like many late-night television chat show hosts. He perches on a retro egg-shaped chair, fidgety and genial, always smiling, often crossing and uncrossing his legs.

'Well, folks.' He smiles and takes a sip from a champagne flute on a spindly gold table next to him. The studio is decked out for Hallowe'en: there is a skeleton bending over the table behind him, cobwebs and drippy candles in every available spot. 'It's time.' A thrill of sound passes through the audience. 'Let's have a look in our green room, shall we?'

The camera cuts to a sofa and a chair, a plain wall behind it. On the sofa sit Richard, Oscar and Bex. Two smile and give a little wave. One stares off to the side. The other guest, an American pop singer, leans towards Bex from his chair, as if he has been talking to her, but she continues to stare past him. The camera cuts away as she moves to stand up.

'Ah, yes – there they are looking . . .' Jasper seems lost for words until his face brightens. 'Looking so very bloody young, yeah? Hate them, hate them.' He shakes his head and the audience laughs. His own face is unnaturally smooth and wrinkle-free, his hairline recently magically regenerated. 'So for those of you who have been living under a rock for the last few months, my next guests decided to do a little summer project last year and film in a creepy old hotel with a dark past, never guessing that their movie would become a sensation and that they would also, sadly, lose their closest friend in the process. Without further ado, I'd like to welcome three intrepid young people who have taken the film world by storm. One word: Ravencliffe!'

The audience claps and the lights swoop and whirl for a few seconds. Jasper stands as the three of them walk onto the set. Oscar and Richard are arm in arm with Bex, who is in the middle, a show of solidarity, of friendship . . . a way to keep her with them. Richard has on slim black trousers and a freshly ironed shirt, Oscar's denim is stylishly distressed, and Bex is in a short, glittery black dress but her lipstick is smudged and she is wearing her scuffed purple boots with thick hiking socks. Her legs are pale and she has a bruise on her shin.

The three sit on a sofa that looks like an open hand, the seat a green velvet palm with fingers stretching up as the back. Mock cobwebs have been thrown over it. Jasper motions to the audience and a hush falls. He lets it settle for a moment. Bex shifts. Richard interlocks his arm with hers again.

'Well.' Jasper leans back, stroking the stem of his champagne glass. 'We all know how much of a horror film buff I am.' Jasper is also the host of the channel's prestigious film review show. 'So this is a real honour, to have you on the show, especially on Hallowe'en. Perfect timing.'

There is laughter though Jasper has not said anything particularly funny. Richard smiles, as does Oscar. Bex does not until suddenly she flicks her gaze around her and then gives a harsh sound approximating laughter a few seconds after everyone else's has died away. Jasper considers her and then darts a look at the production team out of shot. He leans in.

'I have to be serious here though, for a moment. One year on from that night and it looks unlikely that Leo's body will ever be found. How are you all coping?'

There is silence. If you look closely at Bex (and many people have, many times) you can see that she flinches, a brief jolt of her head. Oscar opens his mouth to speak but Richard talks over him. 'Honest answer, we're not coping, Jasper. We are in the middle of all of . . . this . . . and all we want to do is hunker down and grieve for our friend.'

'Of course. But let me, if you will, bring you back to that night. What did you think, setting off to Ravencliffe in that boat? What did you expect?'

'I don't think that thinking came into it much.' There is a flutter of subdued laughter. Richard's fingers dart to his face, tapping lightly at the cheekbone under his right eye. 'We were a bunch of bored idiots, daring ourselves to do something stupid.'

'Teenagers, eh? But that place you found – it is horror film perfection. Ravencliffe, folks. Big old hotel on the cliff, gardens and stuff all down the cliff face, meant to be a swanky Victorian spa resort, y'know the thing – women in hoop skirts taking the air, promenading and the like. We have a photo for you . . . yeah, there it is on the screen, that's actually a still from the film. But then the whole idea falls apart, something to do with the railway line . . .'

'Yes. There was meant to be a new railway line being built to reach Cardigan, where the hotel was, so it would be in the perfect spot for visitors, but those plans were delayed for whatever reason. Building the hotel had left Morwood, the owner, with loads of debts by then anyway—'

'Wait. Cardigan?' Jasper swivels in his seat to glance at the audience with a raised eyebrow. 'What kind of name for a town is Cardigan? Is it next to the town of Sweater, just up the road from the tiny hamlet of Pullover?'

There is laughter. Richard fixes Jasper with a look. 'Actually, the Welsh name for Cardigan is Aberteifi, which means "the town at the mouth of the river Teifi". And I don't know where the word Cardigan comes from but it's got nothing to do with clothes—'

Jasper mimes an elaborate yawn and then smiles. 'No one signed up for a language lesson, Rich. Back to the hotel. So, in despair, Morwood shot himself right in his own office. The place was then abandoned. The shots you took . . .' Jasper kisses his fingers like a chef tasting a brilliant meal.

Richard sits straighter. 'Yeah, we're proud of those.'

A strangled laugh comes from Bex. Both Richard and Oscar turn their heads to her. She is not smiling and those vacant eyes of hers remain as empty and desolate as the rooms in the Ravencliffe Hotel. She begins to pick off the beads at the bottom of her skirt.

'Look, we never expected to be film stars yeah?' Oscar jumps in, even though Richard frowns at him, his fingers pressing against his cheek as if his face hurts. 'But you've got to make the best of it.'

Richard speaks quickly. 'The film is a tribute to Leo. That's the important thing.'

'Bex.' There is a sharp glint in Jasper's eyes. 'We haven't heard much from you. You were the last one to see Leo alive.'

The camera moves to a close-up on Bex's face. Her hair has been quickly styled into a half-up, half-down ponytail but sweat has made little curls stick to her forehead. She pulls another bead from the skirt of her dress and lets it fall to the studio floor. There are now lots of them at her feet, like ants. Her eyes focus on Jasper.

'It's been a total shock for all of us, we—' Richard begins.

But Jasper cuts him off. 'Bex? You were the last one to see him.'

'I don't think—' Richard again but Bex wriggles free from his grasp and bends to scoop up all the beads she has thrown on the floor, sliding off the seat so she is kneeling to get every last one, counting under her breath.

'Bex, honey? You don't need to do that.' Jasper's eyes gleam with delight as audience figures dance across his vision.

'Bex? What're you doing? Get up!' Oscar whispers to her, trying to drag her upright by the arm, but she jerks her elbow away from him. She studies the beads in her palm and then she stands.

'Can we stop filming for a sec—' Richard begins, but at that point the first bead has been deliberately flicked into Jasper's face. Bex picks out another one with her fingertip and takes a step closer to the talk show host, who gives a short laugh.

'Hey, hey, hey! Settle down, missy.'

Another bead is flicked into his face. And another. And another. The vacancy in Bex's eyes hardens and focuses as she picks out bead after bead and Jasper raises his interview cards to his face, angling away, still trying to smile. Bex counts to herself, never getting beyond four.

'We should go to a break now!' Richard lunges out of his seat but Bex sidesteps him, chucks the rest of the beads at Jasper like confetti and stalks off set.

The screen goes black.

Chapter 10

Under the spotlight, Bex felt sweat trickle into the hollow of her throat.

She stood in Morwood's study. Ten years ago, when they had sailed across to the hotel, this room had been their goal. Find the study, film there, tell all the ghost stories of the place, dare the spirit of Reginald Morwood to come and swallow their souls and then, when that did not happen, eat snacks and go back to their bunkhouse a few hours later, tired and cold but with some footage they could use to impress their future university Film Studies tutors.

There were the empty bookcases next to the wooden panelling which curled away from the wall as if it was trying to distance itself from the place; there were the gaslights in sconces, the dirt and leaves and carcasses of little dead animals on the floor. There was the desk, scratched and beaten with splintered edges.

It was made of cheap plywood.

They had done a good job, Bex had to give them that. It was almost as she remembered it, though fear and adrenaline had left a migraine tinge to the whole place for her that could never be recreated. They were filming a teaser trailer, the executive from the production company had called it, something to whet the appetite of the fans, to announce what was coming. It was easier and quicker to record this on a soundstage so they could get some 'buzz' for the project whilst the location team worked their magic in the real Ravencliffe.

The word 'buzz' made Bex think of her intercom and the eye watching her.

There would be many more eyes soon. In the darkness around her, lots of people scurried, talking in low tones, tweaking something on the set, something on her, moving cameras on rigs that glided at speed, one minute far away, the next right in her face.

Her dress itched. She would have objected, but changing it would have caused a delay and she wanted the whole thing to be over as soon as possible. They were going for a gothic theme, it was clear – something with a nod to the Victorian, even though she had spent the original film in jeans, a jumper and those purple boots. Her long black lace dress made her look like a porn star version of a nineteenth-century school ma'am. Someone had placed around her neck a glittery acrylic version of the Ouija board planchette, that little bit of wood people used to spell out messages from the dead. It had been no use telling them that they hadn't even used a Ouija board that night. At least she had made her thoughts clear about changing her hair. No return to red curls, not for her, on that she was firm. They could dress her however they pleased because clothes could be easily discarded but if she went back to red she'd be stuck with that hair for a good while. The intricate updo they'd chosen was ridiculous and pulled at her temples.

This was going to be the first time she met Oscar and Richard again.

The intervening weeks between this moment and her decision made standing in front of her intercom had passed in one shake of a snowglobe, except it wasn't a tiny Leo in it, but a tiny her, lifted and spun as her world went upside down and everything blurred.

'It'll be a moment in cinematic history – the three of you

meeting up again for the first time!' Marsha had told her once she had arrived at the studio, presumably the reason they had kept them apart until this day.

Oscar first.

He stepped over a camera cable and bounded on set as if he was the game show host, about to spin the wheel that would suddenly appear from a bookcase somewhere. Bex felt every lens in the room train itself on them.

'Bex.' He had taken up the offer of a new hairdo, Bex thought as she looked at him. The boy-band bleached tips she had seen a few weeks ago at the convention had been toned down, the tan evened out, the whiter than white smile less of a contrast. His costume had clearly been taken from the same nineteenth-century-set porn film – a frock coat and tight-fitting trousers in black velvet. 'I mean . . . wow . . . it's been so long . . .'

She realised that for him, it had. He didn't know about her yearly visits to the convention, most of those involving him making a guest appearance, apart from the one time when he had been arrested for drink-driving. She also realised that she needed to say something and not just stand there sweating.

'Oscar.'

The tan did not hide the lines on his skin. They weren't yet thirty but he looked sun-worn and she didn't blame him for spending as much time in the daylight as he could, because for them, the shadows were much darker than they could stand.

Then he moved to her and too late she understood that he had been going in for a hug. She had already angled away, thinking he was going to walk past her and so he ended up clutching her side-on, her head awkwardly pressed into his shoulder. She wondered if he had changed much from the brash eighteen-year-old she had known.

He bent to her and whispered, covering his mic, 'I'm glad you came.'

Time had clearly made him sentimental, because, ten years ago, he would not have been pleased to see her. He never had been. She smiled for the cameras and pushed herself out of his grip but he kept hold of her hand, clutching it between both of his.

'So. Ten years,' she said, her brain unable to give her anything more profound.

'My God – I mean . . . look at you. It's been a . . . well . . . hasn't it?'

'Hasn't it?'

'That's great!' A voice called out from the darkness behind the lights. Calling their stilted stab at a conversation 'great' was definitely stretching the definition of the word. Bex squinted into the glare. 'Lovely stuff. Get into positions for Mr Deyes.'

A make-up artist darted towards her, but Bex batted her away. Her face could only absorb so much blotting powder and pretty soon she was going to end up looking like one of those white-faced mime actors. Oscar took a spot behind her, close enough for her to feel him breathing on her neck.

And then he was there. Richard.

He did not bound on but stepped over the various trip hazards with a deliberate care. She had not had much time to think about this; about seeing him again. Her ex-boyfriend, the man who had, with a lot of help from Oscar, created the film whilst she had been mourning Leo, both of them selling it to the highest bidder and in the process selling her, her face, her feelings, to a wider public who had picked it all apart with glee. There had been rumours that it had all been scripted, that they were actors, that Leo would reappear in a month or two, that they would then all show the world the hole in the top hat through which they had pulled the magic rabbit.

After a while, Bex had lost track of the rumours.

'Rich!' Oscar went over to him, his arms outstretched, ready to attempt another hug, even though the last one had gone badly, but Richard kept him at arm's length, grasping his shoulders. His smile when it came was clipped and tight.

This was not the Richard she remembered. Ten years ago, he would have stridden onto the set, the charm drifting from him like a heady aftershave, one that worked so well it made people forget the whiff of arrogance that was a bitter undertone. He looked pretty much the same despite his shorter, still glossy, brown hair and the bloodshot in one eye, but everything had a sharper angle: his jawline, his frame, his gaze.

The scar had faded but Bex remembered blood, so much of it, sticky on her hands, smeared onto her jumper.

'Bex.' Richard moved past Oscar and came nearer.

'Rich.' If any person watching was unsure of their names, they certainly weren't by now, Bex thought. There was a terrible stretched moment where neither of them moved and then Oscar squashed them all into a group hug, pressing Bex and Richard together with one eye on the cameras. She would have pulled away and it felt like Richard was about to do the same but then he stooped to her, his arm gentle across her back, his face close to her neck. If she closed her eyes, she could pretend she was eighteen again, before Ravencliffe, before the summer that changed it all, when she had been a shallow teenager with a handsome boyfriend.

A sharp edge dug into her middle.

'Leo.' Richard leant back and showed her the picture frame he had in his hand, an ornate silver thing. 'I thought he should be with us.'

This was going to be the problem, Bex realised. For the whole of this reunion she was going to have to work out if what either of them said and did was a truth of sorts or simply for the camera. She hadn't remembered being so aware of it, when they had filmed at Ravencliffe first time around, mostly because they had never thought anyone would see the footage and then things had got so out of control there was no time to second-guess anything.

Bringing the photo was the exact right thing to do. That was what made her suspicious.

Richard placed the frame onto the desk and Bex tried not to

look but couldn't help herself. She gazed at Leo's photo and dug her nails into the palm of her hand, blinking back tears. They would not have her tears. They had had everything else, but her tears for Leo were her own.

'Right – lovely.' That disembodied directorial voice boomed out again. 'We'll set up for the establishing shots.'

The three of them stood, mostly still, mostly silent, as the cameras glided around them and the lights flashed in their face, lit them up from behind, dimmed and brightened and glared and dazzled. Hands moved them, adjusted clothing, brushed hair, made them sit, stood them up again.

It took what seemed liked hours.

When it ended, they were abandoned and people moved to the screens, viewing the day's work. The lights lowered and then overhead bulbs came on casting an unforgiving bright glow. Bex could see a bit of fraying lace on her cuff, the parts of the desk that had not been painted to the edges and the scuff marks on the floor. She saw that Leo's photo frame was not ornate silver but silver paint on cheap wood and she scratched some of it off with her nail as Oscar cleared his throat behind her.

'This is weird, yeah?' He laughed but the laughter died away, embarrassed at itself. 'Gotta be honest, Bex, we didn't think you'd show, did we, Rich?'

'And miss all the fun?'

'Look, we each have our reasons for being here, whatever they are.' Richard unbuttoned his frock coat and loosened his cravat. 'Let's just do this, as respectfully as possible and then—'

'I'm never doing anything like this again.' Bex unclipped the back of the photo frame as she spoke, taking out the photo and slipping it into the pocket of the jeans she wore under the dress. Then she ripped off her microphone. 'And we need to talk.'

Chapter 11

It was the easiest thing in the world. All she had to do was show them the lighter and explain.

Richard and Oscar gazed at her.

'Microphones off.' Bex tugged on Richard's.

'So? What did you want to talk about?' Richard threw his microphone away to the side of the soundstage, got out his vape pen and sucked on it, a sweet cherry smoke drifting towards her. Oscar followed suit and tried to stick his hands in the pockets of his too tight trousers but only his fingers could fit.

'I . . .'

The lighter was right there, tucked down her cleavage, one use for the ridiculous top they had made her wear. All she had to do was show it to them. Dressed in their black clothes, they were three lace-bedecked ravens under the bright overhead lights.

The thought was a beak pecking at her brain – *one of them could have sent that package to her house.*

'Given up smoking?' Oscar nodded at Richard's vape pen.

'Given up lots of things.' Richard's scars had faded to almost nothing, Bex noted. 'In fact, might as well be honest because this process, apparently – it's all about owning your truth. I was all for this. The ten-year thing. I need the money.'

'Whoa, man. The rumours were true then? Y'know about . . . you losing your shit? Gotta respect.'

'Well, no, Oz. Not really. I've got no respect for the man I was. Or the man I am, in that case.'

'Wait, what? You blew *all* of that money on . . . what? Drugs and alcohol?' Bex didn't bother to coat her disapproval in a polite tone.

'Well, you're not the only person who couldn't cope with . . . everything that happened, Bex. You act like you are but . . . anyway, I got in over my head.'

Bex felt the anger die within her, a flame choked out with too much kindling. It didn't matter. They had been headed back to that place the moment they left it ten years ago. Richard continued, 'So – I'm out of rehab and pretty much bankrupt but I want to pay for my little girl's future.'

'You have a daughter?' Bex tried to imagine Richard holding a little girl in frilly skirts and a pintucked bonnet.

'Yeah, her name's Ruby. She's five. Here . . .' From out of a battered leather wallet he took a photo. Bex leant in and saw a cute kid in bunches wearing a puff-sleeved dress and a massive ice-cream smudged smile.

'She's adorable.'

'Yeah. She really is. Her mother hates me which I don't blame her for at all. I haven't really got anything right with all of this. The money can change that. Or start to, at least.'

Out of the corner of her eye, Bex saw something large and black swooping towards them.

'Hey!' She hitched up her skirts and marched towards the unfortunate young man holding the boom microphone, who had been trying to catch their conversation. 'Fuck off! This is private, you hear me?' She swiped at the furry object of her disapproval and it made a muffled thunking sound. 'Private! Fucking vultures!'

'Ms Harrison.' A woman came towards her and Bex recognised her as the one from her Zoom call, the executive in charge of the reunion show. She had a shock of cropped white hair and huge plastic-rimmed glasses in red. 'I'm Marsha, yes? We've already met. Put the microphone away, Neil.' Neil did so, but it was rather large so he could only stand sheepishly with it upright at his side like a furry and therefore useless spear. 'Please continue your private conversation.'

Bex glowered. 'We have to know when we're being filmed. At all times. This isn't some sick fucking reality television show.'

'Quite.' Marsha spoke with a soft lilt as if trying to soothe an unseen baby. 'But let's tone down the language, hmm? I prefer a serene, nourishing working environment.'

'Well, don't stick a fucking mic in my face without me knowing and I won't have to swear.'

Marsha smiled, a tight, mirthless thing, and turned to an assistant with an overstuffed clipboard.

'All right, Bex?' Richard came closer, but not too close because she still had a look that signalled thunder. 'No need to get worked up, yeah? We're all getting used to each other and how this thing will work . . .'

'It's not going to work, is it?' Bex muttered.

'Hmm?'

'It's not going to f— flipping work.' She cast a glance to Marsha who didn't appear to notice. 'All of us. What we're doing, going back there. It's a nightmare waiting to happen.'

'No, no, not at all—'

Oscar tugged at his cravat and joined them. 'Bex, like – nice as all of this is, catching up, kids, and the rest . . . you said we needed to talk?' He looked at his watch, hidden under a large cuff. 'It's just I've got a photo shoot in an hour.'

'Hey, man. Don't be rude. This is a moment, yeah? This is *the* moment. The three of us back together. Leo. Ten years. This is moving forward whilst keeping our hearts in the past . . .' Bex had a feeling that Richard had memorised this speech beforehand. 'Bex, over to you.'

This was the moment.

She told herself to turn her back so no one else could see, beckon them closer and show them the lighter. But did she trust them? Had she ever trusted them?

Instead she scratched off a sliver of paint from the corner of the desk. The fraying edge of her cuff caught on a splintered edge and she let it tug loose, making the lace on her sleeve sag a little. It had all begun here, in this study. Until they had seen what had been placed there on the desk, until that point, they had just been having a silly, goofy night. This study had changed everything.

Oscar cleared his throat.

'Yes.' Bex jerked her arm away and she heard material tear. Smoothing the Ouija board planchette around her neck with her thumb, she looked at Oscar and then at Richard. She didn't know these people. She knew who they had been at eighteen, but eighteen was plastic, it was pliable, a dough not yet baked into a person. For all she knew, one of them could have sent her the lighter. They could have pushed Leo from that spot on the steps (even though he had been on his own), they could have swiped the lighter from his dead body as a trophy (except that body would have been seen on the rocks below) and then ten years later sent it to her to goad her, to play games.

It was not likely. But it could join every other theory about Leo – each of them as unlikely as the next.

'Well?' Oscar checked his watch again, though that was probably more to show it off to the others. It had a massive, complicated dial more intelligent than him.

'I just wanted to say the same as Richard,' Bex began in a rush. 'Y'know . . . this is a moment, yeah? Moving our hearts forward . . . or, or back . . . whatever it was . . .'

It was a relief to be interrupted. Marsha came towards them flanked by three young people. She stopped a few yards away and called over, 'Is your private conversation finished? I don't wish to intrude.'

She said it in a very polite way, but Bex had a feeling that her words were cruise ships, gleaming up top with a motor underneath that could slice a person in two.

'Yeah, we're done.'

'Lovely. I'd like to introduce you to your personal assistants for the rest of this shoot. They will be with you every step of the way.' That sounded horrendous, Bex thought, considering the people before her. They were so young they couldn't have been long out of school. 'They are here for your every need and whim and will support you night and day. Bex, meet Holly.' Marsha pushed forward a Goth Barbie with unnaturally dark hair and a tenuous grasp of eyeliner application. 'Holly, meet Bex.'

Holly gave a wide smile and, regardless of the eyeliner, Bex could recognise that gaze. Her heart sank.

'Ms Harrison. I . . . I mean this is . . . I'm an admirer of the film!' She offered her hand to Bex and, when Bex took it, she shook her whole arm so hard she thought she might have dislocated a shoulder. That was all she needed, Bex thought, as she wrestled her hand free and tried not to let her smile falter. A bloody super fan.

Chapter 12

Bex, ten years ago

As I sit next to Leo in the library with the papers spread around me, the idea becomes less of an idea and more of a plan.

A supply teacher started it all off. Last year, faced with a room full of teenagers and no prepared lesson for history that day, that teacher decided to shove on a video with a vague link to the subject: *The Most Haunted Places in Wales*. Ravencliffe had instantly caught my attention. I was already obsessed with my books by Stephen King and Peter Straub, tales of ghosts and demons and terror, and there, a two-and-a-half-hour drive away, sitting on the clifftop, was my very own horror film set. Strictly out of bounds. A ruin. A wreck. A challenge.

Caerphilly library isn't very busy on a Saturday morning. It is a Lego brick of a building, badly clad and badly insulated, the one big room carpeted in the scratchiest tiles available to humankind. It is soon to be abandoned for a shiny new structure in the town centre, a flagship place with its own witch's hat turret roof, all glinting glass and soft grey stone. The librarian is much warmer than the old heaters puffing out stale air around her. Dressed in big bright jumpers and fleecy boots, she reads a never-ending conveyor belt of detective crime fiction. Once I'd described the old hotel to her, she had tapped away on her computer and ordered in the documents now spread around me.

I am in my own little papery heaven.

'I can't believe I get to study the original architect's plans. See? It's not that far,' I say to Leo, who pushes his glasses up his nose and tries to stop paper from slithering to the floor. My friend since we were little, he is sweet-natured and soft-spoken, sharing my love of horror novels and obscure indie bands. Sharing everything, really. Rain runs in rivulets down the windows and beyond; there is mist and a hint of the mountain that broods over our town. 'A little road trip, a bit of filming, see what we can make out of it? It'll be fun.'

'West Wales? Old hotel? It'll be creepy. I love it . . . wait.' Here he makes a show of looking around and then under our table. 'You're sure Rich isn't coming? Sure he's not here right now? You two are, like, attached together nowadays . . .'

There is an edge to his voice that he doesn't try to hide. I am already regretting sleeping with Richard. Not the sex, the sex is good but . . . well, everything else. I sigh and give Leo a shove. I know exactly what Leo thinks of Rich because it is what I should be thinking of him, if only that weak, fluttering feeling in my stomach when I see him didn't get in the way.

'Very funny. No. This is just us. A Bex and Leo Double Feature.'

'Fright Night!'

Summer is that mountain outside the library window – it looms. We have sat our exams and now the only thing ahead of us is a prom where most of the girls in my year are planning to wear the tiniest amount of bejewelled material that they can get away with. We are free except for the reckoning day of our results. A haunted hotel in the middle of nowhere seems like the perfect way to take my mind off that. If I am lucky, I think, I might get eaten by ghouls and never have to face my father.

Because all that is left is not just results. All that is left is an entire future plotted by my parents: university degree, teaching qualification, teaching career, retirement, pension, burial. A map. My parents really like a map. When we go on holidays, the same holiday every year to a cottage in North Wales, we always take the same route and stop in the same service station at the exact mid-point, go to the same tourist spots and eat at the same restaurants. It is the missionary position of holiday-making.

This summer, though? This summer is a holding room, a waiting space before the next bit of our lives begin.

'I'll drive,' I say. 'You can be in charge of snacks and entertainment.'

Leo smiles. People say that someone's face lights up when they smile but that isn't what happens with Leo – he lights you up instead. I want to squeeze his baby cheeks. Out of everyone in our sixth form, Leo definitely looks the youngest with his smooth skin and big eyes. He will be asked for ID before buying a drink until he's probably in his forties.

'Haribo and jelly babies and chocolate mice! We can stop somewhere for a picnic. It'll be good to get out of the house.'

I'd met Leo's dad a few times. His mum had died recently and, well, his dad had kind of died with her too, really. I'm not sure he ever noticed what Leo was doing – he could have high-kicked his way into the living room wearing sequins and feather wings and his dad would have nodded and not taken his eyes from the television.

Something about Leo brings out the best in me, whatever I can call my best. So we plan and draw up a list of supplies and are generally having a great time until the library door swings open.

'Harrison!' Richard always does that – calls you by your surname or gives you some fool nickname like even your name is his to bloody control. He bows elaborately and then kisses my hand. 'At your service, m'lady.' Oscar follows him in.

I tell myself not to look at Rich. I can remember how much

of an idiot he is if I don't look into his eyes but that is hard when he has hold of my hand and then plonks his arm over my shoulder as he sits next to me, all floppy hair and well-developed forearms. I guess I am disappointed in myself. I always thought I'd be with a guy who was less . . . *Richard-ish* . . . about everything, someone who reads books and likes punk bands, but it seems my pheromones or hormones or chemistry or something thinks differently.

'Oh my God.' I wriggle my shoulder out from under him. He just smiles. He likes it when I am – in his words – spiky.

'You know you don't have to revise anymore, right?' Oscar flicks at a piece of paper. They have both come from a Saturday morning rugby match, still dressed in their sports kit, but Oscar's is too big for him, having once belonged to his older brother. Mike, the brother, is captain of every team, head boy, star student, raiser of money for charity, first of our school to go to Oxford. The brothers even look a bit similar except Oscar has more spots, bleached blonde hair and a nose that takes over his face. He will always be trying to fill out his brother's clothes.

'We—' I begin.

'It's nothing special.' Leo interrupts me and frowns in a way to remind me that this trip is just the two of us, the chocolate mice and our Panic! at the Disco CDs. He flips his lighter round and round in his hand, the only one of us who smokes. He believes it makes him look older than he seems, but he could have puffed on a pipe and worn a fake beard and he still would have looked about twelve.

'This is the old Ravencliffe place. We saw that vid on it in history, didn't we?' Oscar thumbs through paper, dragging the sheets out of order. I am surprised he remembers the hotel. 'The guy who shot himself?'

Richard takes a closer look at the mix of original documents and books we have been studying. 'Oh yeah . . . the owner, right? That place would look amazing on camera. You know, like one of those urban exploring adventures . . . I could do it as a Film Studies project for my uni course next year.' I note the way there is no uncertainty in Rich, no doubt that he will get the grades to do his fancy degree.

'Like *The Blair Witch Project*, yeah?' Oscar laughs and fiddles with one of the sheets of paper. 'Freaky bloody film.'

'I bet these two loved it though, didn't you? Witchcraft in the woods and all that. I bet it'd be your dream to go over to the hotel and, I don't know, try to' – here Rich puts on a deep voice – 'communicate with the spirits . . .' They both laugh again and Leo and I flick a little glance at each other which Rich catches. 'Hang on – is this what all of this is about? Are you planning a visit? A little jaunt . . . without me?'

'No,' says Leo.

'Bex?'

I cannot help myself. I am a moth. Rich is a dazzling light and I willingly bash myself into it, bash the sense out of my head and the control out of my tongue. I can see Leo's expression darken as I speak about what we are planning, our trip, but Richard's attention is a heady thing, like the last half of a cider bottle which you know is going to be empty soon and then all that's left is the hangover.

We lose control of the trip. By the end of that library session, Richard is driving, Oscar is planning a frankly hideous selection of R&B 'choons' and most of the boot space is likely to be taken up with beer.

'It's a good job we'll be there to protect you from the big scary monsters,' Oscar says.

'Oh yeah? You, protect me? The boy who can be defeated by a peanut?' I retort. Rich smiles and smacks Oscar in the shoulder, who blushes and shoots me a frown. Every year our school has EpiPen training paid for by Oscar's parents, which we don't mind because it means we miss a lesson; possibly being able to save Oscar's life is merely a by-product of that.

'Pinky promise to save me from the monsters, yeah?' I hold out my little finger to Leo, trying to bring him back to me, despite the fact I know I've done exactly the wrong thing by inviting these two on this trip that was meant to be the Bex and Leo Double Feature. I wish I could take back my words.

Leo does not offer his pinky finger in return.

After messing with the Ravencliffe research I had spread on the table, pretending to read it but really making paper aeroplanes out of some of the pages, Rich and Oscar leave, trailing a fug of Lynx deodorant in their wake. The clatter of rugby boots makes the librarian frown and Leo glares at me so hard I feel myself redden.

'Why did you do that? I thought the trip was just going to be us?'

'Leo—' But he stands and grabs his bag. It's natural, I remind myself, that he's a bit more clingy with me, after his mother dying, I get it. I should have patience, try to understand, but his next words infuriate me.

'I should've known,' Leo says. 'What do you even see in him? Well, yeah, I know what you see in him, just like all the other girls—'

'Hey—'

'—but I thought you had more sense.'

He leaves me with those stinging words. And there, sitting at the library table surrounded by all that information on Ravencliffe, I'm not scared of any monsters waiting for me at the hotel. No, what frightens me the most is that I might have lost Leo.

Chapter 13

The car had a new leather smell that was so overpowering Bex had to open her window. It was also huge, the kind of thing in which you could successfully survive a zombie apocalypse with room left over to set up a whole new civilisation afterwards.

Next to her, Holly deep-breathed into a brown paper bag.

'I'm so sorry. I get a bit travel sick,' she said between gulps, the bag inflating and deflating like a puffer fish.

'No problem.' Bex eyed the complimentary champagne. It was ten in the morning – who needed champagne at ten o'clock on a Wednesday? The Welsh countryside flashed past her, blobs of white sheep on fields so green it felt like they were a special effect of some kind. The land on her side was already dropping away into a vista of hills and valleys, stitched together by hedges, and she knew what that meant. It meant they were close. She pressed a button and the window whirred up.

To say things had happened quickly would be an understatement. June had turned to July and then flung itself into August. There had been a few days at a hotel, without Holly, to allow her to tie up any loose ends that Bex did not have. Her house and her plants were sorted, her mother already settled in with her box of Mills & Boon and her steam mop, ready to spring clean the whole place so hard she would involve all the other seasons too. Bex's bland hotel room had become a train and then this car and the sound of a paper bag crinkling. Out of curiosity, Bex peeked to see if the champagne was open. It was.

Holly made a retching sound, her voice muffled by the bag. 'Oh God, so sorry. I think it's the dark glass on the windows, it's making it worse.'

If the champagne was open, then it would only go flat if no one drank it, Bex thought as she picked up the bottle to read the label. It looked expensive. After all, she was unlikely to ever again find herself in a chauffeur-driven car loaded with free alcohol. Might as well take advantage of it.

'Want some?' There were glasses too, not the plastic kind you brought to picnics. She pinged the glass to check and then had to ping them another three times to make four. Four was safe. Bex needed safe for this trip. 'Are you even old enough to drink?'

Holly raised her face from the paper bag. She wore a pale foundation so it was hard to tell if her skin was that colour through choice or sickness. 'Oh – yes, I'm eighteen.' As Bex went to pour a second glass, Holly stopped her hand. 'But no, thank you. I'm on work hours. And also, I don't think it'll help my travel sickness.'

'Fair point.' Bex topped up her own glass some more and then took a sip. It was dry and crisp and tasted as expensive as the bottle looked.

'I wear all the bands and it doesn't do a bit of good.' Holly offered her wrist to Bex who saw it was indeed full of elastic and magnetic bands. The rest of her outfit made her look like a depressed bee, striped black-and-white tights under a black pinafore minidress. 'I've even taken some herbal thing that's meant to help . . . it smells of old socks. Sorry. Anyway! Itinerary. But before I start can I just say again—'

'No.'

'Oh. Right . . .'

'If you say it's an honour to meet me one more time, I may have to . . . I don't know, pull your nose or something.'

'Right. Sorry. Okay then. It's just, the film – I mean, I've seen it so many times, and all my friends have too, I mean we weren't old enough to see it first time around, which really sucks, but it's our favourite horror film of all time. It's not fake, yeah? Oh, and Ravencliffe, I mean that is just the perfect place – it's on a cliff and there's those statues, oh and the maze and the things that happened there when it was being built, I mean—'

'If you say "I mean" one more time I will pull your nose too.'

'Ah. Sorry—'

'Oh God, stop saying sorry!'

There was a pause and then Holly cast her a sideways glance. 'Would it be easier if you write down all the things I might say that could annoy you? It'll probably save us time.'

For a second Bex thought she was being serious but then she saw Holly's face. She laughed, despite herself. 'You'd end up silent.' Holly smiled.

The first glass of champagne had disappeared with speed. A second would be fine because the stuff was mostly bubbles and therefore largely made of air, hardly any alcohol at all. The only way to get through this filming would be to ride it on a wave of fizzing, sparkling inebriation.

'Some things for you to know. We've secured Jasper St Clare to be the host of the reunion show. In fact, he contacted us—'

'I bet he did.'

Jasper St Clare. In his stupid swivelling seat with his smug smile and calculating stare. She actually couldn't remember much about the original interview the three of them did with him only a few months after the film came out, that time was merely static on her radio waves. But she did remember the way those beads pinged off his unnaturally plastic skin, how good it had felt to flick her finger and send them hurtling towards him. The shape of those beads had reminded her of a chandelier at Ravencliffe, teardrops with wicked pointed ends. It was a memory that ended in blood. Only a few days after that interview she had holed herself up in her house with the wall, all offers of interviews, appearances, sponsorship, sequels and merchandising firmly and without any trace of doubt – declined.

'He's very excited, apparently.' Holly tapped something on her phone. Her fingernails had little cobwebs painted onto them.

'I'm assuming wardrobe isn't going to give me anything beaded to wear?'

Holly nodded, all seriousness. 'It was in your notes. We're mostly dressing you in a straitjacket. Designer, obviously.'

Bex gave Holly a good long look; Goth Barbie had some personality under all of that make-up. She got herself comfortable in the leather seat, deciding that she might just enjoy some of this girl's company if she could keep up the snark. The champagne bottle couldn't have been that big because it emptied far too quickly and those bubbles began to go straight to the blood capillaries in her face. She slipped her jacket off her shoulders, unsure how much time had passed. There were a lot of buttons on her passenger door so it was a complete guess when she hit on the right one to open the window. The dark glass whirred down, a black curtain dropping to the floor, the theatre show about to begin because there, on the cliff top, was a nightmare made of brick and marble and stone.

The hotel.

Chapter 14

Luckily, the car travelled a lonely stretch of road so, when it stopped with a jerk and the passenger door flew open, there was no other traffic to worry about.

Bex fell to her knees on the tarmac by a grassy verge. Palm flat on the rough surface she told herself that the ground was right there, that she had not been tilted and tipped upside down, that some great hand had not rummaged about in her insides and then grasped her heart so hard she felt her eyes were going to pulse out of her head.

'Breathe, breathe.' Holly's voice was very far away and that made sense because the car was so big, she probably couldn't get round it, but then Bex felt warm fingers press over hers and realised that the girl had to be much nearer than she thought. The pressure on her hand was good, she needed all the ballast she could get. 'Calm breaths . . . in . . . and out . . . in . . . and out . . .'

Bex did as she was told, counting in groups of four until each time she got to the fourth count she felt a little calmer. Each breath loosened that grip on her heart, each one made her feel heavier and heavier until she felt safe enough to take one palm off the ground without floating away like a tattered feather.

In hindsight, the champagne had probably been a mistake.

A straw pushed itself at her lips. 'Here, you need to drink something other than alcohol.' Bex dutifully sipped. 'This is my fault. I should never have let you finish the whole bottle and then, I didn't realise we were so close – oh God, I'm a terrible assistant! You should ask for a new one . . .'

Holly spoke many more words but Bex could not keep up with them as they tumbled over her. If she kept her head down, she would not have to see it again but it didn't matter: she knew it was there, that it had already sensed her, like a bird of prey spotting something delicious in the grass below.

'I'm fine.' She slumped off her knees and sat on the ground, drawing her legs under her chin. Holly crouched next to her, big wide eyes made comic by that flamboyantly awful eyeliner.

'Look, I mean – we're meant to go to . . . that place . . . straight away. There's a trailer set up for you, they've cleared room for a camp so we can stay on-site the whole time but . . . I'm not sure, maybe you'd want to . . .' Holly tapped on her phone. 'Look, there's a B&B close, I mean, you don't have to, but we could take the night, re-group, start afresh in the morn—'

'Yes.'

* * *

Bex had never seen so many novelty teapots. She and Holly sat in the guest lounge surrounded by a horde of china, held back by the glass of the display cabinets.

'There's a Marilyn.'

'A Dalek.'

'Laurel and Hard . . . tea . . .'

'Is that meant to be . . . Einstein?'

To achieve this tannin oasis, Holly had had a whispered discussion on her mobile phone and Bex had hoped it was Marsha on the other end having to bend to someone else's view of what a 'peaceful and nourishing environment' looked like, even if it was for only one evening.

A tiny old lady wearing a massive set of pearls that could probably have been wrapped around her waist two times came in with nominal control of the tray she held.

'Here, Mrs Bloom, let me.' Bex bounded over and rescued the cups and saucers before they ended up on the teapot-print carpet.

'I didn't want to send you girls off to bed without a little refreshment. And call me Miriam.' Miriam tapped Bex's hand away as soon as she had placed the tray on a table, busying herself with pouring and steeping and swilling. Her accent was smudged by a soft Welsh burr. 'You were lucky I had a room free, my lovelies.'

Bex imagined a Mr Bloom, hastily chucking teapots out into the corridor to get to the bed in the now-booked room. This B&B was on the same coastline a little further down from Ravencliffe, set just above a row of holiday cottages. The coast reared up from there to the cliff where the hotel stood, now only a faint black outline against a blacker sky. A floor-to-ceiling picture window gave a view of the wide beachy smile of Poppit Sands and beyond it the Irish Sea, moody clouds bullying a white-faced moon. Bex knew this jagged bit of coast. It was ingrained into her brain like an etching, knife-sharp: the dark, pockmarked rocks and hidden coves carved by hungry waves, the boom of water and the scream of gulls.

Bex drank the tea from a cup so delicate she was afraid that holding it too tightly would crack the porcelain. For Mrs Bloom, tea was not a hasty teabag in a mug, no, there was a mini milk jug, a silver sugar bowl with tiny tongs, a plate of biscuits and each of them had doll-house-sized spoons to stir their brew. Bex was a bit disappointed that their teapot was plain white.

'We're only here for the one night, we're doing some filming up at the hotel.' Holly dropped a sugar cube into her cup, stirred and then chinked the spoon against the side of her cup.

'Ah, yes, the old Morwood place. I heard all that brouhaha was starting up again.' Mrs Bloom perched on the edge of an armchair. Bex wondered if Holly knew what 'brouhaha' meant. 'Not that I'm in a position to mind. We still get visitors every year, young people who look a bit like you, missy.' Here she looked at Holly and made a vague gesture to her face, her black dress, striped knee socks and clumpy boots. 'Of course, the Coast Path runs along the edge of the land, so we get ramblers too, decked out in all their gear. They can't get in though, site's been fenced off for almost as long as the film's been out. Expensive fences too. Bats, apparently.'

'Bats?' Bex had lost the thread a bit and was imagining construction bats in hard hats knocking up some fences . . . awkwardly because their wings kept getting in the way.

'Protected species, I heard. They're roosting somewhere on the grounds, though if your lot are filming there again then something must have been worked out.'

'Yes. I heard Marsha talking about that.' Holly took a biscuit. 'The inspector's had to check no bat roosts were being disturbed. All clear.'

When Mrs Bloom left, giving them a smile and telling them to stay up and gossip for as long as they wanted, Bex fiddled with the sugar tongs. 'Sorry . . . about this.'

Holly stretched her legs out onto a waiting footstool. It had a spout. 'And miss out on this teapot utopia? You did us a favour . . . but seriously, I get it. It's a weird, disorientating thing that you're doing, y'know, after everything that happened . . . it's a bit like that scene in the film where Richard gets really anxious, when it's just the two of you—' Holly's words stuttered to a stop in the face of Bex's frown. 'But . . . umm, yeah, you were there, so you don't need to . . .' Holly cast about for a change of subject. 'Oh look, that one's an Elvis! Elvis Pres-tea!'

For a while they sat, benignly watched over by painted eyes.

'I'll talk to Marsha. Make sure you don't get into any trouble,' Bex said, twiddling her tiny spoon. 'And thank you.'

'No problemo.'

'I'll get my shit together tomorrow, I promise.'

'Ah, don't sweat it. Enjoy the teapots. Maybe drink a bit less champagne though, even if it's free?'

'Wise.'

That night Bex tried to sleep under a thick, garishly patterned duvet in a frilly room where even the headboard was swathed in a flouncy fabric. This may have been one night's reprieve but she could not put it off any longer. Despite her best efforts, she couldn't help but think about how it had all started back when they had been eighteen and about to get into a boat that would take them to the hotel. Whether she was ready or not, the car would come for her tomorrow and she would have to face her past, and all the ghosts that waited there.

Chapter 15

Bex, ten years ago

Standing on the jetty that night, with a strip of sea in between me and the hotel I'd read so much about, I can already tell that the boat is going to be too small for all the male ego about to be packed into it.

'Are you just going to stand there?' Richard aims this at Leo, as he lugs his rucksack into the boat. My boat. I found it, got it from a friend of my dad's who was into fishing and lived near the hotel: a scraped and battered thing with an engine that coughed consumptively. He had left it for us, tied to the small jetty facing the opposite shore where the hotel clung to the cliff.

Leo hangs back.

'What's he meant to do? You're in the way.' I give Richard a nudge. He is wearing a thick, dark woollen coat, an item of clothing more suited to a crisp city night, not this secretive jaunt to an abandoned place. At least there is a beanie hat stuffed into his pocket. The jetty on this side is nothing more than some planks of wood a few minutes from the bunkhouse where we stayed and we are all trying to get our stuff into the small boat, stepping on each other's toes.

I may have lost all control of the trip but I refuse to be the pathetic girl, the nervous one, too afraid to do stuff. If the boys are going to do something, then I will too – in a better outfit and with good hair. My purple boots are the perfect style for stomping and that is what I want to do – stomp all over this great wasteland of a summer between sixth form and university. We have all done Media Studies for A level, so we think this qualifies us to be the next Quentin Tarantino ready to play about with cameras in the supposedly haunted hotel.

Around us, light drains from the sky as the sun sets. It is a time for shadows and whispers and the rustling of small things in the undergrowth that are waiting to bite.

'Think we'll see Reggie himself, stumbling around with his ghostly brains half hanging out, waiting to kill us for trespassing on his land?' Oscar throws his bag into the boat and jumps in after it, sprawling on one of the benches set into the side of the vessel. Reginald Morwood, the man who built the hotel and then, when it all went wrong for him, shot himself in his study. I feel sorry for the servant who had to clean up his brain splatter from the wall afterwards.

'Well, he'll definitely spot you with that hair.'

'Fuck off, Bex,' Oscar says, the tips of his bleached blonde dye job almost gleaming by the light of the moon. He likes to think he is stylish. The rest of us disagree. To anyone looking at us it would seem as if we are great friends. Unified. But it isn't like that. It always has been Richard and Oscar. Leo and me. Two sets of people made into an uneasy four.

I follow Oscar, keeping the wobble out of my stance as the boat rocks beneath me because there is no way I am going to look even a tiny bit weak, a tiny bit vulnerable, a tiny bit girlie on this trip. Richard has tried to get me to wear just a vest under my leather biker, which is ridiculous. It may be summertime, but it's summer in *Wales*. At night. In an old, cold building. I know he's just looking to get a shot of my nipples poking through the thin material. Sod that. I'm wearing a vest, but it is a thermal one and I've got a jumper on over it. Richard had sighed when he'd first seen me.

'Come on, Leo my boy, jump in.' Richard holds out his hand for Leo to climb aboard after me and then takes it away just as Leo leans his weight towards him, making him lose his balance. He nearly goes head-first into the bags on the floor of the boat but I step in and catch him by the shoulder.

'You can be a real dick – Dick,' I say as Leo ignores me. His bright green raincoat looks like an outfit you would choose for a five-year-old to go splashing in puddles, and a book pokes out of its pocket. We are still not on the best of terms after that day in the library, though at least he didn't pull out of the trip altogether.

'I'm okay, it was just a joke.' Leo shrugs and looks for confirmation from Richard, who smiles and drapes an arm around his shoulder. It has to be a pheromone of some sort, I think, watching Richard ruffle Leo's hair and then turn his attention to his camera. There has to be some sort of subconscious cell-level something going on that makes me still feel a bit like my internal plane has dipped suddenly when he looks my way. It isn't even about a bad-boy phase because Richard really isn't a bad boy – merely an arrogant, careless one.

'Wagons roll!' Oscar yells as Richard turns the key in the ignition and the boat's motor hems and haws and finally decides to spring into life. There is another route in from the mainland, but it's a steep climb along a path now claimed back by the forest, easy to get lost in and hard terrain: too hard for us. We have no choice but to walk up the steps from the hotel's old jetty. Of course, to make life easy, we could hike across Poppit Sands and then use the Coast Path to get to the hotel but Rich is not interested in easy. He wants adventure, something that looks good on film, and a boat ride does that. It will be a twenty-minute journey from the jutting tip of the cliff where our bunkhouse is over to the curve of coastline that holds the hotel.

'Do you know how to steer a motorboat?' I ask, because I do. My dad had taken me fishing sometimes, possibly in this very boat.

'Yeah. Watched a vid. Point it at the steps and we're good.'

I leave him to it. Oscar has a camera: 'Should we, like, introduce ourselves, for the watchers?' Typical Oscar, dying to talk about himself.

'No!' Richard yells above the sound of the engine. 'This is organic, fluid . . . this is natural. We do what we feel, in the moment.'

'Well . . . *in the moment* I want to introduce myself.'

Richard and Oscar had provided the cameras, two of them. Richard's one was, of course, much more expensive. I had suggested simply filming on our phones and had been met with a barrage of reasons I should be ashamed of myself, as a prospective Film Studies student, for thinking something like that. 'Only an amateur would film on their phone, Bex.' This had been followed by a lot of talk about camera specifications and I had zoned out.

The water slaps against the boat, sending little sprays that I let my hand trail through. I am tired and grouchy from two nights of bad sleep, the four of us in a bunkhouse room, the closest affordable place to Ravencliffe. Richard had made it sound like a holiday but sharing a room with three boys is not the kind of holiday that has ever appealed to me. I am sure I smell of hair gel and Lynx Africa. Even Oscar had sensed my annoyance and dragged Leo off for some 'sightseeing', as he had called it, the day before: 'Give the lovebirds a bit of time to themselves, eh?' he had said. It would have been better if he'd taken Richard and left Leo with me.

'No one's going to see this, apart from maybe some university admissions tutor . . .' I say.

'What would you rather be doing, Bex? Worrying about what

your parents will say when they realise you're not going to get straight As?' Richard calls back to me.

Bastard. He always knows which buttons to push, the good and the bad ones. Results Day is coming for me and it is safe to say that I've lost my grip on my studies. I could blame Richard for that but I'm master of my own ship and I'd screwed up its course all on my own. I'm probably not going to fail, but I am definitely going to be mediocre. My dad does not like average, especially when it comes to grades.

The last of the sun's fire leaves the sky and the darkness creeps in. It is a darkness that seems to come from the very cliff itself, a black, forbidding wall of rock that towers over us the closer our little boat gets to it. But I feel no premonition of danger, no chill hand of fear holding me back. There is nothing to suggest that this night is going to be anything other than cold and a bit tedious whilst we watch Richard try to get some arty tracking shots of abandoned rooms and weed-choked gardens.

After around twenty minutes we reach the small jetty. It would once have been polished and primed ready for the private boats of the select few Victorian holiday-makers who could afford the most expensive suites, hoping for a peaceful break at the Ravencliffe Hotel. Beyond us is the crashing expanse of the Irish Sea. The waves are so loud, a booming possibly amplified by the hollow cove where the jetty sits, and the noise fills my head.

Richard jumps up ready to wind the rope around a waiting stump whilst the rest of us hoist bags and the two cameras we have brought with us. Snaking away up the cliff are the steps cut into rock.

'Shit.' Oscar's gaze takes in the cliff face and the steps cut into it, steps that wind all the way up to the building at the top, past little plunge pools and the remains of flowerbeds. He pales, I think, though it is hard to tell under the fake tan.

'You okay?' Leo stops and turns to him, frowning.

'I didn't think it'd be . . .' Oscar gestures weakly at the cliff.

'I told you about the steps!' I sigh. 'I said we'd have to go up them. It's a cliff, Oscar – how else d'you think we were getting up there?'

Oscar takes a step back and scratches at his throat like he is struggling to get a good breath.

'Bex!' Leo shoots me an angry look and goes over to Oscar. 'He can't help it, can he?'

Vertigo. We all know Oscar is scared of heights, ever since we were twelve and we had been taken on one of those school activity weekends. When we tried abseiling, Oscar had spent the entire time clinging on to a bit of rock, sweat dripping from his chin whilst Leo, who had aced that particular activity, bounced around him like a friendly spider on a web, trying to get him to move.

'I . . . can't . . .'

'Look, how about you stay with the boat, yeah?' Leo pats his arm. 'I mean, I was always a bit worried about just leaving it here unattended. You can make sure it's all ready for us when we get back. See, there's a blanket for you and you can read my copy of *The Shining* whilst we're gone. It's good. It's scary.'

'Perfect!' Richard is already bored and itching to get going. 'Scaredy-cat Oz here will wait with the boat. Let's go.'

'Wait. Your phones. You haven't brought them, right?' Oscar asks. We all shake our heads.

The mobile phone issue had been discussed before we set off. 'There won't be any signal,' Oscar had said, 'so it's a waste of rucksack space bringing them. Leave them at home.' I had been about to point out that they don't exactly take up that much room when Richard had got in on the discussion. 'Bringing your phone to the haunted house is hardly in the spirit of the thing, is it? Not very *raw* . . . or *real* . . . and anyway, I have the perfect solution!'

Back in the boat, Richards smiles. 'Why use a phone when we get to use *these*?' He rummages in his rucksack and hands out walkie-talkies with the enthusiasm of a Boy Scout leader. Actual walkie-talkies like we're six.

'Rich—'

'Nope. I won't hear a word against these. These, my friends, are cool. You should be thanking me for bringing them.'

Only I know that my phone is tucked into the bottom of my rucksack. Even if it doesn't currently have any signal – I feel better for knowing it is there.

We pick up our bags and torches. We have those ones that strap around our heads, like miners, but it messes up my hair so I shove it in my pocket and use a handheld one instead.

'Here we are.' Richard speaks for the camera. 'Ready to face the curse. Personally, if the vengeful spirit of Reginald is watching us tonight, wanting to claim a soul as penance for trespassing on his land, I'd like to ask him to take Leo first. Easy meat.'

'Hey!' I punch his arm and he grins. Leo rolls his eyes. Jumping from the end of the jetty onto a wide flat rock, Rich swings his rucksack onto his shoulder and takes the first step up.

We are prepared. We have our stuff and our bags and our cameras and our silly stories of curses and legends. The night lies ahead of us, dark as a ripe plum waiting to be bitten. I begin to climb.

Chapter 16

Bex, ten years ago

Below the three of us is the boat, bobbing in a squid ink sea. Oscar makes Richard take shots of him in a pensive mood, one hand on the motor, before we leave him behind. The steps are a very long, winding way, taking us on a steep path through desiccated gardens and a few small, blue-tiled pools with plants creeping up through the mortar. There are the jagged remains of the spindles that would have held up a low stone wall meant to stop unwary guests from toppling off the steps to their doom. In Morwood's head when he had been designing this part of his hotel, he had imagined elegant relaxation, people wandering through the colourful flowers, lazing in the pool and watching the sea.

I know. I have done my research. Though my grades have slipped a bit this year, I have always loved being able to take notes, colour-coding things with an array of highlighters. I had to give the architect's plans and old papers on the building of the hotel back to the library but I made copies, and I discovered a local internet history site dedicated to the place. I downloaded old letters from Morwood to his acquaintances, telling them of his big plans – so much paper, I had only read about half of it.

Around us the wind howls. It wants to push us off our perch, make us plummet and end up splashes of red blood on slick wet rock.

I don't believe in ghosts but I have read enough horror novels to know that places soak up human emotion, and, over time, that can fester, warp and twist with age into something . . . malignant. Amityville, The Overlook, Hill House. That's why I want to go to the hotel, to feel a bit of something like that because I've never felt it before. Experiences. I want to experience everything all at once, and the world has so much of everything, I feel like I'll never get through it all.

But Richard is only interested in my nipples. 'This is the spot. *The* spot! I need a money shot.'

The money shot. Honestly, he really does think he is Tarantino.

'I'm not taking my jacket off, you total perv,' I yell to him as I round the corner of the highest step, looking up at him and not my feet. 'And anyway, you know that if I did, I'm wearing a T-shirt bra under my jumper so there wouldn't be any nipples on show, no matter how cold the wind is.'

He shrugs and smiles in a way that is meant to show he is being ironic and cool. 'Can't help it if I think my girlfriend's attractive and want to show it off, can I?' There is quite a bit wrong with this sentence, mostly the 'my girlfriend' bit. I lost my virginity to Richard, but that was a choice made because he looked clean and smelled good and had a bit of a glint in his eye. No big deal. Some girls make a massive fuss of the whole event, like it is life-changing or something. I don't want to be his girlfriend. I don't want to be anyone's girlfriend – that seems like a lot of work I'd rather not put in. 'I'll have to provide the nipple shot myself . . .' Richard takes off his jacket and puffs out his chest, pouting a little.

Leo doesn't laugh. 'Peter Manning died here.' He turns away from the sea and faces the hotel.

'You know there's another story, right?' I say, catching an opportunity to get Leo's interest so at least he'll have to bloody look at me. I know all about Peter Manning, the tragic carpenter who fell to his death from the edge of this lawn, a victim of the bad luck that dogged this place during its build.

'Hmm?' Richard isn't listening but twisting the lens on his camera.

'About Peter Manning. That he didn't fall – but was pushed.'

Leo is determined to avoid my gaze, but that bit of information gets Richard's attention. 'Say that again. I'll film it.'

I stand on the final set of steps, feeling a bit silly at having to repeat myself. 'It is rumoured that Peter Manning did not fall to his death in a tragic accident from this lawn outside the ballroom window. No, the rumour is . . .' I pause for the camera, '. . . that he was pushed.'

'By who?'

'Well, that's where it becomes a bit hazy. As a pretty uncaring English boss, Morwood was really annoyed by his workers speaking Welsh on-site, thought they could be talking about him or plotting things behind his back and so he banned it. Peter Manning was the leader of a group of workers who refused to obey that, which got him in Morwood's bad books. Some of the accounts say that Peter was a pain in the neck though – flirting with the maids who had arrived to start cleaning the place up ready for visitors. He could have argued with one of his fellow co-workers, or maybe he owed them money – they liked to play poker in the temporary worker camps set up around the hotel.'

I stare down at the churning sea beyond the rocks at the bottom of the cliff, imagining how Peter's small, splayed body rimmed with red would have looked. And, up here, standing where we are, another figure gazing down at their work with the lingering feel of Peter's shoulder blades on their palms after giving him a hard shove.

I have read pretty much every Stephen King I can get my

hands on, soft paperback copies, floppy with age from the library, and chewed through the classics and then the total traumatising weirdness of Clive Barker and all sorts of stuff in between. I am well equipped to come up with a hundred gory theories as to what really happened to Peter Manning.

'Well, RIP, Pete old boy, however you died.' Richard sweeps the camera around to view the hotel stretching up away from us. 'Now – the main event.'

I am so busy gawping at the building looming over us that I don't notice the small pebble I stand on that sends my foot sliding out from under me. As I wobble, I realise with a shock of fear that I am far too close to the edge of the step and the rucksack I'm wearing helps throw me further off balance. There hasn't been time to put my walkie-talkie away and it falls out of my grasp as I yelp and glance at it tumbling down before smashing onto the rocks below. I wonder if I'm about to follow it.

Then a hand clasps mine. My gaze meets serious, bespectacled eyes. 'Okay?'

Leo. I nod. He drags me away from the edge and I could hug him but he's already off, leading us as we climb the final steps. I try to take a deep breath. Waves crash and boom and the noise gets under my skin, into my head and the cavity of my rib cage, the constant rush of sound making me dizzy.

'The walkie-talkie!' Richard shouts. 'You've lost it! I borrowed those!' He pauses and sighs. 'Try not to get yourself killed before we even start, Harrison.'

My brain snags on a phrase I read in one of the local history books about the hotel. A bad luck place, they had called it. My heart hammers in agreement as I push my way through what had once been the back lawn but is now a jungle of tall grasses, the scratchy fronds sticking to our clothes, rustling and swaying in the rhythm of the wind. When Leo reaches the huge window of the restaurant and ballroom he pauses and puts a hand to the glass.

Ravencliffe is mostly a normal hotel built on top of the cliff but then it spills down the cliff face with a few luxury suites and the ballroom/restaurant built out from the rock in levels leading down to those gardens, the pools and the steps. For guests arriving from the dock there is an entrance set next to the ballroom, though the main reception is at the front of the building facing that Italian stone fountain that had never even been switched on.

Richard puts his shoulder to the door. The door ignores him. It is a warped, hefty chunk of iron-braced wood. Richard has never liked being ignored – he kicks it.

'There are steps leading up but . . . oh . . .' Leo trails off.

We consider the steps that would have led up to the top of the cliff and the front of the hotel. Whether someone has deliberately done it, to stop people accessing the place from the cliff, or whether it is the hand of Father Time and Mother Nature, the rest of the steps are a wreckage of boulders and rubble.

It is Richard's decision to break the glass. As he picks up a rock from the broken steps, I have a wild impulse to stay his hand. The ballroom windows have withstood the elements and this cruel wind for over a hundred years and with one swift movement a callow eighteen-year-old breaks all of that. The glass cracks but I feel, still reeling from my accident, a weirdly superstitious prickle that something else cracks with it this night – something we should never break.

We enter the hotel.

Chapter 17

Stone eyes watched Bex and Holly get out of the car. There was more sky than Bex remembered – and the daytime did not help, it did not brighten the moss and cracked glass, the broken tiles and weed-choked gravel. This hotel was a night creature, and it did not like having a light shone upon it.

'Bex.'

Standing at the gates were the mummy and daddy of this monstrous child of a reunion show: Marsha and Jasper. Marsha wore her signature red frames, her hair a snowcap on the oil slick of her fashionably baggy black leather dress. Jasper was exactly the same as the night Bex had thrown beads at him, but that was only to be expected as plastic does not wrinkle. He wore a puffer jacket and boots that could have been used to trek the Arctic, having taken to heart the warning that summer could be changeable on a clifftop in this part of the country.

There was a new security fence stretching away from the old gateposts, marking out the territory owned by Echelon Pictures. They had bought the hotel and its environs around nine years ago, the statement at the time emphasising that it was to stop trespassers trying to gain access and prevent accidents. The Wales Coast Path that allowed walkers to skirt the very edge of the cliff at the back of the hotel had been temporarily closed for filming in the interests of public safety. No one wanted a photographer tumbling into the sea in the pursuit of trying to get an exclusive picture. On the drive in, Holly had pointed out the news crews and paparazzi stationed at the foot of the hill, on the edge of public land.

'So happy to finally see you.' Marsha came forward. Bex could not work out if she had given the word 'finally' an extra emphasis. 'Don't mind the security. There's a lot of interest in what we're filming and, well, we want to keep everything under wraps. Do look out for Artemis, our trained eagle; she will be taking out any unauthorised drone technology during our stay.' Bex glanced up at an eagle-free sky. 'Needless to say, we won't be allowing anyone to film or record anything themselves.' Marsha held out a lockable metal box. 'Everyone's phones and devices are to be locked away until we leave, though of course they can be used to keep in contact with loved ones under supervised conditions. This is very much the epitome of a closed set.'

'An actual eagle?' Holly shaded her eyes and stared at the sky.

'Police forces in Europe have been training them for years, with some success.'

'Some?'

'Well, they are eagles, after all. But we do not need to worry. Artemis is the very best, highly intelligent and highly trained. Only paparazzi camera drones need to worry.'

Bex and Holly dropped their phones into the box and Holly picked up a walkie-talkie from a nearby table, the old-style technology a reminder of the ones the three of them had carried around the hotel on their first visit. Holly's Goth Barbie look seemed to be a permanent style-choice. Today she wore a pair of black jeans hung with chains, her clumpy boots and another Ravencliffe T-shirt, this one a limited edition from a RavenCon a year or so ago; on it an ornate sketch of the chandelier from the ballroom, dripping in blood. Her elfin features were heavily laid over with foundation and that thick eyeliner, making a cartoon version of her face.

Jasper held out his arms to Bex, as much as his over-padded coat would allow.

'Aren't you worried I might start throwing things at you?' Bex said.

'I had extra danger money written into my contract.' His smile was the same: white and sharp and waiting to pounce.

Around them, the grounds had been cleared and the production crew camp had rolled in. The original workers who built the place would once have stayed in canvas tents but instead there were now trailers for wardrobe and cast, a food truck and various covered spaces, the roofs snapping and slapping in the wind as people busied themselves with equipment, cabling, lighting and wires. Bex watched them work. Everything and anything could be a clue and she had to be alert, not get swamped by the memories the place brought back to her, but swim through them, trying to spot the secrets in the underwater murk. Her first thing to do would be to get back down to those steps.

'Look.' Bex came closer to Jasper, enough to be engulfed by his aftershave. 'I don't think I apologised at the time, but I should have. I'm sorry—'

'No need . . . I probably deserved it.' Jasper's expression was almost soft but then that mischief came back into his eyes. 'And it made great telly. Our show's highest viewing figures. Bought me a yacht.'

Holly, who had been monitoring this exchange, tugged on Bex's arm before she could do anything she definitely wouldn't regret. 'Come on. We have orientation.'

* * *

There stood the hotel. A place of nightmares, a place *in* many of Bex's nightmares and a nightmare made real in stone. The carved creatures were forever stilled, crumbling at the edges a little more; the glass was fractured and dirty, each arch on the windows a raised eyebrow, a calculating stare. She came to the doorway. The door was open, the steps pitted and scratched, framing the scene within.

It felt like the moment, ten years before, when Richard had broken the pane so they could climb into the ballroom, the glass shattering along with their lives. Now there was nothing left to break: her, Leo, the future she'd thought she'd have – it had all cracked and fallen away. If she wanted to piece some of it back together, well then, her feet were going to have to take her over this threshold.

Inside was dim and cool, the air heavy with mould and decay. Holly handed her a hard hat, which she put on. Light streamed in through the tall front windows, the dust dancing in their spotlight. On the ceiling two floors up was a silvery painted moon and stars, now even more dimmed with age, but the grand staircase in the middle had kept its sweeping beauty, sending a swirl of steps and landings up and around to each of the floors above their heads.

A large group had formed around Marsha standing on a crate.

'Reverence.' The word was soft and the pause after it unnaturally long. The man next to her took a peek at something on a clipboard and scribbled a few notes. 'This is the word I want you to have in your hearts as we film over the next few days. Reverence. A deep respect for something . . . for someone . . . for Leo.' Bex wanted to reach out and pluck his name from Marsha's mouth, get her hand right down her throat until her eyes bulged and it wasn't just because of what she was saying. What she was saying was right. But the way she stood, surveying the people before her, her hands clasped together like she was a preacher – she was enjoying it. It was her moment. Not his.

As if on cue, at the mention of Leo's name, the lights around them flickered with a low fizzing sound.

'Sorry! Generator's a bit temperamental!' A voiced yelled from the back of the room as they blazed once more but Bex preferred to think of it as Leo's ghost expressing his annoyance with Marsha in the only way he could.

Marsha flicked a glance at the studio light positioned not too far from her and then continued, 'This place is not simply a location, it is not a film set. This place is a memorial. For those of you who do not know the history, Peter Manning, a carpenter who fell to his death here. Reginald Morwood, the owner who shot himself. Leo Finch whose body has never been found. We must strive every hour to elevate this experience above merely a few days' work. We must honour the memory of the spirits here; we must keep their names and their lives and their deaths in our hearts the entire time. In fact, I would like you all to bow your heads and we will take a minute to reflect in silence on what we are about to do.'

Marsha held her arms out and closed her eyes as if summoning the holy spirit. Bex put her hand in her pocket and felt the familiar edges of Leo's lighter as she searched out Richard and Oscar who stood on the opposite side to her, each one with his own version of Holly at his elbow. She caught Richard's eye. The two of them kept their heads unbowed whilst Oscar nearly dislocated neck bones in his eagerness to be the most reverent in the room. She couldn't guess what Richard was thinking from his expression – they had never been one of those couples who could communicate via glances.

'Thank you.' Marsha opened her eyes again and smiled. 'Thank you. I can feel that this is going to be a momentous time for all of us. We are going to do excellent work. Now' – a business-like edge entered her voice – 'some housekeeping. Health and safety. This is an old building, in disrepair. I do not want anyone to get hurt. Please follow the signs. Some rooms and staircases are inaccessible as are parts of the grounds. Please wear your hard hat at all times unless you have been told to remove it for filming . . .'

Bex took the opportunity to move away whilst Holly had a

whispered conversation with a young man wearing many lanyards. She skirted the fountain and the maze, which had, when she had first come here, been a huge overgrown tangle of yew hedge but had been cut back, presumably for this filming. Then she headed to the side steps that provided access to the cliff gardens and the steep path to the jetty. Ten years ago those steps had been rubble, possibly deliberately damaged to limit trespassers but now, Bex noted, they had been roughly rebuilt.

A locked metal gate blocked her way.

Bex sighed. She needed to get down there somehow and have a look around for all the things she had missed that night when she had first visited.

A shadow fell over her and Bex heard Marsha's voice. 'Sorry. We have to closely supervise any activity on the steps. We don't want any more . . . accidents . . .'

'So we won't be filming down there at all?' From where she stood she could see choppy waves, each crest of white a gleaming smile, taunting her. She desperately needed to get down to those paths. Already her plan for this day was being thwarted.

'Certainly not, far too dangerous. Our filming schedule begins in earnest tomorrow, bright and early. With that in mind we are holding a special cast and crew welcome meal in the reception hall tonight, to fuel us for the days ahead.'

'Oh. That sounds . . .' Awful. Marginally worse than poking out her own eyes. 'Lovely . . . but I think I'll get an early night, do some meditation in my trailer.'

She had hoped that mentioning meditating would help her case, but Marsha pressed her lips together and let her fingers rest on Bex's arm, not a touch really, just the pretence of one. 'I think you'll join us, yes? You, Richard and Oscar, you're our honoured guests. It will look very odd if you don't attend. So, I'll see you there.'

Bex would have preferred to have spent her time tracing her steps, following the route they had taken ten years ago through the hotel, reminding herself of what happened and where, searching for answers. Marsha turned, heading in the direction of the maze with her walkie-talkie crackling at her hip before stopping and calling behind her, 'Oh, and the meal will, of course, be filmed.'

Brilliant, Bex thought as she watched Martha walk away. Just brilliant.

Chapter 18

'When shall we three meet again?' Oscar held his arm out as if he was an over-the-top actor declaring his lines. 'In thunder, lightning or in rain? Or . . . in the middle of a clothes explosion?'

Wardrobe. To Bex that meant a couple of drawers of T-shirts and jeans or shorts, or whatever felt comfortable that day. She had long ago forgotten about fashion because having a style relied upon other people watching you – and she had avoided that for a very long time.

But to *Ravencliffe: The Reunion Show*, wardrobe meant a trailer bursting with material and a woman in charge of it all called Diane, who wore a voluminous, brightly patterned skirt.

'You sent no information on measurements or preferred style, so I had to bring options.' Diane unwound one of the many tape measures that she wore like necklaces around her neck and wrapped one rather too tightly around Bex's waist. Her tone required an apology so Bex gave it.

'But you don't need to fuss,' Bex added in a rush. 'I'm happy in whatever.'

Diane paused, frowned and then stepped back from her, crossing her arms. '*Whatever* isn't going to cut it. This is about statement. The world is watching . . . or, at least a good chunk of it. What statement are you going to make? Are you the old Bex we knew, or are you something . . . different . . .? And if you are, what kind of different are you?'

These were a lot of questions and Bex felt like it was an exam she was fast failing. 'Different! I'm different . . . I'm . . . give me a sec . . .' Sweat began to prickle.

Richard, who had been taking note of the conversation so far, led her by the arm to the tiny trailer sofa. 'Just look at some of the clothes and pick what you might like.' He dumped a load of jackets, dresses and tops in her lap as Diane tutted and picked up the items that began to slide onto the floor.

'Careful with the stock, please. We re-use.'

This was the first time the three of them, Richard, Oscar and Bex, had been able to talk together in the same room since filming the trailer. Bex was pretty certain that was by design, that the film company had kept them apart so they would have no chance to work through the awkwardness, the slip-ups and emotional leakage that an audience would pore over in the weeks and months to come. Oscar stepped out of the changing cubicle at the back, which was merely a rail with a curtain, posed and cleared his throat.

'Mate. That is definitely . . . different . . .' Richard couldn't help a half-smile.

'Double denim is very edgy right now.' Oscar looked down at himself. 'But I don't think I'm pulling off edgy, am I?'

'No. But you are pulling off fading-country-star-with-a-wife-twenty-years-younger-than-him . . .'

Oscar took off his denim jacket and threw it at Richard, who caught it with one hand.

'Careful with the stock!' Diane grabbed the jacket from him, gave his arm a light smack and smoothed out the jacket before returning it to its hanger. 'Here. These are you.' She handed Oscar a change of clothes with a steel certainty to her voice. 'Not edgy.'

With one hand, in a lithe, fluid motion, Richard took off his

T-shirt before unbuttoning a new shirt. A needle-scratch memory made Bex blush but their record was too badly damaged to play anymore and all the material on her lap was making her hot. She pushed the lot onto the floor and spoke over Diane.

'Can we have some time alone? Diane, go get a coffee and come back in twenty minutes, yeah? We promise we won't set fire to the stock. And, Richard?' She threw him a look. 'Put a top on.'

Oscar stuck his head out from behind the curtain where he had gone to change. 'Did I hear the word coffee? Can you bring me back one as well, please? I am not getting nearly enough my dose of caffeine—'

'Right, okay—' Bex nearly pushed Diane out of the door and then she turned to the others, feeling like she was back in the classroom trying to get her essay done whilst the two of them threw paper at her. 'This is not funny.'

'You don't like the clothes choices—?'

'No! This!' Bex gestured widely to incorporate not just the trailer but the crumbling building, ratty maze and death cliffs as well. 'The whole thing. This is not funny.'

There was quiet. Oscar pushed the curtain back and it screeched on its rail.

'No one's saying that it is.'

'This is not a . . . a . . . jaunt! This is not a laugh. Look at the both of you, making jokes, trying to charm everyone. This is – I don't know what this is – this is all one bloody great big mistake.'

'Hold up, Bex.' Richard buttoned his shirt and Bex's pheromones stood down from Alert Level status. 'Charming everyone? That's just being polite. You should try it some time. And just because we're being polite and cooperating with everyone and not making a damn scene every five minutes doesn't mean we don't . . . we don't . . .'

Oscar came out of the cubicle in a much better outfit than the double denim; he now wore a dark roll-neck jumper and slim-fitting trousers in twill check. 'There isn't a day I don't think about Leo.'

Richard sat on the sofa and hunched his shoulders.

'It's not just me though, is it?' Bex said. 'You feel that filming here again is . . . wrong?'

'No. Not really.' This soft blurring to Richard's voice was something new, a measured, thoughtful tone with none of the arrogance of before. 'I feel like this is weird and uncomfortable but nothing we do over the next few days can hurt Leo anymore. He's gone. Nothing we do will bring him back either. But we are still here, we're still stuck trying to make sense of it all.'

'We could do that without a camera crew.' Bex resisted the urge to cross her arms, so she ended up clutching her hands together as if she was Oliver Twist asking for more.

'I can't, remember? These cameras are paying my debts.' Richard rubbed at a spot on his neck, the skin reddening under his touch.

Bex had a lot to say about that too but instead she asked the question she had been wanting to ask since she arrived at the hotel. 'Is there anything you haven't told me – about that night?'

'What do you mean? You were there.' The trailer was too small for the three of them, stuffed with heaps of clothes and rails and hangers, so when Oscar stepped towards her and she moved back, she banged her hip against a cupboard. Two against one. Uneven. Leo had balanced them out and now, with him gone they teetered and tilted.

'But did Leo do something I didn't see? Rich – did you spot anything in all that footage when he . . . when he fell?'

'Oh God, Bex – I didn't get through half of all that film in the end, I was still recovering. I had to get Oscar to cut the film for me—' Rich didn't bother to keep the annoyance out of his voice.

'I saw that figure—' Bex began.

'Jesus! Bex – you have to drop this!' In two strides Richard was so close to her she could feel the old connection between them, stinging like salt water on a bitten lip. He took her by the shoulders and held her gaze. 'We were kids back then, with that stupid ghost story that none of us actually believed; we just used it as an excuse to go visit the scary-looking place. There was no one else there that night, no ghosts, no dark figures – nobody. Just us!'

Bex was aware of Oscar watching them, quieter than usual, just like he'd used to smirk at their fights as teenagers. Her voice was soft when she spoke. 'Because a lot of it could all be shadows and fear and a gust of wind or something but there's stuff I just can't explain. I've spent years trying to work it out. You and me and Leo, we were all together and so that only leaves Oscar—'

'Not this again. He stayed with the boat! You could see him; I could see him. He was too afraid to get up those steps. We've been over this . . . lots of times.' The egg whites of Richard's eyes were cracked red. Oscar remained still and observant.

'Yes, so who was it? Someone had to be in the hotel with us!'

'Well, so what if they were? So what if there was someone sleeping rough there who thought they'd scare us, what difference does that make – now?' His grip on her shoulders was beginning to squeeze as if he could push out all of her argumentative words.

'Because they could have killed Leo!'

This silence was more an absence of air. The two men looked at her and then each other and then back to her again.

'Killed him? Bex. I . . . No one killed Leo. God, you know that. He fell, or he jumped and some strange freaky tide thing means his body never surfaced. *You know that.*' Richard gave her a gentle shake. 'Bex? You know that?' She had never seen such hollows under his eyes. 'This is where you make your decision. You grin and bear it and the filming gets finished and you take the money and you . . . do whatever you do with it. Go live the rest of your life. Or . . . or you carry on like this, you let it eat away at you . . .'

He didn't finish that scenario but Bex knew where it led. To a house behind a wall, watching a video of a dead person night after night and throwing away the empty vodka bottles each morning.

'Here.' Oscar finally spoke and stood between them, taking both Richard's and Bex's hands. Richard's hand slid from her shoulder and, as she was wearing a short-sleeved top, down her bare arm, his touch leaving a warmth behind before grasping her hand. 'We get each other through this, like we did before – yeah?'

It took a lot of willpower for Bex to not let her forehead sink against Richard's shoulder.

'Mate – we look as if we're ABBA or something, about to start singing . . .' Richard said and the two of them laughed, breaking their grasp so Bex was left untethered. She took a step backwards, rubbing her wrist. If they were a Seventies super-group, Bex thought, then their pitch was off and they were all singing different lyrics loud enough to make crystal crack.

And Oscar was wrong – that night, ten years ago, they had not got each other through it, not at all. When it had come down to it, when Bex had been covered in blood and screaming Leo's name, she had been alone. So be it. She would find the answers without their help.

Chapter 19

Bex, ten years ago

It does not take us long to start arguing.

Richard and I had argued plenty before that night. The problem is he wants the World According To Richard and I want the World According To Bex. We are discovering that the two worlds do not mesh. God – what am I doing with him? I don't even like him that much, though I've found out that I don't need to like him to want to sleep with him. In fact, *not* liking him often makes the sex better. What can I say? It feels sometimes like there are two versions of me. Sensible Me wants to take Reckless Me's hand and gently lead her to a wall so she can bash her head against it a few times.

We argue in a rotting ballroom. Shredded loops of pink velvet at each window make me think of torn strips of skin and the marble pillars are as cold as ancient bone. The walls peel as if the whole place has a bad outbreak of flowery wallpaper eczema and the floor is pockmarked with holes. Chairs are piled up in one corner and the three of us stay well away from the chandelier that still hangs from the ceiling, a twisted, corroded tangle of metal and crystal.

'We should focus our filming here,' I say. At least here we have easy access to an escape route: the broken window, the steps, the sea, the boat.

'No.' Richard swoops the camera around as if the room is a swaying ship. 'It has to be the study.'

'Where Reginald shot himself,' Leo mutters.

'Exactly.' Richard stops and zooms in on a piece of the tattered wallpaper, making his voice gruff and low. 'Maybe there will be bits of dusty brain matter left. Who knows?'

Leo unpacks the second camera and I watch him film the oddest, sweetest things: a piece of ribbon tied around the leg of a chair, the pattern in the parquet flooring that can just be seen under the grime and decay, his fingers next to a sooty handprint on the wall.

'Lead on, Macduff!' Richard says in a tone that makes me clench my teeth. He doesn't need to do that crap. I can bet my life that he hasn't actually read *Macbeth* and, even if he has been forced to do it in school, he will have been one of those students who daydreams in class and then watches the film version the night before an exam. Pretty people don't need to try so hard.

I take out the copies I made of the architect's plans from my rucksack and roll them out on a bit of floor that looks least likely to give way. 'So. I think Morwood's study was situated on the top floor of the main hotel, above reception, at the front of the building. He had what looked like living quarters too, so presumably he'd planned to stay here and oversee things as his spa resort idea took off.'

'We can dump our bags there, do a bit filming in the study and then explore, yeah?' Richard does not wait for an answer. 'I've got a great idea for this ballroom too. You can dance, Bex. Something balletic.' News to me. I don't dance. In clubs I drink on the sidelines and critique everyone else in a sarcastic manner. If he wants dancing, he is going to have to do it himself. I try to gather the plans back together as he strides off. 'Onwards – reception!'

Another door, covered in flaking gilt, leads to a narrow staircase with a handrail carved in mahogany and then we are in a large, airy room with huge double doors at one end. The reception hall. Mosaic floor, more pillars, wood panelling, a big desk topped in brass and the wide sweep of the main staircase, a curve that swirls around the interior of the hotel all the way to the top floor as a series of stairs and gallery landings. Standing in the middle of the room I look up to the ceiling two floors above me, once painted midnight blue and silver with moons and stars to represent the night sky. The sense of space is church-like, almost. I can imagine someone standing on the top-floor gallery landing, close to that painted moon, being able to look down on the whole reception laid out like a map below them, perhaps leaning on a beautifully carved handrail. Those handrails do not exist up on that high landing, however. I can see that the work had been started on the left-hand side and then abandoned, perhaps one of the final touches that Morwood never got to finish before his plan fell apart.

'Look!' I point.

Perched on each newel post at the beginning of the staircase are two carved ravens, their heads cocked to each other with a beady stare, feathery brows drawn together in what very much looks like disapproval. Given half a chance they would shrug off their wooden stillness and attack.

I touch the carving on the finial. 'Ravens for Ravencliffe.'

The wood is brittle and cracked but the raven's eye is fierce and its wood talons grip tightly onto its plinth. Richard lowers his voice to a horror movie growl and films a close-up of the raven's beak. 'At night they probably fly around this place, looking to eat any unsuspecting visitors . . .'

I laugh. They look as if they would disintegrate if anyone even knocked them. The worst a person would get is a splinter.

A gold luggage trolley, the kind you only see in luxury hotels, has been discarded in a corner and Richard grabs it, Leo filming as he glides the thing through the vast room and then jumps onto it as if it is a chariot. Even Leo, still grumpy with me for ruining his trip, can't help but smile.

'Here, m'lady.' Richard holds out his hand to me and before I can take it, picks me up around the waist and whisks me onto the trolley.

I suppose, from the outside, this would look like a romantic scene: Richard pushing the trolley, making it swoosh around in a circle, and then jumping back on to join me, wrapping his arms around me from behind. The two of us. Love's young dream.

Not quite.

I cling on to the bar as he swings me in a circle so fast it makes my brain believe it is about to leave my body. The bar wobbles under my grip and I try to stand firm as the room whirls around. In the style of *The Wizard of Oz*, it feels like the hotel is going to be swept up and away and we will all be plonked in a strange land with only a yellow brick road to show us the way and a madman at the end of it all. I try to speak and shift so I can jump down before I throw up or my wobbly knees give way. But Richard senses that movement and so he clasps me tight.

Those arms around me are not a loving gesture. They are to stop me escaping.

Suddenly there is a screeching sound and we jolt forward, my nose nearly slamming into one of the gold bars. I hear Rich swear behind me and I twist around to see that one of the trolley wheels has come away, sending us tilting off balance, the metal wheel rim scraping across the floor. A wall looms into view and I brace myself for impact, for pain, but then think, *Sod that*, and half dive, half roll off the trolley, dragging Rich with me. The thing smashes into the wall and we end up in a heap, but at least with all of our limbs intact.

'You all right?' Rich breathes into my face.

I push him away and get up, dusting down my jeans. 'Damn stupid thing to do in the first place.'

I don't wait for a reply but head to the double doors that lead out to the driveway and the fountain, not thinking they would open. They do. A squeal, a scrape and a juddering and there is an outside to disappear into, announced by a howling wind. I need fresh air and a sky above me.

With very little to illuminate it apart from the moon, the hotel is a horror novel's front cover sprung to life. Victorian Gothic, the style is called – I have learnt that from my research. There are those distinctive arches above the windows and carvings on the stone of vines and creatures and weird half-beastie things. Two floors rise from the porch, the roof made up of gable ends and little pointed peaks above the windows and there is even a turret nearest the overgrown garden. I instantly love that turret; it gives a fairy-tale edge to the whole place. But we all know about fairy tales, don't we? They are vicious, dripping in blood.

In front of the hotel is the stone fountain, carved in Italy and shipped over especially for Ravencliffe. The fountain that never was. Never switched on. Never to have water running through it. I'd expected dolphins or happy cherubs splashing stone water, maybe Neptune or a mermaid or something. But the four shrouded figures clinging on to this fountain are grim and anguished, facing where the water would have been in a pose that looked as if they wanted to climb into the bowl, or tear it apart.

Beyond them is the overgrown maze.

And beyond that is a wall of trees, those ones planted by Morwood to screen the building. They are slowly staking their claim to this place, swallowing the maze first but eventually taking back the land where I stand, the driveway, those grimacing stone fountain figures and finally, the hotel itself.

I turn away from it, shivering in the cold that has set in with nightfall, though the day has been summer-warm. A bad luck place, I think again, one where you cannot trust luggage trolley wheels.

This is when I see it. The other two have trailed out after me and I make some kind of noise and point and Richard stops filming the fountain and aims his camera at a window high up on the second floor of the hotel.

Where a light shines.

Chapter 20

There were hours to kill before the planned meal that night.

Bex only succeeded in maiming them.

Wardrobe was done, orientation had happened, make-up wouldn't be until tomorrow and there was nothing else for her to do. Other people scurried around, busy setting up things that Bex did not know needed setting up: lights and sound and cabling and checks. This was how it was to be a ghost, she thought, wandering from her trailer back towards the hotel – the world went on around you, without even knowing you were there, and you were left to walk and try to remember what it felt like when you once had been seen.

She had a plan, however. Whatever it took, she was going to get to those steps because they were important. They were the last place where Leo had been seen and there had to be something there, something the police had missed. At the locked gates she tightened her scarf against the wind; the green material deliberately chosen to remind her of Leo.

'It's not that high.' Richard appeared at her side. 'The gate. It's just for show, mostly. We could climb over it.'

Bex considered it. The gate was a wire mesh affair only coming up to about her chest, padlocked on one side. A little bit of the old Bex piped up. 'You first.'

So he did. In an annoyingly lithe way, he took a bit of a run up, put one hand on the top of the gate and jumped straight over in a fluid motion, landing on the other side and ending in a little bow.

'Show off.'

'Come on then, Harrison.'

Bex knew she was never going to be so elegant but at least the home yoga videos paid off as she managed to hook her knee over the top. 'Don't just stand there – help!' She laughed as she hauled and Richard pulled until they both collapsed on the other side, her face, her, well – *everything* – unexpectedly too close to Richard. She scrambled back, nearly falling off the step.

'Well, that wasn't my most dignified moment.'

'I've seen worse.'

He really had. Some people should never be mixed – and she and Richard had been just such a pair. Gardeners could create new flowers by splicing two kinds of the same species together but her and Richard created a twisted, thorny, stunted thing. With a different flower, who knows how she, or he, might have bloomed?

He offered her his hand and helped her up, the two of them walking down the first set of steps until they came to the bend, passing the raised beds where huge plants and weeds now grew in wild abandon, twisted and tangled. They stopped and gazed down at the sea and rocks below. It was odd to see it all in daylight, not in a star-choked darkness or the grim light of early dawn. As Bex stared out at the sea, the horizon was merely a line, a shading between one type of grey and another. A flock of Canada geese cut across the sky, stately in their formation, intent on a destination, a place of safety somewhere on these cliffs that had only brought terror to her.

'I always thought we should have bought this site ourselves, y'know,' Richard said, not looking at her but back up at the hotel. 'I didn't even realise it could be bought until the film company did and by then it was too late. But it shouldn't be theirs. It should be ours.'

Richard was wrong, Bex thought as a seagull banshee-screeched at them. They belonged to the hotel, not the other way round; it had got them in its clutches as soon as they stepped from the boat.

'Do you want to know what I think about?' Bex touched the rough tip of one of the stone spindles that would have made a balustrade at the edge of the steps but, as with many parts of the hotel, had never been quite finished. 'I wonder what we all would have become, if we had never sailed here. What kind of futures would we have worked out for ourselves? All of us, not just Leo.'

At eighteen she hadn't known what she had wanted to be; though her parents might have had a grand plan for her, she herself had had no certain leaning towards a career or a path. She remembered not being too worried about that, in fact, actually liking it, the idea that a wide road would open up for her after her exams and that road could bend and swerve anywhere. But the hotel had put its great hand over her, like a person would in order to catch an insect and she had fluttered against its skin for the rest of her years.

'We still have time.'

Bex flicked a look to the hotel. Did they? She headed down the steps, past the small, empty pools where people had meant to laze and watch the sunset, brushing her hand against plants that had meant to be lovingly tended by a troop of gardeners. Richard followed. She kept away from the edge, remembering how her foot had slipped that night and how she had watched her radio fall into the sea. From where they stood they could see that the jetty had completely collapsed in on itself, broken splinters of wood littering the rocks. It was clear that the film company had decided to fix only what was needed for this reunion show and the rest was left a ruin.

They stopped at the final curve; the last place Leo had been seen.

Perhaps she had expected that simply being here once again would unlock something, some hidden memory that would allow the night to spill its secrets like a gutted fish. Or that, standing here now she would uncover some vital clue that the police and all those millions of people watching had missed. Instead there was only those crumbling stone spindles, the churning sea below and a sky the colour of smudged pencil.

'What happened to him, Rich?' She knew it was pointless asking the question again, but she couldn't help herself.

'Oh God – I wish I knew. Even if it was horrible. Even if it was the worst thing I could imagine, it would still be better than never knowing at all . . .'

'Please tell me.' Bex turned to him and gripped his arm. 'Please. If you know something—'

When he turned to her, Richard's face was tortured. 'I don't. You have to believe me.'

Edging nearer to the drop, Bex stared at the rocks and waves, the cliff wall a sheer plunge under them. Lower down, and too far away for anyone to reach from the step, was a kind of natural ledge but it went nowhere, just a home for gulls and bird shit. A few flat rocks reached up to it from below. Leo couldn't have jumped down onto that ledge like some kind of ridiculous superhero. And why would he have wanted to?

But why would he have wanted to kill himself?

Bex had read about suicide, how, for some, in the days leading up to an attempt on their own life, the suicidal person seemed almost happy, calm at last to have found a solution to their pain. Perhaps that was how Leo had felt. The idea that he had been suffering and had never told her was almost as bad as the fact of him being gone. After all, he had lost his mother only months before they had set off for the hotel and his father had hardly been much of an emotional support. Had she not been a good enough friend? Thinking back on that time, the girl she had been and the cross words they had exchanged in the library . . . she wasn't sure of it . . .

'I know them all, the theories. What he might have done.' Bex watched the waves whirl and swirl, spitting up white froth between the rocks.

'Yeah. Me too.'

She thought of the lighter in her pocket. 'There's something we missed. I know it.'

There was nothing more to say to that so Richard pressed his lips together and then made the slow climb back to the top, Bex following. The coastline had been searched in those days after Leo went missing, police crew and divers exploring the numerous small coves and crevices in the slick rock. All to no avail.

As the two of them neared the gate, a familiar face waited.

'You shouldn't be down there.' Oscar stepped back to allow them to climb over and his face became almost pixelated through the mesh, like that other face Bex had paused on each night in her house, creeping close to the screen to see the squares of colour that made up skin that had once been alive.

'What're they going to do? They need us to film their precious show.' Richard bounded over the gate once more and then the two of them dragged Bex across.

'It's dangerous down there, you heard Marsha – you could have got hurt.'

'Oz, man. Chill.' Richard slung his arm around Oscar's shoulders and Oscar scowled – it was a familiar expression from their schooldays: annoyance that he wasn't being taken seriously but also secretly pleased that he was the cool kid's friend.

Bex walked away without a goodbye, her mind churning. She could feel her time here slipping away, like rockfall from this cliff. Days. She only had days and she had no idea where to start or what to do and she needed to get herself together and get organised. There were still hours before dinner so she decided to head back to her trailer and study the hotel's floorplan for the billionth time to work out which rooms to search tomorrow in between filming.

Cliff rockfall, when it happened, only took a few pebbles to get the whole thing started. That was what she was, she thought as she gripped the handle of her trailer door, she was a pebble, a small object, but, in the right conditions, just big enough to bring a landslide crashing down.

Chapter 21

That night, they ate with the dead.

There was a ghost at this feast. A seat had been left empty next to Bex.

Of course, Marsha had made a speech, a re-hash of the one from earlier. Bex used it as an opportunity to take a look around the two long trestle tables that had been pushed together and covered with cloth then festooned with bits of branch and flowers in a haphazard, barn-wedding kind of vibe. The meal had been set up in the reception hall, the stairs winding around the space, each of the two galleries above them swirls on a hideous, flaking cake. Candles glimmered from corners – artificial ones, Bex noted; no one wanted to burn down the place that was going to bring them all a hefty pay cheque – and a few hurricane lamps were scattered about. Despite her thick coat and woolly hat, Bex could feel the cold almost seep up through the floor – icy hands waiting to grab her by the ankles and drag her under the earth.

There was a feudal seating plan. At the top table sat Jasper, Oscar, Leo and Bex and then the order of importance dwindled down the length of the trestle tables. Bex could hardly see who was at the other end and neither could the cameras which were, of course, trained on the Ravencliffe Three. Catering had been given a reprieve for this meal and, somehow, the film company had got towers of pizza boxes delivered to this desolate spot. Richard helped hand them out.

'To Leo,' Marsha said.

Opposite her, Richard raised his eyebrows along with his water glass and nodded to Bex, who grabbed her wine.

'To Leo,' came the reply.

Bex kept her gaze away from the empty place setting. The stunt reeked of Marsha and her bloody *reverence*. Bex was beginning to think that word meant 'something that will look good on camera'. In her jeans pocket, under her coat, there was the hard lump of the lighter. One of the people around this very table could be the person who sent it to her with that message: *It's time the world knew what really happened to Leo Finch.* So, what had happened to him? Who, out of all the people here, knew? And, most importantly – how could she find out?

Next to her Oscar pitched his idea for a prime-time game-show to Jasper, who nodded half-heartedly and kept topping up his drink. Perhaps, from his viewpoint at the jetty, he had seen something that night and had never told them. The idea of Oscar *not* saying something though, of actually avoiding attention – well, that was very hard to imagine.

'But the best thing, out of all of this, is that I get to see my friend Bex again.' Oscar turned to her, his hand edging towards hers. She had seen a DVD copy of the only film he had ever been in after *Ravencliffe*; his acting was nowhere near good enough to keep up this level of sincerity.

She smiled, very aware of the cameras set up around them, but moved her hand out of reach to unfold her napkin. 'Oh yes, the best thing,' she repeated.

'Because, it doesn't matter how long we've been apart, something like this, like what happened here . . . there's a bond. An unbreakable bond.'

Bex was suddenly reminded of one of his television adverts: he had been stuck to a ceiling to prove how great the glue was. An unbreakable bond. She smiled again, more at the image in her head, and Oscar, catching Jasper about to sidle out of his chair, grabbed his arm and turned his attention back to him.

What exactly had she thought she could achieve here? Bex wondered, fiddling with the edges of the napkin? That she would arrive and instantly become some kind of supercharged Miss Marple, working out a missing persons case a decade old, in the middle of also filming a show? She pushed her wine glass to the side and poured herself more water from a jug on the table. Or had she thought that as soon as she neared it, the hotel would unfold for her, like a monstrous doll house, opening up so she could poke through all of its dusty secrets?

Richard got up and sauntered down the table, ostensibly to reach across and take a slice of pizza. Bex recognised that move. The way he kept eye contact with the woman he reached across, giving her a smile as he bent over her – it was the kind of move that could get a guy into trouble these days, Bex thought, as she saw the woman flick back her dark hair, realised it was Holly and watched her return his smile, not with one of her own but with something glimmering in her gaze that did not suggest he was heading for a workplace tribunal. The candlelight, the easy familiarity in the tilt of her head and the angle of his body, it was one of Bex's mother's Mills & Boon covers sprung to life.

She would have to have a word with young Holly about the perils of . . . well, the Richards of this world. But was he a peril, anymore? Bex checked herself. Most eighteen-year-old boys were a peril to either themselves or someone else, but ten years had gone by since then. She knew nothing about this Richard: bankrupt and father to a little girl.

The light from the candles wavered but in a weirdly set way, the LEDs designed to flicker in a rhythm that was meant to soothe but instead made the whole room feel like it was running a bad signal that might blip out at any time.

Blip. And there she would be back at eighteen, with sea mist clinging to her hair, Richard darting around with the camera, Leo studying a twig or a bit of faded wallpaper, the echoing of their voices.

Blip. And she would go back further still, to a man sitting in his study, his greatcoat wet from the rain, looking her straight in the eyes as he put the gun to his mouth and then a loud bang, a jolt and those eyes glassed over.

Blip.

A slice of pizza appeared in front of Bex. Tapping her fork against her paper plate four times did not work, so she did it again, and again, quiet, subtle taps, hoping no one would notice. But then she was stuck in it, that counting, and none of the combinations of four felt right, none of them made her heartbeat slow so she swallowed and tried again, forcing herself to concentrate on the numbers, one two, three, four, but it wasn't working, it wasn't working at all—

She stood up. Knowing that this could make the director's cut she steadied the chair which had half-tipped over behind her and muttered to her plate, her glass and the table in general that she needed some fresh air.

That was when Oscar began to choke.

Chapter 22

The table stilled for a moment and all Bex could see was Oscar gasping for air as he clutched at his throat making a terrible retching sound.

Then people began to move and shout and there were hands grabbing his shoulders and someone spilled a wine glass near her, the red of it seeping into the cheap paper tablecloth and Bex remembered a night ten years ago where she had had blood on her hands, the sticky chill of it as it dried.

'Jesus! His allergy! Did someone give him nuts?' It was Richard's voice that galvanised her, got her creaky brain whirring once more and also her limbs, pushing people out of the way and lunging for the bag Oscar had slung over the back of his chair. Richard had always made fun of him for his man-bag, calling it his handbag, asking if it was where he stored his tampons, but they all knew, under the bravado, the real reason he carried it around with him.

In school they had had lessons, but school was a long time ago and a lot had happened since.

Richard was at her side. 'Do you remember how to do it?'

'Yes. I think.'

'Then do it.'

She could hear Marsha calling an ambulance but she knew that was far too many minutes away, especially along that long, steep, secluded road, even if it had been recently cleared.

They were now in their own little circle, everyone else having moved back to give them room. Oscar sat in his chair, each retch and rattling choke making the metal chair legs beneath him screech against the floor in commiseration.

'Is there a first-aider?' she heard a voice shout.

Bex rooted through Oscar's bag, throwing out a book, something on how to unlock your inner tiger, a metal water bottle, a proper old-style Filofax and finally . . . there it was, a slim black pencil case. She flipped open the plastic tube.

'Blue to the sky . . .' Richard began.

'Orange to the thigh . . .' She finished the rhyme they had been taught at school, the classroom carpet tiles scratchy on her knees, practising with empty trainer pens until they got the hang of it.

She removed the blue plastic cap. Middle of the thigh, that's where it needed to be, a quick swing. Oscar's mouth had puffed up, his eyes watery but fixed on hers. He tried to speak but she rubbed his hand. 'It's okay, Oz. We got this. Like at school, yeah?'

He nodded, his breath coming in tight little gulps, and she decided to stop thinking about it and let her forearm swing, the orange tip of the EpiPen slamming into his leg. Click. And hold.

One . . . two . . . three . . .

And done. She threw the pen away from her and massaged the spot on his leg with a trembling hand. In fact all of her had suddenly gone off kilter and she had no strength to help the others as they wrapped a blanket around his shoulders; she did not even have the energy to get up off her knees. She could close her eyes and sleep right there.

'Good job, Harrison.' Richard's arm held her around the waist and hauled her up. For a second she let herself rest against him as her legs and arms recalled their roles and her brain stopped whirling. Four. She hadn't counted to four when administering the EpiPen and now that seemed like a bad omen, though Oscar's eyes had already cleared and, despite the swelling on his face, his breathing had lost that deathly rattle. She pushed herself away from Richard and picked up Oscar's abandoned paper plate.

'How did his food get contaminated?' she demanded. 'You all knew. You must have known. There's like . . . rules for this kind of thing. What did he eat?'

The plate was of little help. Only crumbs remained and the rest of the table was a mess of bottles, knocked-over glasses and crumpled napkins.

'He just had that one slice of pizza. I remember him saying he was watching his weight so he'd stop there. Cheese and tomato I think, I don't understand—' Marsha held two blankets in her arms, the material slipping out of her grip.

'This isn't bloody good enough, Marsha! Something like that . . . it could kill him! What kind of show are you running here?'

For once, Marsha had nothing else to say.

* * *

An hour later, on top of the cliff, surrounded by sky and trees and lots of empty land, Bex was trapped.

Darkness had fallen like a shroud. The ambulance crew had shown up for Oscar, who, by that time was a more cushioned-faced version of his former self. He assured them, through swollen lips, that he was fine but Marsha had insisted on them taking him to the nearest hospital to be checked over.

'Buff . . . you . . . on . . . sar wiffout me?' Oscar had managed to ask.

'No, no – absolutely. Not one camera will roll until you are back on set,' Marsha had said as he was wheeled away before she turned to an assistant and ordered her to make up alternative call-sheets without him just in case.

Out in the dark night air, Bex stared at the maze. It was not the overgrown tangle she had pushed her way through ten years ago – now the entrance was a neatly cut mouth waiting for her. No. No, it was not a mouth: it was only twig and leaf; it did not have any sentient thought of its own. It was simply a place. But she knew that she did not believe that anymore: this place meant them harm, she could taste it in the air, like salt on the breeze.

An accident, what had just happened to Oscar – that was what everyone was calling it. Unfortunate. Regrettable.

Bex knew better. This place would pick them off, one by one, like bits of lint on an old jumper.

A darker shadow detached itself from the maze and Bex felt her scalp tingle. An otherworldly glow seemed to radiate from it.

Blip.

Back she went ten years, about to rush after a figure only she had seen. Deep in some animal part of her brain she knew that this shape had been waiting for her, a thing made of bad deaths, the spirit of Morwood himself, come to claim her just like the curse said he would.

The shadow remained still for a few moments . . . and then it waved.

'Oh hey! Bex!' Holly's voice.

The blood that had thundered in Bex's ears sheepishly sidled back to other organs.

'For fuck's sake – you didn't half scare me, lurking about like that.' Bex watched as Holly rushed over to her.

'I wasn't lurking. Well, yes, maybe I was. I needed a break from the chaos so I convinced Luke over in security to give me my phone for five and I checked out the latest *Married at First Sight.* Have you seen it this year?' She waggled her phone at Bex.

'No.'

'You should! It is, like, over-the-top dramatic but you really get to know the contestants and . . . anyway, my fav is still in so – phew!' Up close, with Holly's face lit by the glow of her phone screen, Bex could see that her lipstick had smudged, probably from eating earlier, the red smear reminding Bex of another face in another time, the blood running into a mouth trying to speak. 'Is Oscar going to be okay?'

'I think so. Have you seen Rich?'

'He's helping clear up the meal. Keen to lend a hand, that guy. Bit of a looker too . . .'

'Take my advice – he's a train wreck. Stay clear.'

'Bex?' Marsha's voice. Bex sighed and turned. Backlit from the candles, Marsha stood in the stone porch next to one of the pillars. Bex couldn't see her face in the dim light. 'You're needed inside.'

The woman was like some kind of souped-up house mistress from an Enid Blyton novel, Bex thought, always showing up to spoil any fun, even though Bex was far from enjoying herself.

Holly stepped forward, sliding her phone into her pocket so Marsha wouldn't catch sight of it. 'We were just going over the itinerary for tomorrow, weren't we, Bex?'

If Holly was waggling her eyebrows at her, it was too dark to make it out. 'Oh yes – the itinerary, can't drag me away from those things. Love them.'

Holly spoke over her. 'I wanted to make sure nothing goes wrong for the start of filming, yeah – call me a control freak! We'll be done in a while and then we'll come in.'

Marsha stepped down from the porch, her heels crunching on the fresh gravel laid only a few days ago to allow easier access. She was dressed in a huge black batwing jumper that reached her knees, leather leggings on underneath. It took a lot of money to look that creased and shapeless.

'I know what this is,' she said, taking her glasses off and cleaning them with the edge of her top.

Holly swallowed. 'I mean, I— We were just—'

Marsha put on her frames and threw her head back, opening out her arms to the sky. 'You have to come out here to feel it, don't you? I understand.' To Bex's surprise, Marsha took her hands, hers strong and calloused. Then she spread Bex's arms out as well so the two of them looked as if they were about to start an elaborate Regency dance routine. 'It is right that we should take a moment to . . . feel. What just happened was shocking for us all.' Her voice became brisk once more. 'I've fired Oscar's assistant. Fresh start, eh?'

'I'm not sure that was strictly—'

'There. Just breathe. Do you feel closer?'

'To what?' Bex imagined the ghost of Reginald Morwood rising from the ground to fit snugly between their arms in an embrace.

'Leo.' Marsha made the word a whisper, a prayer, a summoning. Bex snatched her hands away.

At that moment a crackling came from Holly's hip and she stepped to one side. Bex reminded herself why she was here, that this was to find out what was really going on, not get into arguments with annoying directors, or producers, or whatever Marsha was.

Holly walked back to them. 'Marsha, there's a problem up on the top floor. They're setting up for tomorrow but—'

'Why are they still up there?' Marsha lost the breathy airiness to her voice, forgot all about reverence, frowned and stomped away.

Holly waved the walkie-talkie at Bex, a grin taking over her elfin face. 'Dodgy button. It's been crackling all day, making me crazy. Guess it came in useful, though, eh?'

'Thank you. I don't know how much more of Marsha I can take. But won't you get in trouble when she finds out no one's up there?'

'Oh, there's someone up there all right. I saw Tim and Nic sneak up the stairs twenty minutes ago and they haven't been able to keep their hands off each other since we all rocked up here. So Marsha will definitely find *something*, all right . . .'

'Evil. You're cleverer than you look, y'know?'

'That's rude but it's probably the nicest thing you've said to me so far so I'll take it.'

Bex took one last gulp of fresh air and turned to the open front door. It was a picture frame and through it she could see the table and some of the people around it, the whole scene glowing in the candlelight like amber. Bugs got caught in amber for millions of years, frozen in their last moments, and this place had done the same with every bad thing that had happened within its walls: it had imprisoned them all as rotten little insects within jewel colours.

'I'd better get back in.' She didn't move.

'Look.' Holly poked her palm with the antenna of her walkie-talkie. 'Do you want to escape for a bit?'

Chapter 23

Bex, ten years ago

Rich, Leo and I stand on the driveway and gaze at the glimmer high above us in the hotel window. A light where no light should be.

'It could be a reflection on the glass . . .' Leo offers, his voice no more than a whisper.

'Well, yeah. It could be.' Richard steps back to get a wider shot. 'But you'd need to have something for it to reflect off. Only trees face that window. Don't see any lights in them.'

'It's a glow,' I say, my eyes fixed on the spot high above us, afraid that if I look away it will disappear.

'Maybe it's . . . I don't know . . . fireflies . . .?' Leo suggests as Richard rolls his eyes.

The light wavers and wobbles, like a candle, I think.

'Do you think there's someone here?' I ask.

'Living out here, you mean?' Richard trains the camera on me. 'Like a squatter? Pretty out-of-the-way place to squat . . .'

I don't want to meet the kind of person who feels the need to hide out here on their own, living amongst the spiders and decay. Richard heads back to the front door.

'What're you doing?' I follow and grab him by the arm.

'We can't not go and investigate the strange light in the haunted hotel, can we? I mean – this is perfect, it's exactly what our film needs!'

'But, anybody could be in there—'

'Look, it'll turn out to be, I don't know, something boring. And if there is someone, well, there's three of us. Safety in numbers, yeah?' Richard lowers the camera. 'This is brilliant. It's that bit in the film, y'know, where the audience yells at the screen for us not to go in but we do anyway? This is meta. It's perfect!'

Beside me those silent stone figures claw their way around the fountain, and the wind, softened a bit by the building that shelters us, tugs at my hair and my jacket, finds the weak spots in my layers and slides in its chilly fingers.

I blame my brain. I've read about it, how a teenage brain is a thing not done growing, and some vital bits of mine haven't quite settled in – the idea of consequence being one of them. I want to know what the light is just as much as Richard and the idea I could wade into some kind of real danger is only a muddy-water picture.

I follow Richard. And Leo, of course, follows me.

* * *

There is a chunk of fallen masonry on the reception floor: a large white bit of rock that could be used as a weapon. I pick it up, hefting it as if I am judging if it is good to throw.

That staircase in the middle of the reception is a thing of beauty. We turn our torches on it and Richard's swooping, looping filming style matches the elegant, sinuous glory of the thing. It is a ribbon that curves around the reception, all the way to the top of the building, gallery landings on each floor, perfect places for someone to look down on us – though that is a thought I don't need at that moment. Instead, I imagine Victorian ladies in silks and velvet rustling their way up the steps, a pale delicate hand trailing along the mahogany banister. I deliberately do not picture any other kind of face caught in our torchlight, eyes like dark moth markings.

Up the stairs we go, keeping to the edges in case the middle is rotten, until we come to the first-floor landing and then follow the gallery around, with a view of the reception below us. The second staircase leads to the top floor, Richard ahead of us, testing the broken boards. Moonlight shines in through the landing windows, tall arched glass that throws light onto dusty floors. The painted moon on the night sky ceiling over our heads is peeling away.

'To the right. That's where it came from,' I say, gripping the rock in my fist and instinctively making my voice into a whisper. A corridor disappears into the gloom, doorways set into it. I have studied the plans so I know that there are some more guest rooms on the left, known as the east wing, but the west wing on this floor had been planned for staff: offices and living quarters for Reginald himself, the rest of the staff to be eventually housed where the temporary workers camp had been set up during the build.

But we don't need to consult the plans because we can see the glow as we take careful steps along the corridor. It comes from under the door towards the end, the corridor itself stopping at a picture window which has a crack across it like its own jagged smirk.

I had hoped for us to climb up there and for the light to have disappeared, a trick of the eye, a glimmer of nothing, a ghost-spark. A shiver – fast, goose bumps, then gone.

'Shit. It's actually a light.' Richard holds up a hand to stop us.

'Who owns this place?' I stare at that glow.

'What?'

'I mean – are we trespassing? Well, I know we're trespassing, I mean – that could be the owner of the land. They could call the police. I'm NOT getting arrested here—'

'Why would someone who owns this wreck of a building be here in the middle of the night?'

'Let's just go,' I say as Leo hangs back.

But Richard moves before either of us can stop him. That teenage brain again, no care for consequence, only concerned with the here, the now, the excitement of it all. He grasps the round doorknob and puts some force behind his shove, thinking the wood will have expanded in the frame and jammed the door. But it hasn't. The momentum carries him straight in, Leo and I on his heels, me with the rock raised in my grip as if I am about to throw it.

What I find is a study in a state of slow decay, Richard standing in front of Morwood's desk.

And on that desk is a single, recently lit candle.

Chapter 24

Bex, ten years ago

An impossible bloody candle. I stand in Morwood's study and stare at it. It has been placed on a side plate, its wax white and fresh without even one dribble, the flame bright and large.

'Is it real?' I cannot keep my eyes off it, hypnotised by its rhythmical wavering from a puff of air the three of us do not feel.

Richard has his hands outstretched to the flame as if he is warding off a dangerous dog. He reaches out and prods it and I really do expect at that moment for his finger to go straight through, for it to be a spectral fire sent from hell, a curse, a warning, a sign.

The candle wobbles as his finger touches it.

But the alternative – a real candle lit by a real hand – is worse because that means somebody has been in the hotel with us only minutes ago, a quarter of an hour at most. The flame is high and fresh and so is the candle.

'Is this you?' I turn on Richard who is bent, studying the flame, his camera for once hanging loosely at his side.

'Huh?'

'Did you do this?'

'How could I? I've been with you all night.'

I leave the two of them in the study and run into the corridor, back to that landing window, the one with a view of the sea. If Richard can't have done it, nor Leo, then maybe it was Oscar. Far beneath me I see a boat bobbing by the jetty, and in it a shape under a blanket, blonde hair sticking out from the top.

'We would have seen him.' Richard stands behind me but this time there is no embrace. 'That light was in the window as soon as we got near the fountain.' He takes my arm and leads me back to the study. 'To light it Oz would've had to climb the steps and that takes a long time, they're so winding. We'd have seen him, Bex – we'd have still been on the steps ourselves. And he can't climb them anyway, you know what he's like with heights.'

His vertigo. That picture of him hugging the rock face on our abseiling activity comes into my mind, his fingers white against the stone because he clutched it so hard. I cannot deny the sense in Richard's words. But sense is something that has left this room because there in the middle of it is a candle that should not exist, still shining away, throwing shadows in the corners that waver like spirits.

The study itself is as much in decay as the rest of the place, despite its glow. The walls on two sides are bookcases, the books within spongy and soft with mould, the black spots speckling their spines like bubonic book plague. Many of them have ended up on the floor, a pile of them against one corner trying to climb to the ceiling in some sort of bid for escape. The desk has survived but it is a hulking shipwreck, its drawers ripped out, its leather top scratched as if it has been clawed. Behind it is a big window overlooking the driveway, fountain and entrance to the maze.

'Don't!' I lunge for Richard who leans towards the candle. 'Don't blow it out.' It is bad enough having some awful curse candle shining away there in the middle of the room, but it is a thousand times worse to be the people who blow it out, to show whoever is watching exactly where we are and give them a darkness in which to ambush us. 'I want to go.'

'Bex—'

'No! This is creepy and we've got loads of film. I want to go.' The tremble of real fear cannot be masked in my voice.

'It's just some coked-up squatter playing with us!' Richard reaches for my arm and I take a few steps backwards, unaware how close I am to the nearest bookcase. There are wide, thick wooden columns between the shelves and as my arm flails out of Richard's grasp it hits one of these with a slap that makes my fingers sting.

We watched in amazement as the column clicks and then swings open to reveal a very tall, very narrow door to an extra storage space.

'Nifty.'

My fingers tingle then for a different reason other than I have just slammed them into wood. They want to slap Richard for using words like 'nifty' because he thinks they are retro and it makes him cool, urbane, educated. This is not nifty. I watch him press at the other columns which spring open under his hand, each one a narrow secret compartment.

'Leo, let's go.' I tug at Leo's sleeve and he glances between me and Richard like we are his needy, newly divorced parents.

'I don't know, Bex,' he says. 'There's lots more to explore, I guess . . .'

'What? Don't you think this is weird—?'

'Guys!' Richard interrupts, reaching into one of those secret bookcase spaces. 'Look!'

An impulse grips me, that I shouldn't let go of Leo's sleeve; instead I should pull him with me all the way out of this hotel and down the steps and straight into the sea if I must. The only thing I do however is let Leo's arm fall.

Richard brings out a metal box from the hiding place in the

column and carries it over to us, holding it out with both hands as if he is a bloody choirboy at Mass in charge of the sacrament.

Before I have a chance to say or do anything, Richard smashes the thing into the side of the desk, a few times, hard and fast, until its hinges loosen and break, allowing him to open it up. 'I learnt that from a movie somewhere. If something's locked, go for the hinges because they're the weakest point.'

All three of us bend to look at what is inside, the lure of jewels or hidden treasure too strong for even me to resist, despite my wish to leave.

'It's just full of paper.' Richard sifts through the pages with a disappointed look on his face. 'Useless old paper.'

Except I know that some old paper isn't useless – I vaguely remember something about bonds or the like, the kind of paper that becomes more valuable the older it is. People have become rich from such things. I take the box from Richard and begin to read through some of the documents, handling them carefully because they are thin and delicate.

'These are mostly letters? From Morwood to a doctor, it seems, and they're talking about his wife, Jane . . .' The stories of Ravencliffe often do not mention his wife but that is not a surprise – history is a tale badly told by men. Leo and Richard don't seem too interested, Richard riffling through those hidden bookcases and Leo turning to the window. 'She was a lot richer than him, in fact it was probably why he married her. But Morwood is explaining how she's unwell, he calls it hysteria and . . . oh . . .'

'What?' Richard begins to tap on some old panelling.

'Morwood, he . . . it sounds as if his wife is refusing to ask for more money from her father and this doctor . . . it looks like the two of them are planning to . . . have his wife committed . . .'

I have read about stuff like that. Rich Victorian husbands, wanting divorce, wanting change, wanting to wreck a woman's entire life with one flourish of their pen, could have their wife committed to an asylum on gossamer grounds. They could happily move on whilst their wives rotted in the dark, labelled crazy.

'Whoa.' Leo stands next to me and looks at the letters over my shoulder. 'Nice guy.'

'Maybe she was, y'know . . .' Richard signals crazy with a wave of his fingers near his temple and then trains his camera on the letters as he arranges the paper into a more attractive shot.

My look bounces off him. 'There is literally no such thing as hysteria, it was a made-up condition used to control women. In fact, film me saying this – it's important.'

And it is. There in that moment I want other people to know about Jane, that she existed and the injustice that happened to her because I am sure, when I get home and do a bit of digging, I will find that Jane had spent the rest of her days locked away and that just doesn't seem fair.

'I'm going back to the boat,' I say, collecting the papers and returning them to their box, which is slim enough to fit into my rucksack.

A howl of wind rattles the glass in the window and makes me turn to it before I can even hoist my bag on my shoulder, once again grabbing Leo's hand.

Through the window, down towards the maze I see what a lot of people would say is a shadow, or a tree moving in the gale, or any number of things but I know it is none of those. I know what I see. A blurred dark figure out in the shadows, shrouded in a huge coat, head tilted as if he is a curl of coarse hair snug in a locket.

A dead man.

Chapter 25

The people in the pub did not stop and turn to look at the interlopers. That would have been too obvious. They were sneakier than that, darting glances from the sides of their eyes, or using the mirror above their table to study them. The pub was called Smugglers' Rest, though the smuggler in the painted sign didn't look very rested, straining as he was to cart a heavy bag full of shipwrecked goods into a cave.

Holly was surprisingly resourceful. Bex had watched her smile at Luke the security guard as she returned her phone. It was clear that the young man would have done much more than give her a bit of technological contraband if he had the chance. After all, the security was meant to keep the people outside out, not the people inside in – they weren't prisoners. Luke had stroked his patchy baby beard and had been only too eager to pull the gates open for them, especially when Bex had been introduced.

'Oh man – I've seen the film! Some fucked-up shit went on here, yeah?'

She had posed for a selfie and done her best to give a smile that wasn't merely a rictus.

When out of Luke's sight, Holly then dangled a car key in Bex's face.

'How did you get that?'

'Marsha forgot to bring her extensive vitamin collection with her and sent me to the nearest chemist to pick up emergency supplies. Luckily, I only get travel sick when I'm a passenger. So I just . . . temporarily forgot to return the keys.'

'Sneaky.'

'Thank you.'

'You're old enough to drive, right?'

Holly had rolled her eyes.

The car park was a roughly cleared patch of land near the gate, tree stumps still sticking up like mole heads in odd places. The space was far too big for the cars in it, a few trucks and a couple of those four-by-fours like the one that had brought Bex to the hotel. She had expected a pack of photographers at the foot of the hill, but there didn't seem to be many around at this time of night and the car windows were darkened anyway. She had ducked down as they passed them. Soon the two women had arrived at a pub not that far from where they had stayed at Mrs Bloom's B&B.

'What do you want to drink?'

'A cider and black please.' It was the drink they had had most often that summer of being eighteen. Not because they liked it, but because it was cheap. Sat at a sticky table, Bex sipped at it, her eyes stinging more from its sharp bitterness rather than any nostalgia. Around them a few older men contemplated their pints and the football match on the television held up by a wall bracket that was itself fixed with duct tape and glue. There was dark wood panelling, threadbare seats, a dusty display of crisps and the smell of damp clothes, damp dog and dampened expectations of life in general.

'This is lovely. I can't believe I'm having a drink with Bex Harrison! Like *the* Bex Harrison! No one will believe me!' The brightness in Holly's voice did not dim as she unstuck her coat sleeve from the table. Then she sniffed at Bex's glass. 'Dear God, you used to drink this?'

'Yeah, I don't know how I did it either.' Bex picked at a button fixing the leather of the seat to its frame. It fell off under her touch and rolled into a corner. 'You should get paid extra, y'know – for having to deal with me and my freak-outs.'

'The Bex Bonus.' She smiled and sipped her lemonade.

Bex smiled. 'Yeah, that sounds about right: the Bex Bonus.' She searched about in her brain for some suitable small talk. 'What do you want to be when you, y'know, grow up? Because you're about twelve, right? You look about twelve. If this was the kind of pub that cared, you'd have been refused service.'

'Well, I'm actually eighteen and I want to be involved in this kind of thing as a career, you know, telly and film, so when this job came up it was perfect because I could scope out who does what and what looked like a good way to start. And get paid for it. Well, get paid a bit anyway . . . And – it was Ravencliffe! Half of my chat room applied for this job!'

Bex put her drink down and stared at Holly. 'Holly – serious question. Are you a Raven?'

Holly pointed to a badge peeking out from the collar of her black denim jacket. Bex saw a little beak and two clawed feet. 'Proud corvid right here. And I know you and Richard and Oscar, you think we're dumb and obsessed and, well . . . some of us are, gotta admit . . . but it's just love, isn't it? We're passionate about the film, about this place. About the people in it.'

Pushing her drink away from her, Bex leant back in her seat and it let out a gentle puff of musty air, a ghost sigh. 'Y'know, that's not quite it. I don't think you're sad, it just scares me, the way you're studying us, like we'll – like I'll – let you down in some way. It's a lot of pressure.'

On the television above them, the football match finished and the three old men on the table nearby got out a pack of cards. They were the three wise monkeys come to life: one with his false teeth threatening to slip out, one with his hearing aid and the final one with his wire-framed glasses. Speak no evil, hear no evil, see no evil.

'Last orders, ladies!' the barman said. 'Or you can stay for our poker lock-in. The elite table's over there. Watch Alf, he cheats.'

Holly raised her eyebrows. 'Want to get something you can actually drink and then get fleeced by these old dudes?'

Bex did.

* * *

When they had returned the car to its spot and snuck back into the hotel Bex found her trailer, locked the door and drew the curtains.

It was perhaps odd to keep all the cast and crew on location as they filmed, living in this mini village of trailers with little pathways between them, but Bex actually liked hers. It was snug and small and she could lock the door against anyone or anything that she didn't want to face, or, if the worst came to the worst, she could up sticks, hitch a car to it and disappear. The inside was decorated in wipe-clean neutrals. There was a big enough bed at the back, a tiny kitchen up front and a tinier shower and toilet which all worked – she had seen how the trailers hooked up to the water. Generators hummed to themselves near the perimeter fence next to jerry cans of petrol and other fuel canisters. She could easily live somewhere like this. The only downside was that there would not be enough room for her plants.

Around her were spread a selection of the photocopies from the morning spent in the library with Leo ten years ago. Her tired eyes slipped from them. The maze, that was what she would focus on tomorrow, maybe that would turn up something useful. Switching off her lamp she pulled back the curtain from her tiny bedroom porthole and gave the hotel one last look, half expecting a light to be flickering from one of the windows as it had done ten years ago, the beacon that had drawn them to disaster.

There was only darkness.

Chapter 26

The next morning became an artificial night. Bex woke under pieces of paper as bedsheets, feeling as if she had not slept at all. When she walked into the reception hall it had blackout drapes over the windows and studio lights glaring, the daylight outside only a memory.

'We are going to split all of this into three sections,' Marsha explained to them, a voice behind the migraine lights. 'Starter interview with Jasper on the stairs here. Low key. Then we tour the building, visit some of the main rooms. Final interview in the ballroom.'

It was a fever dream. Bex watched as Jasper did his introduction in a pool of illumination. The shadows around him were poured ink, waiting to write awful new stories about this place, but he was oblivious, a wide smile on his smooth face, with his smoothly pressed shirt and even smoother words that slipped away from Bex before she could understand what he was saying.

And then they were on.

The three of them entered from different directions and Bex moved through the awkward hugs and greetings with what she suspected was not the most natural of smiles. She tried again but her mouth muscles had forgotten how to do it and she feared she looked more like she was about to bite someone.

At least she wasn't wearing a beaded dress. With Diane's help, she had decided on the Bex she wanted to be for this show and that Bex wanted to be comfortable and wearing shoes which, if she needed to run, would not be a hindrance. Slim-fitting jeans, a looser top made of a silvery cobweb fabric over a vest worn underneath and her own green scarf. There wasn't much different about Different Bex at all. Finding she had got rather fond of it, she kept the Ouija board planchette necklace from the promo trailer tucked into her neckline, the acrylic warm against her skin.

They sat on the stairway steps, that sweep of mahogany that still held its beautiful curve despite the rot and ruin around it. There were cushions laid out for them to sit on, but the poses were uncomfortable and wherever Bex moved a sharp edge poked somewhere. She was glad that she hadn't gone with a skirt as, by this point, the viewing public would have had a good look at her knickers. There was a sofa but it had been deemed unsuitable and had been pushed back against a far wall. Perched on the newel posts of the staircase were the two wooden ravens, looking appalled at the noise and light of the crew and all their equipment.

'Okay – cut!' Jasper called off into the darkness.

'Jasper?' Marsha's voice came back at him. 'You can't just yell cut whenever you want. You do your job and I'll do mine, yes?'

'Can't be helped, lovey – got to click my spine back into place.' The crunching sound set Bex's teeth tingling. 'Bloody stupid place to sit, don't know why we can't use chairs like civilised people.'

'Because this isn't a civilised place . . .' Marsha kept her voice as falsely sing-song as Jasper's so it sounded like they were both in a musical where the rest of them hadn't been given lyrics.

Bex took the opportunity to stand and let some blood flow back into her legs. Marsha at least was right about one thing: there was no civilisation anymore. What had once been envisaged as the pinnacle of modern rest and relaxation, an oasis for care-worn rich Victorians to promenade and swim and enjoy the view, all that had been scraped away and the bones that were left were brittle and pockmarked.

Before Marsha could continue, the whole room plunged into darkness.

'Sorry!' A voice called out and Bex heard Marsha curse, despite her earlier statement that swearing was discouraged in her reverential working environment. 'It's the generator again!'

'Everyone stay where you are – I can't see a damn thing!' Marsha yelled.

'Sorry!'

With the blackout drapes at the windows this was a kind of darkness that Bex had never experienced in the hotel before. She could not see any sinister shadows at least but then she realised that the black itself was just one huge shadow pressing close to her face, like a monster sniffing her out. There were murmurings and the shuffling of feet, a metallic clang and the soft whisper of the edges of curtains dragging in the draught, a dragging that could be clothes, could be the hem of a greatcoat worn by a dead man shuffling towards her—

A warm hand grasped hers and the lights came back on.

'Okay?' Oscar squeezed her hand and then let it drop before wiping at a smudge on his shoes which he had spent most of the interview admiring. 'Thank God this isn't live, eh? I'd be a nervous wreck.'

'Right! Time for the trolley section,' Marsha called out.

'What trolley?' Bex turned to Richard.

'God, Bex, you have to wake up! Start listening. The luggage trolley, remember, from the film? It's still here.'

'You are kidding me?'

The cameras started rolling and Jasper clapped his hands together. 'Okay, okay. This reception hall was the scene for one of the most well-loved scenes in the film. A little slice of happiness before . . . well, all the rest happened. And I'm talking about one thing . . .' He went to jump up, remembered his back and made it a slower, more careful movement. 'The luggage trolley.'

For a second Bex would have sworn that the thing glided in on its own, a creature come to life, waiting for its return to glory but then she realised that someone out there in the shadows must have pushed it on. Jasper caught it with one hand and brought it to a stop.

'Oh wow.' Richard smiled and his was genuine, his mouth muscles behaving better than Bex's.

It couldn't have been the same one, Bex thought as she got up and went close to it, spotting its newly fixed wheel. Surely that one had mouldered away by now, fallen apart, its metal rusting to jagged edges. She wouldn't have put it past the film company to build a new one and then spend a day kicking the hell out of it to make it look old.

'Now, we've had it fixed and checked over so it's all perfectly safe. How about a spin around the room for old times' sake?' Jasper gave the trolley a wiggle and the wheel wobbled.

'Oh – I don't know—' Richard began.

'Yes.' Bex spoke over him. They looked at each other.

'Really?'

'Yep.' Here at least was one moment she could try again – here she could go back and enjoy one scene from the film, unlike the first time when her smile had actually been a rictus. She grabbed Richard's hand and jumped on, relishing his surprised expression.

'Clear a space, clear a space . . .' Jasper said, flapping his arms to the camera crews and sound technicians, who hurriedly moved or kicked away cables and tracks. With everyone occupied Richard took the opportunity to rip away his microphone, leaving the battery pack on the stairs and did the same for Bex.

'You know I hated this the first time around. I just wanted to get off,' Bex said.

'You did? Shit. I thought it was romantic. Well, until we nearly hit the wall.'

'Millions of people agreed with you though, so you were right.'

He fixed her with a look that hovered somewhere around amusement. 'You wanted to dump me before we even left for our trip.'

'You knew?'

But Richard didn't answer. Instead he ran with the trolley, swooping it in an arc as he picked up speed, swinging it in a circle as Bex held on. And this time she did not want it to stop, she did not grip so tight she could lose the feeling in the palm of her hand, even though for the first few seconds she braced herself for the judder of the wheel coming off. No. This time she wanted to let go, to be flung out in a glorious, dizzying swirl of chaos, so hard it would jolt her right back through the years to this time ten years ago when the worst thing she could think of was breaking up with her boyfriend. Flashes of faces and lights and peeling wallpaper whizzed past her.

'Here.' She held out her hand to Richard.

'Sure?'

'Yes.'

So he gave the trolley one last push and jumped on behind, this time not wrapping his arms around her but reaching over her shoulders to hold onto the bar. If she wanted to move her head a fraction it would fit snugly into the curve of his throat; if she leant back a millimetre, she would be supported by his chest. The world spun around them, blurred out so the faces and lights and wallpaper, the whole hotel and everyone in it, for a few moments, was nothing but a foggy backdrop. When he spoke, Richard's words were warm breath in her hair. 'I wish things had been different.' Bex did not know how to respond to that, so she took his arm and wrapped it around her waist as the spinning world slowed, pressing her hand on top of his. Maybe for those seconds they really had been swept into the past where another future beckoned, one where, when the world came to a halt, they could see each other properly for the first time behind the bravado and arrogance and pride.

Wheels creaked and slowed and Jasper appeared out of the darkness to grab onto the rail, ghost-white teeth and bright silver hair, a newly minted shining phantom. The world settled around them, slotting everyone back into their allocated roles, each one of them a neat dovetail joint. Bex could feel Richard breathe behind her and she closed her eyes. She did not let go of his hand.

Jasper cleared his throat. 'Magical. Just magical. Hate to interrupt but we have a *lot* more to come. Not least something we haven't even told these three.'

Bex's eyes flew open.

'That's right. A surprise! Hold on to your hats, people, you are going to love what we have in store for you!'

Bex doubted that.

* * *

Filming ate the whole day in one gulp.

There had been no way to escape and try to get to the maze, or look in any of the other rooms in the hotel. Bex's idea of searching out answers was fast becoming a plan written on cheap paper that was already tearing at the edges. She had to try harder tomorrow, she decided as night came and she crashed into sleep, staying under its weight until an insistent thumping on the door woke her up the next morning. She blurrily tried to scramble out of bed, reaching out for the glass of water she had left on the ledge by her pillow the night before. Her hand found something else instead, something that should have been tucked tight in the pocket of her jeans.

Cool hard plastic.

A smiling dead face, taken from where she had left her clothes in a pile on the chair and deliberately moved so it would be the first thing she saw when she woke up.

Leo's lighter.

Chapter 27

Bex, ten years ago

A bloody dead man, out for a bloody stroll. There are pictures of Reginald Morwood. Stern, stiff portraits in sepia, a man with a thick head of dark hair, wire-rimmed glasses and a moustache. He looks as if he's a normal person wearing one of those comedy masks.

There is one picture of him outside Ravencliffe, taken at its completion with his workforce standing with him. He was forty-eight when the hotel was finished, a man in his prime, believing the riches were about to start pouring down, and he is stood with his thumbs in his waistcoat pockets, presumably opening them wider for the coins about to go rushing in. Moustached, bespectacled, he wore a greatcoat, the kind with that mini-cape thing at the back of it, meant to help the rain slide away. It is a distinctive style of coat, one I have never seen before, outside of that picture.

But I look out of the study window and see, stalking across the gravel beyond the strange fountain and heading into the maze, a tall figure, the coat flapping behind him.

'There's someone out there!' I point.

'Holy shit!' Richard gasps, taking a few steps to the window. 'Fuck – I missed it! Holy . . . shit!' He moves fast, snatching the camera as he yanks Leo by the arm and pulls him towards the door making a whooping noise. 'Let's get him!'

Before I know it, I am left alone with the cursed candle and the shadows.

I hesitate. In front of me, through the window, is the dark driveway, that fountain with its crawling, creeping statues and the entrance to the maze into which I just saw that figure disappear. Behind me is the impossible flame wavering in the draught.

Darkness, or light – which one to choose?

It is probably symbolic that I plump for the dark. Grabbing the second camera that has been left on the desk I run, out of the study and down the stairs, checking from the landing window that Oscar is still in the boat far below us, a small figure under the blanket. I reach the main staircase and end up at the double doors, shoving them open as I dash out to the drive.

'Did you see it?' I barrel after them and pause, moving the camera round to take in the whole scene: fountain, drive, maze, trees. No stalking figure. But I know where he is heading.

'Wait!' I call to Leo disappearing into the maze, Richard out of sight. As I near the entrance I forget about wanting to leave, forget about the impossible candle, forget everything except that I am alone in the dark, abandoned by my friends.

The maze is elegantly designed in concentric circles that lead to its heart where the plan had been to hold afternoon tea for some of the guests. Chaos has claimed that order. Now the untended yew hedges are trees, overgrown and wild, reaching towards each other to block paths and confuse anyone foolish enough to wander in, bony branch hands snagging clothing and hair. The flagstone path keeps some of it back but it is clear that I am going to have to push my way through.

In I go.

It is hard work. Spiking, scratching, stabbing, the trees are a jostling crowd, moving against me, trying to push me back. I keep my gaze on the path and my hands in front of my face, protecting my eyes from sharp twigs and branches that want to blind me, my torch only illuminating more narrow yew leaves for me to push through.

'Leo? Richard?' I yell. 'Wait for me!'

It is a stupid thing to do, to go chasing after this person with only a camera. Being a teenager is like being drunk, that edge of drunkenness that threatens to tip from toasting and sloshing cups together into something darker and wilder.

Yew leaves are poisonous, I know. If eaten, only a small amount is enough to kill a person and these toxic leaves crowd in on me, trying to force themselves into my mouth, my eyes, my ears as I push and crawl through. I imagine this place simmering in its poison for hundreds of years, the venom seeping into the earth and the trunks of the trees that had once been hedges, its malignancy growing.

I force my way around a corner and freeze, my heart thudding.

A still, pale face waits for me.

It is funny what fear does to you. I don't say 'Hello?' in a weak, little, wavering film heroine voice. I don't stumble backwards and end up on the floor. My hands don't shake. There is a ringing silence as, briefly, the rustling around me halts, the trees themselves paused and watchful.

But this is no spectre. Telling my hand to move, I train the camera on it and zoom in on its stone face, or where the face would have been if it hadn't thrown an arm over its eyes as if blinded by some invisible light. It is a sister to the statues on the fountain, same flowing robes, same strange, tortured pose, embedded now into the overgrown maze like a splinter in swollen flesh.

Nowhere in the plans have these statues been mentioned. It is an odd, macabre thing to have in the maze, something designed to frighten, to repulse – surely at odds with the idea of a hotel meant to relax and heal. And it isn't just one, there are lots of them, each one a heart-in-the-throat moment as I labour my way through the maze, each face looming out at me as if to warn, to frighten, to reprimand.

Ahead of me is a clearing, the flagstone path widening into a circle – a stop-off or dead end, I presume.

Another statue, the yew branches reaching around it in a deadly embrace.

Then it twitches, a horrible jerking movement.

A dead man waits for me. There is the greatcoat, its hood pulled up so his face is in shadow, even when my trembling, bouncing torchlight finds him. In front of me is the person I think I saw from the window. This time the rustling and scratching around me does not stop but grows wilder, louder; I feel the feathery tips of the yew leaves brush against my neck, my cheek.

He stands.

I stand.

I attempt to speak but those hot confident words of earlier have melted away. There is a menace to this still, silent, watching figure, something that paralyses me for a second, even though my thoughts race. I can't hear Richard or Leo behind me. I don't even know where they are and I am alone here with this . . . whatever it is: ghost, demon, man.

He stands.

I stand.

Then he moves again. It is almost as if the trees drag him into them, closing over him – there one minute, gone the next – and a clamp loosens around my throat.

I follow. I don't believe I am even thinking properly, my feet move on their own, my brain stunned like those snakes you see being charmed in India. The ghost/demon/man plays a tune in my head and I dance to its rhythm.

Which is all a fancy way of saying it is yet another stupid decision.

Sometimes I think I hear voices, Leo and Richard, snatches of words and the sound of footsteps moving fast, loud one minute and faint the next. Little twigs and branches from the hedges get stuck in my hair, cobwebs cling to my face and pushing my way through is beginning to make my arms ache. Stone faces loom out of the murk to glare at me or jeer, I can't tell which.

Finally the maze spits me out at its bull's-eye, a large circular stone space, the trees held back. The figure should be standing here, waiting for me once again.

I am alone.

Out of breath, scratched and tired, I yell in frustration. I can see where I had come from, my torch illuminates the broken branches, and there is no other exit. The figure has melted away like smoke but the idea of smoke makes me think of that impossible candle burning high above us in the hotel. Impossible candle. Impossible figure.

There is a sudden rustling behind me and I jump forward, catching my foot on something sticking up from the ground and then for a few minutes I don't remember anything at all because I stumble and fall and smash the back of my head hard.

The blackness takes me.

Chapter 28

Bex, ten years ago

There is a hand on my shoulder and the taste of metal in my mouth.

'Bex?' Leo's voice.

I try to sit up because, to my great surprise, I am face flat to the floor, grit on my cheek.

'Leo?'

'Don't move too quickly, you've hit your head by the looks of it.'

Edging up on my elbows I pat my temple and wince. The camera is a few feet away from me and Leo's face swims wide into my vision, huge eyes, square glasses and those chubby cheeks.

'What the fuck did I trip on?'

'Umm . . .' Leo looks around. 'I came up behind you and I think it scared you so bad you fell over this thing . . .'

On the ground is a large circle of inlaid wood set within the stone, the pattern soft and rotten in places. I run my hand over it, confused. 'It's flat?'

'No – this . . .' Leo points to one side where a low metal rail forms a semi-circle around one half of the wood.

'What is it?'

'I don't know.' He tugs on it and it doesn't move. 'Maybe there was another weird statue that stood here, and this rail was in front of it? You okay?'

I touch the sore spot on my temple and close my eyes whilst my body works out which bits hurt and which don't.

'I think so.'

'You gave me a real shock, seeing you fall like that.' Leo puts his arm around me and squishes his face next to mine, a bit too close to my throbbing temple for comfort but I don't push him away. This is an olive branch.

'Can we just leave now please?' I wiggle my feet, feeling one ankle twinge where it has been caught by that metal bar.

Leo moves his face away and presses his lips together, picking up the camera and tightening the strap. 'I don't know.'

'What do you mean, you don't know?' I pull away from him. 'There was someone in this maze! They ran in here before me and I followed them but now . . .' We both look around at the distinct lack of another person standing with us.

'So where did they go? There's only one way in and out.'

'I . . .' That is the question. Impossible candle. Impossible person.

Closing in around us are those trees with their dense foliage, an easy place for hidden eyes to watch us. I don't shiver because I've never once shivered when afraid, but I do sit up straighter and test the weight on my ankle.

'You saw him too, right, from the window?' I ask Leo who dips his head to scrape at something on the wooden flooring beneath us.

'Umm . . . no . . .'

'What? But you weren't stood that far from me!'

'Yeah, but by the time you pointed and I looked out at the maze, whatever you'd seen had gone . . .'

Whatever I'd seen.

'I did see something—'

'Look – Bex. This is a creepy place, right? And it's dark and there was that stupid candle and we're all a bit jumpy so I can totally understand . . .'

I finish his sentence for him: *I can totally understand why you've gone a bit crazy and hallucinated the ghost of Reginald Morwood . . .*

I stand up. The ankle feels a bit weak but I can walk it off as I go back down those steps, to Oscar waiting in the boat. 'Come with me or not, but I'm leaving.'

'If it had just been us on this trip things would be different . . .' Leo mutters.

I stop and suppress the frustrated noise in the back of my throat. 'Oh my God – I get it, okay? I'm sorry. I shouldn't have told them about it. Point made. But what was I meant to do? He's my . . .' I falter.

'See? You can't even say it. You can't even say that Richard is your boyfriend!'

I stop at that.

'I—'

'You can't say it because you know he's not right for you, you're not right together. You're ashamed of the whole thing and that's just cruel, Bex. I mean, I don't really like Rich but he probably deserves a bit more respect than that.'

'You don't know anything about him!'

'Neither do you!'

The yew branches rub their leaves together in glee as we fall into an angry silence. Of course, what is unspoken between us is what we've never really talked about at any length, and probably should. His mum. Her death. We've tried, a few halting, stunted conversations that Leo quickly cut off. I should try again, I think, though no words come to me.

'Oh, come on. Let's get back to the driveway.' Leo walks off without waiting for me.

It is worse going back. The maze clutches on to us and I have no strength left in my arms. The branches want to drag me deep into their rotten wooden heart and each time the looming, leering faces of the odd statues make my heart pound. Leo leads the way. Through the tree canopy above us, I catch a glimpse of the impossible candle burning high in the window and there are times when I imagine we could wander forever, always thinking we are just about to escape, the two of us becoming another story to add to this place.

Finally, Leo spots a wider gap in the hedge and the glimpse of a fountain. 'Here! Bex! Here!' His voice is ragged with relief and I could kneel and kiss the gravel driveway, could even kiss one of those horrible statues crawling over the fountain. But I don't have time to kiss anything because an almost otherworldly howl comes from the direction of the hotel.

'Where's Richard?' Leo asks.

Chapter 29

'Where's Richard?' Bex slammed open the door of her trailer, nearly hitting Holly in the face as she took a step backwards, slopping the contents of a mug over her sleeve. 'Or Oscar. Where are they?'

'I – umm—'

'Who has a key to my trailer?' Bex took a few paces and glanced around as if the person who had moved the lighter onto her bedside table was hiding out of sight. She could feel the smooth plastic in her hand and she saw Holly's eyes flick to it, before she stuffed it in the top pocket of the cotton pyjamas she wore. 'Was anyone hanging around my trailer last night? Have Richard or Oscar been here this morning?'

'Wait, Bex! The others are in make-up. What's happened?' Holly vainly looked for somewhere to put down the mug, in the end choosing to plonk it on the floor.

That question made Bex pause. Around her were more trailers and vans, only narrow walkways between them, a temporary suburb sprung up next to the hotel. The slice of sky that Bex could see was the colour of old bandages, wrinkled with cloud streaks. Though it was summer there was a chill bite in the air.

What had happened? Thinking on it now, as Holly's walkie-talkie crackled, a static blast of sound, could she even be sure that she hadn't moved the lighter herself? She had had some wine in the pub last night but nowhere near enough to trigger a binge blackout. People could move and walk in their sleep though. It wasn't entirely out of the realms of possibility that she had got up in the middle of the night and, her brain overwhelmed by the events of the last few weeks, moved the thing. Maybe it was her subconscious's way of saying: *Get on with it. Don't forget that this is why you're here . . .*

Holly rubbed at her sleeve and shot Bex a wary glance. 'I think there's a set of master keys to the trailers, but Marsha would have those. Have you lost yours? Don't panic if you have, we can get you a spare, no problem. Look, do you want a cup of coffee before we go into make-up? I brought you one but . . . well . . . you're going to have to suck my sleeve to drink it. I'll get you some breakfast from the truck if you promise not to throw it over me and . . . umm . . . why are you staring at me like that?'

Underneath Holly's coat with her now coffee-soaked sleeve, she wore a black T-shirt with a line drawing of a candle and four familiar faces in its glow. It was that T-shirt that convinced Bex.

'Come with me.' Bex took Holly by the arm and headed for a gap between the trailers.

'Hey, no – wait, we can't – you're meant to be in make-up right now . . .' Holly tried to steer her in another direction but Bex would not be steered. The mini estate of trucks disorientated her for a few minutes until she found a path out so that in front of them was the fountain and the driveway. She turned to her right.

'Oh, we can't go in there just yet. Out of bounds—' Holly began.

'I don't care.'

The maze. It had been recently cut back, the trees returned to hedge proportions. Bex guessed that was the film company's doing, that they probably wanted to shoot something in here whether it was out of bounds or not. Its entrance was a gap in the greenery pockmarked with decay and dead foliage. The pruning had stripped away the maze's veneer of beauty and now it showed its real face – dry and dying. If Bex was going to have to start confronting some ghosts she might as well begin with that dark figure she had followed here ten years ago, the one that vanished and that no one else had even seen. That the maze was currently out of bounds was even better – there would be no one around to hear what she had to say.

'Oh my God!' They rounded a corner and Holly stumbled straight into one of the maze's waiting inhabitants, the statue in flowing robes with an arm thrown over its face to shield its eyes. In the darkness, when Bex had been here before she hadn't been able to take in the details – the claw-like sharpness to its fingernails, the way its mouth stretched in what could be a shout, could be a snarl. Holly peered at it. 'I mean, I knew they were still in here . . . in fact the maze scene is one of the best in the film, in my opinion. The sense of fear, of us being trapped with you . . . here . . . with these things looming out.'

'I always wondered why Morwood had them put in. I mean, this was meant to be a spa resort, a place for people to relax – not to be scared out their wits.'

'Maybe it was a prank? Like the London Dungeon – it's really popular, isn't it? I went there one time and I thought I would totally be okay but it was actually really scary and . . . yeah, anyway – Victorians, eh? Weirdos. You know, I'm going to be in trouble if I don't get you to make-up soon. We've got a tight schedule today.'

'Don't care.' Bex pulled her on, not that Holly was putting up much of a fight anymore.

'Wait! I want to get a pic of me with this one . . . oh, damn. We don't have our phones. I'm definitely coming back and getting some shots. These things are insane.'

Bex knew where she was going this time. She had watched the film often enough to remember the order of the statues so she navigated by them, hideous route markers. Daytime stripped the maze of some of its terror and now it could have been like walking through the London Dungeon but a version when the overhead lights were on and you find it mostly sticky tape, bad wigs and a poorly hidden speaker system. Even the statues themselves didn't seem to have their hearts in it anymore: their elbows and edges fragmenting, their poses softened by moss, weeds growing through the cracks of their palms making them awkward posy holders.

'Umm . . . you're not getting us lost, are you?' Holly asked.

'Nope . . . in fact – yes! Here we are!'

Dead centre. Centre of the dead. A round hedge wall and that strange wooden circle set in the middle of flagstones with its low rail as a half-moon on one side. The last time she had been here, Leo had stood beside her. She almost expected to spot a new statue here: him, frozen at the moment of his disappearance and spirited here to stand amongst the others. But that would have made this a silly ghost story, and Bex suspected that what happened here was going to be much more frightening than any spectre could be, because it involved the real monsters: humans.

'I want to tell you something.' Bex watched Holly walk over the circle and crouch for a closer look at it. 'Something you can't tell anyone else.'

'You do?' Holly couldn't keep the note of excitement out of her voice.

Before she said anything, Bex did the calculations again. She couldn't tell Richard or Oscar about the note and the lighter because it was likely that one of them knew much more than they were letting on. She couldn't trust them. This girl though, with her wonky eyeliner and coffee-smelling coat, she had only been a child when it all happened, there was no reason not to trust her and, this was the key part: she knew the film – possibly better than Bex herself. She could help.

Most importantly though – and much to her surprise – she liked the girl.

So, as each of them stood on the opposite side of the circle, she tried to explain about the note she had been sent and how she suspected that a mysterious someone knew much more about Leo's death than they were letting on. When she finished and waited for Holly's response something inconceivable happened: Holly remained silent.

'So you . . .'

Pause.

'Then . . .'

Pause.

'You think . . .'

Pause.

'Wow. Oh my God. This is huge! Oh my God! Do you think that Richard or Oscar are involved – is that what you mean? Oh . . . my . . . God! Shit!'

Holly's voice became louder and Bex hadn't even told her about the lighter, or got it out of the top pocket of her pyjamas. Instead, she made the mistake of stepping over the low rail and onto the wooden circle so she could reach out and try to calm her down. The mistake wasn't stepping over that rail; it had caught her out before and now she was suitably wary of it, no, the mistake was putting her foot onto a rotten bit of wood which softly crumbled and gave way, taking her ankle down with it.

Chapter 30

Fifteen minutes later, faces peered downwards.

'We are not liable for this.' Marsha turned and eyed Bex who sat on the ground rubbing her ankle. She and more members of the crew had been fetched by Holly. 'We told you all to stay out of the maze as it wasn't safe. My instructions were clear. There were signs.' She brandished the laminated cardboard she had swiped from the entrance of the maze. 'You see. No liability.'

'What's down there?' Jasper tried to raise his arm but his puffy coat was so thick Bex marvelled that he could move at all. Holly knelt and dug her fingers into the rotten, soft pulp left behind by Bex's foot smashing through it. Luckily she had put on boots, not slippers, when she had rushed from her trailer a few minutes earlier, otherwise some of those nasty wooden splinters would be sticking out of her foot.

'I know, right? I think there's a space under there, a . . . a . . . hole!' Holly said.

Everyone let those woodworm words burrow into them.

'A hole? Like . . . a grave?' Bex tried to stand on the same ankle that had been attacked by this patch of ground ten years before.

'We should be filming this!' Jasper shouted to someone, who scurried off.

'Well, no – it could be anything, I didn't mean it was a—' Holly backed away from the hole.

Hiding space. Pit. Grave. The image popped into Bex's head like a burst blister: a picture of a skeleton curled up, knees to chin, as she had seen in ancient burials.

'Wait! Wait!' Richard's voice caused an instant quiet. He had appeared on the scene at the same time as Marsha, Jasper and Oscar. They were all wearing pyjamas and sheepskin boots, except for Marsha who was fully dressed. She probably went to sleep wearing leather, Bex thought. 'This was here before us, remember? It can't be anything to do with . . .' He trailed off and locked gaze with Bex, who gripped that strange low rail as she attempted to stand but then stopped and stared at it.

'This rail.' She bent closer to it. 'We never found out what this was for, did we?'

'In the film didn't Leo say it might have been part of a statue or something?' Holly offered.

'Yeah, that was it. But I think he was wrong.' Bex shuffled around on her knees so she crouched behind the brass rail, careful not to put any of her weight on the wood circle. 'If there is a hole underneath here then this isn't a rail but . . .'

She remembered Leo uselessly pulling on it that night and expected nothing to happen just as hidden and long unused hinges began to creak.

'. . . a handle?'

'Oh shit! Oh shit, oh shit, oh shit, oh shit!' Holly reached over to help Bex pull, but a leather-booted foot stamped down hard on the bar.

'Absolutely not.' Marsha kept her boot on the brass rail. 'Under no circumstances do we open . . . whatever this is.'

'Not until we have a camera here.' Jasper glanced over his shoulder. 'Camera!'

'No. Not then.' As Jasper was about to speak, Marsha held up her hand. 'I said no. Clearly the ground here is dangerous and we don't know what we could be disturbing.'

For once, Marsha sounded sensible and this was such a shock to Bex that she narrowed her eyes and kept a grip on the metal bar. 'This opens for a reason though! We can't just leave it here—'

'Look, it was hard enough to get permission to film because of the bloody bats. We have a schedule and a show to get through. I don't have time for this and whatever new problems it'll bring and we definitely do not have the insurance for it. We only tidied the maze up to get our overhead shots, there was never any intention to film here . . . It's probably . . . well, I don't know what it is, but it isn't our problem.'

'Didn't places like these have ice storage?' Oscar piped up. He had a pink half-moon-shaped eye pad stuck under each eye, the kind used to help reduce puffiness. It looked like the swipes of army camouflage that soldiers wore, if they were trying to blend in against candy floss. 'Having ice in the days before freezers, it was seen as fancy, I think. So this could have been where they kept some ice? Yeah?' Bex watched as he smiled at his historical fact. He had never seemed that interested in learning facts when they were eighteen, she remembered. His History GCSE grade was proof of that.

'There you go. Ice. Boring. Now read the sign, people – this maze is strictly off-limits.' Marsha brandished the laminated cardboard again. 'Anyone who comes in here without permission and breaks their leg will stay that way until we wrap.'

A skinny young man appeared with a camera and Jasper gave him a nod. 'I think you're missing a trick, Marsha, my love. This is exactly what our audience want to see. Fresh secrets from the hotel of horrors, that kind of thing. It doesn't matter if it turns out to be ice storage or whatever, we can fudge that bit but the thrill of opening it, the drama – it's telly gold!'

'No.' Marsha flicked her fingers at the camera man to swat him away. Then she turned to Bex. 'Now we need to get you attended to. Can you help her up please? Let's hope you haven't done any real damage and your ankle doesn't swell because Diane will kill me if we have to change footwear options.'

There was a flurry of activity and Bex found herself standing and then limping away, her arm held by Holly. Jasper rolled his eyes and sighed theatrically, muttering something, before catching Marsha's gaze and checking himself. She began to herd them out, flapping her arms at everyone and shooing them off.

'Wait!' Bex called behind her. 'We have to open this – it could be vital in Leo's missing persons case.'

'All the more reason to leave it well alone until the correct authorities can be informed. Which they will be – once we've finished filming. Now that's the last word on the matter. It is all in hand. We have work to do.'

Each statue that Bex passed on her way out seemed to point back to where they had come from. Dead centre. A hole in the ground. Bones in the earth. First the lighter being moved in the night and now this – they felt like signs, markers on a path that led her on, one she had to follow, not be led away from by the elbow like a hospital patient. She wrenched her arm out of Holly's grip.

'My ankle is fine. I just scraped it.' Not quite true. An old pain throbbed once more but she ignored it and waited until everyone had scattered to their various jobs around them. Only the stone people scaling the fountain were left to overhear. 'I have to know what's in there.'

Her mother had told her that, when Bex had been a child, she used to have tantrums when they went out shopping, the full-on kind that involved throwing herself onto the ground and flailing chubby arms and legs. That was what she felt like doing now. Scream and scream until someone did what she wanted.

Holly probably thought she was being subtle as she craned her neck from side to side to check they were alone. She might as well have held up a notice that said: Deeply Secretive Plotting Going On Here! 'What're you suggesting?'

'Tonight. I'm going back to open it up.'

Holly pressed her lips together and paused for a few seconds. Bex thought her frown meant disapproval so she was surprised at her next words. 'It's a heavy trapdoor. You're going to need some help.'

Chapter 31

The artificial night continued in Morwood's study, where thick black material had been stapled to the windows to help continuity and give the appearance that filming had happened after sundown.

Without the impossible candle burning away, the room was shabbier and smaller with fewer shadows. The desk remained in the middle, scratched and broken, the place where Morwood had signed the contracts for the exciting features his hotel would boast. Presumably, Bex thought, it was also the place where he wrote those letters to that doctor trying to get his wife committed so he could dump her in an asylum somewhere and probably find a new, richer spouse. A true Victorian gentleman.

'So, how does it feel?' Jasper ran a finger along the leather inlay of the desk. The original plan had been for only her, Richard and Oscar to tour the house but after an hour of them saying, 'Umm' and 'Ah' and failing to formulate a coherent sentence, Jasper had been drafted in.

'How does it feel?' Bex had been doing that, repeating the question back to him and she saw his nostrils flare, but she couldn't help it, it gave her time to think. 'It feels like no time has passed. I don't know about you two . . .'

'Yeah. This is where it all started, really, isn't it?' Richard glanced at Oscar, who nodded. 'Here, when we saw that candle.'

Except he was wrong about that, Bex thought. It hadn't started with the candle. It had started before that with the shattering of glass as they had broken the ballroom window to get in. For her, that was where it began. They broke something of the hotel's and in return, it had decided to break them.

'Well, I guess that's not strictly true.' Jasper's mouth smiled but his eyes bored into Oscar. 'After all, Oscar – you weren't here, were you? What were you doing when all of this was happening?'

Oscar blushed. 'I was asleep in the boat at the jetty.'

'Not asleep the whole time though, were you?' Jasper's razor question was designed to slice.

'That's—'

Jasper faked a yawn but then smiled and patted Oscar's arm. 'Only kidding! But seriously – how does it feel to be the one who missed out?'

'Hey—' Richard began but Oscar put a hand on his shoulder and cleared his throat. There was quiet as he thought of his response.

'I've had to make peace with disappointment,' he said in a low tone. 'Not me being disappointed, that's not what I mean. Everyone else's when they see me, that I'm not Bex or Rich . . .'

Bex had never really taken any time to think about Oscar, other than he had been lucky not to have been involved, but looking at his crestfallen expression now, she realised that maybe she had been wrong to simply dismiss him. He had suffered, maybe not as much as the rest of them – but he had certainly suffered, in his own way.

'Because my story – it *is* dull,' Oscar continued. 'The boy who stayed with the boat. I never even made it up the steps to the hotel. So, yeah, you're right to yawn, Jasper. It is boring. I'm of no interest to anyone really.'

'Ah, mate, that's not true.' Richard gave him a playful punch on the arm. 'You're one of us.'

'The Ravencliffe Three,' Bex muttered, watching Richard get Oscar in a headlock as he laughed, the two of them tussling.

'Ah now, no time for horseplay.' Jasper smirked and waggled his fingers at a person standing in the doorway. 'You haven't seen this for ten years . . .'

For one heart-expanding, throat-closing moment Bex expected to see Leo walk towards her, not the Leo she had known but one ten years older, with a few lines around his eyes and the same wide smile that lit up his whole face. The entire thing would be explained – somehow – and everyone would hug, tears in their eyes. Final scene. End credits.

Someone handed Jasper an object wrapped in black velvet. He unpeeled it with the care of a museum curator, only missing a pair of white cotton gloves.

'Oh, you are kidding me – it's not real, right?' Bex stared.

The impossible candle. Or, at least, it looked like the impossible candle. It must have burnt out that night years ago – certainly none of them had gone back to it. What was being held like a baby bird in Jasper's hand was a misshapen stump.

'The actual one,' Jasper whispered. 'The production company found it here on the desk where you left it when they made this place secure to stop memorabilia hunters. I think everyone would like to see if it still lights.'

Richard and Oscar remained silent.

'No.' At least that was what Bex hoped she had said. Her voice had become hoarse. The warped, brittle chunk of wax didn't look as if it could burst into flame.

'I know. Delicious, right? I'm sure that's what everyone would want to see.'

'We don't know why, or how, that thing's still here – shouldn't we leave well alone?' Richard crossed his arms.

Bex pushed the sound mic out of her way. 'Turn the camera off, we need to talk. Marsha?' A shock of white hair and a flick of a black cape ducked out of the doorway. Bex elbowed through the crew and looked into an empty corridor with its carpet rolling up at the edges like small pink tongues. By the time she turned back, Jasper already had a match cupped between his fingers and she knew she wouldn't be able to reach him in time.

It wasn't slow motion at all, in fact it happened so fast that she had barely taken a step forward before the tip of the match met the stub of a defeated wick.

The flame died in an instant, barely a flicker of light.

Richard got there before her. In one movement he grabbed the candle out of Jasper's hand and then closed his fist around it, the wax breaking into powdery chunks which he dropped on the floor and ground under his heel.

'No.'

All that was left of the candle was dust but the damage had been done. It had been lit. It had glimmered if only for a second and as Bex stood there whilst other people argued over old wax, she thought she could hear the distant sound of cracking glass once more.

Chapter 32

Bex, ten years ago

As Leo and I run from the maze towards the hotel and Richard's screams, it feels like I am slipping on a downward slope of events, down, down, holding on to anything I can, trying to catch my breath and keep my wits about me. No time to think, just events flying past, stinging my face with whiptailed flicks.

We follow Richard's yells through reception and up the stairs, past those landing windows where Oscar can be seen bobbing oblivious to it all in his safe little boat. Arriving at the doorway of a room on the top floor, on the same level as Morwood's study, out of breath, my ankle throbbing, I expect demons, an attack from a crazed coke-addict, or squatter or whatever my imagination can conjure up.

When I realise what is actually happening, I make sure to film the whole thing.

'Get it off me!' Richard shouts, cowering in the corner.

'It's just a bat.' I try to get a shot of the darting, flitting little shape as it throws itself around the room. Leo attempts to catch it in the beam of his torch but it is too quick for any of us. 'It's more scared of us than we are of it.'

That is the kind of thing my mother would say. I think of her briefly in her sensible shoes, sitting on her wipe-clean sofa watching game shows, eating a TV dinner on a tray next to my dad doing the same thing. But I also think of her love, a love that wants the best for me, even if she doesn't know how to imagine what that best would look like. I want to be done with all of this and sit with her to watch *Wheel of Fortune*.

'Get rid of it! Fucking rat with wings!' Richard continues to crouch, his hand over his head as if the tiny bat is an army of them, all about to dive-bomb him.

There is no impossible candle in this room, so any light comes from our torches or the moon outside, a sliver of luminous rock mostly covered by tattered clouds. I catch a glimpse of flowered wallpaper hanging in shreds as if the flowers themselves have died and are wilting off the wall. There is a faded carpet here too, swamp-coloured, though that had probably not been the original hue. As I run my torch over the curved walls, I realise that we are actually in the turret on the side of the hotel, the one I had thought so romantic-looking when I'd first seen it. One window faces the driveway and the other the trees to the side of the hotel where the maze is. A sizeable fireplace juts out with some patterned tiles still clinging on to it.

'Bex, don't just stand there!' Richard flaps one arm towards me, keeping the other one clamped to his head.

But this is comedy gold. The darkness needs a bit of light every so often, that is how the best horror stories are constructed. I should know, I've read enough of them. This is the comic relief and there is no way I am going to put the camera down and miss it. Leo takes off his coat and attempts to herd the bat towards the window as if it is a sheep, or no, actually it is more like the bat is a bull and he is the matador, the kind of matador who squeaks every time the thing gets near him. But, all credit to him, he eventually gets the little creature close enough to the window for it to realise that the broken pane is an escape route away from these hulking, noisy humans. Off it flits into the night sky, probably to get some bat therapy.

Richard sinks against the wall. 'Thank Christ for that.'

'Why were you up here?' I ask, putting extra steel into my voice.

'Huh?'

'I only went into that damn maze because you and him ran off into it. Why didn't you wait for me? Why did you leave me in there on my own?'

'You weren't on your own – you had Leo!'

'I . . . I . . .' How to explain it? A shadowy figure led me on a spooky dance to the middle of the thing where I promptly tripped over and nearly concussed myself.

'I wanted to see if I could get a good shot of the whole maze from up here on the top floor, maybe with you guys in it – but the trees were too tall.' Richard stands and brushes down his jeans. Then he looks at me properly for the first time and frowns. 'Hey . . . are you okay?'

I give my temple a cautious prod and it tells me in no uncertain terms that it doesn't like being prodded. 'I tripped and hit my head.'

Richard takes my hand in a gentle grip. 'It looks pretty mean.' He smooths the hair from my face and gazes at me in what might be a deeply romantic way. Little scratches and cuts make my hands sting.

'Yeah, it doesn't feel too great. Rich, I want to go now. I don't know who that was in the maze, or even if I hallucinated it but I'm tired and my head hurts and I twisted my ankle and I really, really don't like this place and it seems to me . . . it doesn't want us here . . .' It sounds stupid as soon as the words leave my mouth but by this point I don't care about being clever, I just want out.

I expect more of a fight, because when Rich wants to do something he is a tanker ship unable to turn but his expression softens even more and he strokes my cheek before he lets his hand fall away from my face. 'Yeah, okay, Bex. We've got lots of footage now anyway. Let me get a few more scene-setting shots and we'll call it a night.'

The wind rattles the window in its frame, a moan of disappointment, as if the building itself is not happy about letting us escape.

'Umm . . . Bex? Rich?' Leo stands in the doorway, peering at something on the wooden door surround. 'You might want to come and see this.'

I really don't want to. What I want to do is avoid whatever it is that Leo has spotted, just walk past it with my head turned away, hands over my eyes.

Richard has no such feeling. 'What?' He moves to the door and pulls me with him.

All I see are two sets of bolts. Nothing extraordinary in them, they are of average size, rough to the touch. But it isn't the bolts themselves that are the interesting thing, no, it is where they are placed.

'See? They're not on the inside of the door, for privacy or whatever. They're on the *outside* of the door like you would if you wanted to . . .' Leo stops, realising what he is about to say.

I finish his sentence for him. '. . . lock someone in.'

Chapter 33

Bex, ten years ago

We all think we know the story. The thwarted businessman, Reginald Morwood, with his bad-luck build and unsteady carpenters falling from great heights and then, just as the dream of his spa resort is in reach the train company snatches it away from him. Gun in mouth. The end.

Except we are looking at the wrong story.

'Why would Morwood want to lock anyone in up here? Is that the kind of thing Victorians did to their servants?' Leo runs his finger along one of the bolts. There is a smudge on the sleeve of his green raincoat, a splayed handprint.

'I don't know, Victorians were oddballs, weren't they? I read they used to make jewellery out of dead relatives' hair.' Richard turned the porcelain door handle which had a cracked blue pattern on it. He hadn't read that fact anywhere; I'd told him when I'd been reading up on Ravencliffe and Victorians in general. However, the reminder of a lock of dead hair brings back the picture of that crooked, stooped figure standing by the maze and I quickly try to shove it out of my mind.

'This doesn't feel like a servant's room . . .' I gaze around at the vestiges of the original decoration left under the rot and mould and decay. When I look at the wallpaper closely, I can see in the few flowers left that their petals had once been edged in gilt. The bed is also not the kind of thing designed with a servant in mind. It is no four-poster but it has a high headboard intricately carved in fruits and sinuous leaves, the vines thick, the fruits plump. There is no mattress left and I can see the wooden slats, each one jagged and cracked as if someone has taken their foot to them and stamped right through.

But it is the fireplace that convinces me. It is tall and made of marble, the kind of thing that withstands the ravages of time. I could have given it a wipe clean and it would have shone in the almost opal glow that marble has. On it is a small wooden trinket box, carved in the shape of a heart, with *Cariad* etched into the lid, the Welsh word for love. I open it only to find it is empty. Around the grate those remaining tiles are delicately painted, each one a scene from some myth or legend that I do not know, the people dressed in togas pointing to things and reclining in a way that suggests they are important or gods and goddesses because normal people didn't have time for lounging in those days, too busy dying of the plague or slaving for their masters or something. My knowledge of the classics is hazy.

'I guess this could be the housekeeper's room?' I crouch and trail my fingertips over those tiles telling me stories I do not know. They are furry with dust. 'Housekeepers and butlers, the ones in charge – they got a better class of accommodation.'

'Why would anyone want to lock their housekeeper in?' Leo stands at the window, possibly looking for his new bat friend who is flitting around out there telling his family about the stupid humans he has just met on his travels.

'Can we just radio Oscar now please? We can grab the last shots as he gets the boat going.' I don't care whose room this was, I don't care about anything apart from being far away from that maze and the impossible candle still burning below us. If I have to, I will walk the Coast Path back to our bunkhouse on my own.

An ally, that is what I need at this point. Leo is at the window so I go over to him, running my torch along the deep wooden windowsill that he leans against. 'That's how the bat got in.' He points at a broken windowpane, its jagged edges glinting in the light of the moon, or our torches.

'They probably roost up here.' I imagine an attic room bristling with little leathery wings, claws clinging to rafters, furry bodies wrapped up tight. In my imagination each creature becomes a tiny shadow in a greatcoat, its waxed material tucked in close like a cocoon.

I try to think of something to say that will break this frost that has formed between us but no ice-pick words form to help me. When Leo glances at me there is a certain sadness but something else is mixed in too, some expression I cannot fathom. He ducks his head down to the hole in the window.

I scrape my fingernail along the windowsill in an idle way, not even looking closely at what I'm doing. However, there on the wood are scratches, not the kind made by bat claws but those made by a knife, by a human hand because those scratches are not merely indistinct lines and whorls, they are shapes. They are letters.

I hover my fingers over them and beckon Richard over. 'So that's a J and an M. Then there's a heart, like you'd draw on your pencil case in school. Then an . . . R . . . yes, an R and another M.'

'JM loves RM.'

Leo stares at me, his face ghostly white in the torchlight. 'RM is Reginald, yeah?'

I cast my mind back to the various reports I had read about the hotel, all of them about Reginald, his dream, his build, his mistakes, his hotel, searching for a name. And then I snag on it. 'Jane!'

Richard turns the camera on me. 'What?'

'Jane! That was Reginald's wife, remember – the one that he mentioned in those letters? He was about to have her committed. JM loves RM. Jane loves Reginald. Of course, if he'd planned to live here then she would have had to come with him . . . oh my God!'

I can tell that Leo has realised too by the way his face falls, and how he glances at, and then walks towards, the door, the one with the bolts on it.

'What?' Richard is barely listening, tapping on the screen of his camera.

'His wife. This is his wife's room . . . *with locks on the outside.* She was in his way, refusing to ask her father for more money. Morwood wasn't going to wait until they stuffed her into an asylum. He used to lock her in, Rich. He kept her prisoner here!'

And at that, as if on cue, the door itself comes to life. Leo is on the other side of it, examining the bolts, when it slams shut and I can put that down to a gust of wind from the broken windowpane, but I cannot put the next thing that happened down to chance.

We hear the bolts outside slam into place.

Chapter 34

Filming in Morwood's study ran late and by the time they finished, Bex's cheek muscles ached from smiling and her dry lips kept sticking to her teeth. All she could think about as she walked back to her trailer was night, the darkness that would fall and allow her to sneak back to the maze and to that pit in the ground so she could finally find out what was in it.

'Was the damn candle the surprise Jasper mentioned?' she had asked Marsha as the crew had packed up around them in Morwood's study.

'Jasper wasn't meant to tell you about that.'

'So it's not the candle. What is it?'

But Marsha had only smiled and walked away.

There was a knock on her trailer door. Bex twitched her curtain back a fraction and swore.

'Bex?' It was Richard.

This was a problem. It wasn't meant to be him at her door at gone midnight. She and Holly had a plan and Richard appearing was not part of it.

'Bex – I know you're not asleep, I just saw that curtain move. Let me in.' His voice slurred and he thumped on the door. She quickly turned the handle so he wouldn't wake anyone else up.

'Jesus, Richard! Why are you here?' she asked as he slumped against the doorframe, wearing a creased T-shirt and jeans. She noted the bottle dangling from one hand. 'How much of that have you drunk?'

'Enough.'

'Aren't you meant to be, y'know . . . on the wagon?'

'Well, I fell off and it ran me over.' His slump turned into a slide and then he sat on her step, head bowed before saying in a small voice. 'I didn't know where else to go.'

It was his tone that did it. Eighteen-year-old Richard had never not known what to do. Certainty had been in his blood, in fact he had overflowed with it to the extent that he had always had some left over for others too, never missing an opportunity to tell her what to do. Had she missed something back then, had this problem with alcohol and who knew what else always been there? She cast her mind back and it was a fishing reel, trying to snag on any old memories, parties where he had been too wild, or days when he had been too out of focus. But then she was hardly one to judge, with her recent champagne overload.

'Here.' She took his arm. 'Come in. I'll make you some coffee.'

The trailer had definitely shrunk in the minutes she had been talking to Richard on the step. Now, with him in it, perched on the edge of the sofa, it felt as if every movement of hers brushed up against him, or stepped on his toes. He did not grip on to the half-empty bottle when she slid it out of his grasp.

'I thought I was fine . . . with all of this . . . you know?' He rubbed at hollowed eyes. 'But being here again, it's just . . .'

'A lot.' She busied herself making coffee. The trailer was equipped with a kettle and a box of sachet teas and coffees, the kind that always tasted metallic, no matter how you made them.

'Yeah. It's a lot.'

'But look at me. I'm a fucking wreck.' He did that familiar hair tousle but without the teenage awareness of every young girl around him. 'How pathetic am I? I came here because I couldn't trust myself not to finish that bottle, and then find another one and then go on a massive bender looking for something to stuff up my damn nose.'

'I have some Vicks, if that'd do?' The words were out of her mouth before her brain had had enough time to sand down their edges and she flicked a glance to Richard, who frowned but then gave a soft snort.

'I think I'll just go with the coffee, thanks. Forgot how you were always so . . .'

'Harsh?'

'Yeah.'

Bex opened what was optimistically called the fridge but in reality was probably only about a degree or so cooler than the room around it. It chugged away as if it were about to explode at any moment. She poured some milk into the coffee and watched it cloud and swirl. 'Still am. It gets me through. Here you go, drink up. I'm warning you though, it's hideous.' She offered the mug which had a big yellow smiley face painted on it. One eye had faded away. There was silence as he drank and the mug winked at her.

'Does it? Get you through?' Richard gave his cup a swirl. 'Because, and feel free to shoot me down in flames because I am in no position to be making judgements on anyone, it seems to me you've been hiding away from everything for the last ten years.'

'You're right. I have. It's worked for me.'

Richard sat back on the sofa and continued to stare into his cup, waving his free hand in a small dismissive gesture. 'Okay, okay.'

'What? At least I haven't whored myself out to any deodorant company or meet-and-greet who'd have me, like Oscar. You know he does those things where people pay him to record messages to them? Like a modern-day singing telegram?'

'Well, who's he harming?' Richard did look up here and Bex knew that gaze, even if it was drunkenly softened by the alcohol in his bloodstream. A challenge.

'Or, there's your option, of course. The tried and tested technique of drinking and snorting yourself into oblivion – a classic choice there. I wouldn't even have to be here if you didn't need to pay your damn debts.' These moves were familiar. Back then they had been teenagers pushing each other to see how far they would go, how hard they could press needle words before they drew blood.

When he stood, the trailer collapsed around him, folded itself in like origami so there was only the two of them and all the words they wanted to say. Not just the trailer but the years collapsed around them too and they were teenagers again, with no sense of consequence, only the here and now. Bex was dwarfed, by him and by those decades and she felt the quiet hush of a switch about to be flicked, of the static calm that comes before change.

But he blinked and that challenge softened in his eyes. 'I started because of the pain.' He spoke in a quiet tone. Bex remembered blood smeared on the ballroom floor. 'It was the pain medication that started it all off . . .'

'You can't hardly tell anymore.' She raised her hand to his cheek and he tilted his head down to her. 'This was all my fault, anyway,' she said. 'It was my idea to come here all those years ago. I researched it all – you'd never have thought of doing it without me.'

'No, no, no.' She felt each no as a breath of air, a shiver on the inside of her wrist. 'I didn't listen, it was my fault. You told me you wanted to leave and I ignored you. If I hadn't . . . Leo would still be here.'

But he was wrong. Leo was always there. Right now he was standing to the side of them with a sad look on his face, the one she had seen when she had given their trip away that day in the library. She would have told Richard then, about the lighter and the note, about what she was planning to do that night, she would have asked him to come with her . . . but first she would have stepped closer into the hugeness and wholeness of him and let herself be swept away for a few moments.

Instead, there was more banging at the door. Opening it a sliver, Bex squeezed out, seeing Holly on the bottom step. The young woman gave her a little wave.

'Who is it?' Richard's voice called from inside.

'It's just Holly. I sent her to find me some paracetamol!' Bex held the door almost closed, hoping Richard would stay on the sofa.

'In the middle of the night?'

'Well, I can't time my headaches, can I? And she's an assistant, it's literally her job – she's meant to assist.' Then she lowered her voice. 'We have a problem. I can't do tonight.'

'Is that . . . Richard?' Holly's whispering definitely needed work. 'Why is he here?'

'He appeared, look he . . . well, he just needed a shoulder . . .'

'Was that *all* he needed?'

And Bex had a brilliant retort for that but instead both of them were distracted by a high-pitched alarm and shouting voices.

Chapter 35

Water dripped. Bex counted the drops: one, two, three, four, but each time wasn't good enough and so she kept counting in her head, her hands closed into fists at her side, nails digging into her palms.

'Shit.' Richard gazed at the inside of his trailer.

It was clear where the fire had started. There were dark smudges on the wall by the little trailer sink and a deep singed hole in what remained of the laminate kitchen counter, its edges curling in on itself like old, hardened lava. Someone had been passing by as the smoke detector began to screech and had wielded the fire extinguisher, stopping the fire from taking hold. Foam slid off the edge of the worktop. Dripping.

One, two, three, four. No.

'Did you leave something charging?'

'No! We don't have our phones anyway. Shit! My trailer could have caught on fire! I could have been in it! What kind of crappy piece of shit thing have they given us to sleep—'

'Mr Deyes!' Marsha appeared at their side and considered the wrecked kitchen counter with them, her bright white hair rather flattened by her pillow. It seemed Bex had been wrong about her sleeping in leather: wrapped around her was a purple fluffy dressing gown and her wellies had bees on them. A chemical burnt-hair smell clung to Bex.

'I could have been in here!' Richard rounded on Marsha.

'I'm well aware, and once all the safety protocols have been worked through, there will be a thorough investigation into what exactly happened here.' Marsha fluidly slipped into the curt and business-like tone of an executive who has learnt the rule book entitled *How to Deal With On-Set Events That Could Get Us Sued*. She paused. 'You smoke, don't you, Mr Deyes?'

'I'm trying to give up. I don't understand what that has to . . . oh. Are you saying—?'

'No one is saying anything. That is my point. No one should be making any sort of wild claims or assumptions about the dangers of cigarettes or vape pens until all the due processes have been worked through, yes? Now, I don't know about you, but I am cold and could do with a cup of tea. I'll get catering to make us some, we'll fix you up with a space to sleep, Mr Deyes, and then we all need to get some rest. We have another busy day ahead of us.'

Ten minutes later, Richard and Bex watched as someone placed plastic bollards and tape around the perimeter of the trailer.

'Marsha's probably busy laminating some new Keep Out signs as we speak,' Bex tried to joke.

'I could have been in there, Bex.' Richard's hand trembled, making the surface of his tea ripple slightly.

There wasn't anything to say to that and Bex could feel tiredness weighing her down like long skirts in water. She watched Marsha in her purple fluffy robe at the catering truck and she had a sudden urge to take cover, to run and find somewhere small and quiet where she could curl up away from all of this.

'I feel it now,' Richard said. 'I never did before, I just thought you were being overdramatic and annoying but . . . you were right. I feel it. This hotel . . .'

'It doesn't want us here.'

'First Oscar, now this. Do you think . . . Do you think someone is targeting us?'

Bex pictured Oscar's wide-eyed stare as he had realised that he could not breathe. If what Richard said was true, then she was next. But she couldn't take anything anyone said at face value in this place, no matter if they still made her stomach dip. She took a step back from Richard and kept her voice neutral. 'Why would we be targeted though? Unless one of us knows more about what went on that night than they're letting on . . .'

It was too dim to really see Richard's expression and he glanced away from her. 'It's not the trailer that should have gone up in flames but that bloody place.' He turned to the dark mass of brick and stone and despair behind them. Three lives gone. Peter Manning, broken on the rocks below, Reginald Morwood, his brains splattered on the wall behind his desk . . . and Leo.

Bex walked away from the trailers, heading towards the hotel with the maze at its side, that weight of exhaustion beginning to tangle her brain, dragging her thoughts down into the murkiest of depths. Her plan for exploring it tonight was not going to work. There were too many people around and she seethed at having to wait another day.

There, at the entrance of the maze, was a shadow upon a shadow and Bex stared at it as once again the world folded in around her like paper. There was just her and that shape, one she had seen ten years ago at this very spot. She blinked again and the shadow could have been wearing an old-style greatcoat, the hood pulled up so no one would be able to see its face, if it had one.

This would not start again. Not this time. Bex began to move towards it, making herself walk tall and not take her eyes from . . . whatever it was. She had followed it once before into that very maze and then it had followed her, to stand outside her house on a normal street in a normal city. It was time to find out what it wanted from her. Whatever it was, she would give it. She would give anything.

Away from the trailers, away from Richard and Marsha and the rest of them, she moved towards the dark, quiet waiting maze. The shadow was roughly human-sized but no matter how hard she gazed, it was a blank of black, as still as every waiting statue on the fountain nearby and those patiently standing in the hedge-lined corridors ahead of her.

Footsteps and fingers on the bare skin of her arm made her scream in a half-strangled way. She whipped around, knowing as she did it that it was the wrong thing to do, that she should not take her eyes away from that shadow, that she shouldn't let it slither away.

'Bloody hell! What's been going on here?' Oscar peered at her with a sleep mask pushed back on his head. 'Why is everyone awake?' The silk of his pyjamas gleamed like oil in the lights.

Too late, Bex snapped her gaze back to the maze entrance, knowing that the shadow would be gone, just a trick of the light. Oscar continued speaking to her, but his words were merely radio static. She just had to get through one more day, a macabre greatest hits of the rooms they had visited in the film and then she could come back here, with Holly to help. She could walk through that entrance and pick the twigs away that caught in her clothes. She could ignore the statues, find the maze's rotten heart and tear it open, or tear it apart.

Just one more day.

Chapter 36

Bex, ten years ago

'Leo! Leo! Did you lock us in?' I run to the door in Jane's room and slap it with the palm of my hand before grasping the doorknob and turning it, a useless thing to do because it isn't the handle that is the problem. The problem is those bolts outside.

But Leo does not answer.

'Leo, mate! Let us out!' Richard joins me.

There is only silence from the corridor outside.

'He wouldn't lock us in! Something's happened! Leo!' I bang on the door again.

'Leo! For fuck's sake! This isn't what we planned!' Richard yells.

'Yeah well, our plan was stupid. It was a stupid thing to do, to wander about in here. We don't even know if it's safe. LEO!' I bellow.

Silence.

'Fuck off, Bex – we all agreed on the plan.' Richard turns on me. 'You found it, this hotel, Miss I'd-Give-Stephen-King-A-Blowjob. This was your fucking idea!'

'My idea? You and bloody Oscar took it over as usual.'

'If you didn't want us here, why'd you invite us?'

The words are out of my mouth before I can stop them. 'It was a mistake!'

Richard's face falls. 'Nice.' We face each other, a little out of breath. He gives the door another shove. 'Real nice, Bex.'

We both stay quiet. I can feel it, how this night has broken apart the bonds that linked us together – the ones already fraying and the ones I had thought were strong.

'I—'

'Y'know, I'm not a moron. It's clear you haven't got the guts to say it so I will. This . . . us . . . was just a couple of disappointing drunk shags so let's call it quits, yeah?'

'Fine by me.'

'Great.'

All the other words we want to say jostle for space between us, hateful, hurtful things with spikes designed to slice and tear. But to our credit, we don't say them. Or maybe not to our credit – after all, we have other things to think about . . . like the still very locked door in front of us.

As Leo has so very rightly pointed out, I know very little about Richard, so as I watch him pace the attic room, face pale, his one arm outstretched, fingers lightly touching the wall, it takes me a minute to realise. 'Rich? You okay?'

'Yep.'

'Because—'

'I don't like small spaces, but this is fine – it's not that small, it's not that small . . .' Gone is the swagger of before and his shoulders deflate as he stops by the window and presses his face close to the broken glass. There is a definite sweaty sheen on his forehead.

'I'm sure I can get the door open. Leo!' I yell again even though I know that silence is going to be the only answer. In my head a thousand horrible things have happened to Leo because that is the only explanation as to why he hasn't opened the door.

Instead I come up with a perfectly reasonable excuse for what has happened. A vicious draught has swung the door shut and then the violence of that action has caused the bolts to shoot across of their own accord, even though that is impossible. Leo did not have time to stop any of it and so, instead of merely unbolting the door as any normal person would do he has . . . he has . . .

. . . fainted dead away and is right now lying unconscious on the floor.

. . . fallen through that floor via a rotten plank, landing in the room below and is just now shaking the dust from his hair and checking to see if all of his limbs are still intact.

. . . been hit on the head by a falling bit of masonry.

'Leo!' Richard thumps the door and then shakes it by the doorknob, before giving it a kick and then sinking into a crouch.

'Rich, we're fine.' I put all of my scant ability to soothe into my words. 'It's an old door, it can't be that strong.'

Of course, I am totally wrong – it is an old door and therefore built of a wood meant to withstand the end of days. Richard sets about battering at it as if he is being pursued by a horde of monsters. He kicks it, shakes it, runs at it and tries to use his shoulder to force it open.

'What the fuck is Leo playing at?' He stops, gulping for air, pushing his hair out of his eyes and then he paces again, this time faster and more fidgety, the camera that he has left abandoned on the windowsill still filming.

'Do you think something has happened to him?' I ask, quiet. Those images play in my head and in each one Leo is alone, bleeding, vulnerable. Worse, he is that way thinking I don't care about him, running our last argument through a brain slowly flickering to blackness.

Richard stops pacing and we face each other, standing in the middle of Jane's room, where she had been locked up, facing a future which was about to become an even smaller place, a grim one in an asylum arranged by a husband she still loved well enough to carve a little heart into a windowsill. JM loves RM. Idiot woman.

Across from me, Richard – the one in our group who always knows everything and, if he doesn't, would never let anyone suspect that – sags. It is the only word for it. It is as if all the bravado, the confidence and swagger have been sucked from him in one quick movement. He opens his mouth and then closes it again, a stupid goldfish. 'I can't be stuck here, Bex. I can't.'

Stepping close to him, I touch his arm. 'It's okay. We'll think of a way out. Let's radio Oscar and tell him where we are – he'll have to get up here to unbolt the door, vertigo or not. Thank God you thought of the walkie-talkies.'

I hope the flattery will puff him up again but he remains motionless against the wall, one hand pressing against it as if he can hold it back. I sigh and take his radio from his pocket, my own dashed to pieces earlier on the rocks. But all I get when I try to use it is useless crackling.

'I'm sorry.' Richard slumps against the door and slides down it until he sits with his knees tucked under his chin. 'About being mean, earlier.'

I crouch next to him, reluctant to sit on the dirty floor despite the mud and grime already smeared over my clothes. 'Me too.'

He smiles a wan copy of his usual megawatt grin, the kind that dazzles its prey and then moves in for the kill. Things are going badly when we start apologising to each other. But we are fine, I tell myself. There will be a rational explanation for this. We will not be left to die and rot here, the mould growing over our bones like an animal's fur.

Without even trying to give an explanation for it, I slide out from my rucksack the emergency phone I'd brought with me. Richard doesn't say anything but, when he sees what it is, he does smile, a weak thing. My feeling of smug superiority does not last, however, when I see the phone is not to be our saviour; the signal strength too weak to make a call.

'This is a nightmare,' Richard mutters. He puts his head on his knees and his shoulders heave.

I study the solid door, shining my torch over it. Victorians made doors to last but I can see, as the light darts over the lower right-hand panel that this one has been patched, maybe at the time, maybe later. That doesn't matter. What matters is that they had used a thinner-looking board, cheaply made, easy to bash in if I find the right tool. I stare back at the fireplace – there, abandoned on the grate is a poker.

That is when we hear Leo scream.

Chapter 37

Bex, ten years ago

I ram the poker again and again into the thin patched panel, splintering it and using the hole created to start prising the board away. Another scream comes from afar and so I wrench and lever, Richard helping, and the nails holding the thin patched plank finally give. This time the wood breaks away, giving a space to crawl through.

We are free.

I would like to say that my only thought is for Leo as I run down that corridor with Richard in tow. I would like to say that my worry for him outweighs everything else. But I'm no movie heroine, I discover. My thoughts are for myself. My fragile layers are like the gilt on Jane's wallpaper flowers and when they are stripped back, there is who I really am, the mortar underneath, a kind that crumbles to black.

The corridor seems darker and narrower than it did when we first walked it. The shadows on either side move with us, though that could be a trick of the light from the torches we hold. I have got my wish at least: I'd wanted to experience the energy that came from a place steeped in bad history. These walls have seen suffering and death and torment – they have sucked it all in like smoke and now they breathe it back over us.

My heart thuds so hard I am soon going to have to stop or choke.

'Leo!' Richard shouts from behind me.

Stairs. First-floor gallery. From the window I watch our little boat, which should have been tied safely on the jetty with a sleeping Oscar inside it, sailing off into the distance.

'Oh my God! Where's he going?' Richard stands at my shoulder.

I don't know. I don't know anything anymore but a hopeful small voice in my brain suggests that Oscar is not abandoning us, that maybe he is returning an injured Leo to the opposite shore.

That he will come back.

Even if he doesn't, we are not trapped, I reassure myself. We can still walk the Coast Path which winds along the cliff to our bunkhouse or cut across the beach at Poppit Sands. It will be a slog, but we can escape.

Richard speaks but I cannot hear anything above the noise from my blood pounding in my ears. If I keep moving I will be okay, I think. If I keep moving, these strange, sinuous shadows in the corners of my vision will not close in on me and that scream that I'd heard will turn out not be Leo's but a fox or something. I leave Richard behind.

Main staircase through to reception. I skitter to a halt in the ballroom.

Just me and the hotel. Darkness. Silence. Dust. The smell of rot. My own breathing, harsh and gasping. Through the huge picture windows I can see only a black sky and that sliver of moon. The wind gets in through the hole we smashed in the glass and it is a tortured screech of sound, a wail from the souls trapped in this place making the old chandelier rattle.

It is a fucking horror film.

But I haven't seen the half of it.

Outside the ballroom window a light flicks on. Wobbling. It jumps about for a few minutes until it settles long enough for me to work out what I am seeing.

A tall figure rises from the high grass at the top step like a corpse from a grave. The long grasses of the old lawn lean towards it as if whispering hideous secrets in its ear but there is no greatcoat, no hood hiding its features. Instead there is a flash of green.

Leo.

Alone.

He is not with Oscar on the boat and I feel relief that he is still with us.

It only takes seconds. I step closer to the ballroom window, intending to pound the glass and yell his name, just as Leo's torchlight flicks off and the blackness takes him. As I resolve to clamber out through that jagged hole in the glass, a terrible cracking sound comes from above.

I look up to see exactly what it is that is cracking, tearing itself away from its fixings, helped by age, by rust, by that wind rushing in through the smashed window, by the very vibration of our footsteps running about on the floor above it. The chandelier. Helped by the hotel itself, determined to smash us to pieces.

Richard throws his camera out of the way and runs for me.

My life does not flash before my eyes. I simply see the chandelier above me, that mess of metal and dangling crystal, I see it judder and then tilt, snapping away from its moorings on the ceiling, not falling completely but sending a hailstorm of glass raining down on both of us. Richard reaches me, bowling me out of the worst of it, sending us both hurtling to the side of the room where we land in a heap.

It takes me a few moments to sit up, to check myself, to pat my face and legs and body for wicked shards of glass sticking out, to convince myself that I am uninjured apart from a few light cuts and scratches and an ankle that now throbs angrily.

It takes me those moments to realise that Richard is scrabbling beside me, his face turned away from mine, crouched over himself, ragged sobs heaving from him.

I think it is the shock of everything, of having a massive great chandelier almost fall on our heads, but then he looks up and, with a shaking hand, brushes his hair from his face.

A face now running with blood.

Chapter 38

Bex, ten years ago

Pretty boy Richard. Richard who could charm a girl with a half-smile and a twinkle in his eye.

No more.

At first I see only the blood. One half of his face is a mess of it, thick and running, and perhaps it is my brain trying to give me manageable little bites of horror, because I think, with that amount of blood, he must have a head wound.

Then he shifts and something glints, that twinkle in his gaze comes horribly to life, and my brain finally allows me the full picture in glorious technicolour.

A shard of glass sticks out from his eye.

No one prepares you for something like this. There's no lesson in school, apart from the odd first-aid class where you prat about with grubby mannequin torsos and learn how to bandage an arm. No one tells you what to do when someone reaches out a bloodied hand to where they think you are but miss because they can't see past the great big piece of chandelier that is stuck in their actual eye.

Richard is every horror novel I have ever read all rolled into one.

I will never read another one.

As he tries to speak, blood runs into his mouth and he chokes instead.

'Don't move,' I manage to say, clutching his hand.

I don't know if trying to take the piece of glass from his eye would sentence him to death through loss of blood alone and probably shock. I can only bring myself to look at his injury in quick glances. The glass is about two inches long, a shattered bit from one of the lower pieces of the chandelier, teardrop shaped.

I can no longer see the end of the teardrop.

The eye itself is swollen flesh and blood and my glance bounces off it. I think again about grasping the bit of glass I can see and then giving it a quick hard tug, but the thought makes my stomach feel as if it is trying to squash itself into my throat.

The bleeding. I can help with that.

Abandoned at one edge of the ballroom are our rucksacks and I stumble over to mine, hearing the shattered crystal crunch under my feet. My fingers, wet with Richard's blood, slip off the zip but I manage to get it open and start rummaging through. There is a scarf, but it is an open-weave thing, like crochet, designed for fashion, not warmth, and it would soon become saturated with blood. I spot Richard's beanie hat still in his pocket and wrap the two items together as makeshift wadding. Checking my phone I see the signal is weak.

'Hold these on your cheek, under your eye.' Pushing the material into his hand, I then guide it to his face. 'We have to get you up and I'm going to go outside and phone for help. You need a hospital.'

I am now playing a part. This film we'd set out to make, it has sucked us all in and here I am playing the plucky heroine, the one who always knows what to do, who holds it all together whilst hell dances around her.

'Mmphf . . .' The sound is unintelligible but the action is unmistakeable.

He points to the camera lying abandoned on the floor a few yards from us.

I shouldn't be shocked. It is what he has come for, after all. 'Something real, something raw.' I can imagine our university tutors in interviews yet to come, asking us about this moment, nodding as we talk about our commitment to the piece, to art, a commitment sealed by blood. They will admire us. They will think us crazy. At first I refuse but Richard gets agitated and I am afraid he will further injure his eye.

So I film him.

Only a few seconds. Shaking, struggling to keep the camera steady, an awful gasping sound coming from me, I point the camera at him and let it run.

When I try to help him up, he cannot stand. I consider dragging him out and attempt to get a grip under his armpits but can only manage to stagger a few feet before I have to let go.

There is no choice.

'I'll go and call for help. I'll come back, I promise.' I don't think he even hears me but just moans slightly and I manhandle him over to the wall so he can slump against it, blood smeared around him as if he is an artist creating an abstract painting.

I run. Climbing through the hole we made earlier in the window, my leg muscles are water but it is good to be running, to be moving away from the hotel, down the first set of steps and onto a path lined with wild shrubbery and plants. I think I am running away from the worst of it, that nothing else can happen.

I am wrong.

Leo.

I turn on the path to the last but one set of steps before the jetty. There he is. I see his camera fall from his grasp and lunge towards him, my already sore ankle sending a jolt of pain that makes me stumble as I hit the ground.

It can only have been a minute at most as I haul myself up. One long glance down. One glance up.

He is gone.

I cannot move. Not in a 'paralysed with fear' way, though that would have been understandable. No, I think I simply shut down, my body refusing to do anything whilst my brain tries to make sense of the empty space where my best friend had been.

When I do move, I drag myself to the step where Leo stood, not even a low stone wall to act as a barrier from the sea and rocks, just those stone spindles. Before I get to it I force myself to my feet and then it only takes a few yards to look over the edge, expecting to see his body below me. Four steps.

I count them: one, two, three, four.

Slow.

Each count is a chance to get it right; if the numbers are said in a certain way like a spell . . . things will be different.

I see only rocks and sea. No body. No sign of Leo at all, he has simply been erased from the scene like a special effect, the kind a video editor would add in post-production.

But I can't stand around staring at the sea, there is Richard to think of. Somehow I get to the jetty. When I try to use my phone, my fingers are slick with blood and mud, they slide from the smooth screen but I only have to tap three times: 999. There is nothing else to do but wait. Emergency services come then, a huge whirring insect of a helicopter cowing the waves and sending spray into my face. Bustle. People shouting. Eventually Richard is brought out on a stretcher.

No Leo.

No Leo.

No Leo.

What else is there to say?

I do not understand how Leo has disappeared. I do not understand half of what happened tonight. There is a story here, probably more than one, and I need to know them all. I need to layer them all on top of one another as if they are tracing paper so I can see the pattern form and work out what I've missed.

Because I've missed something, I know it. There is a lie, a secret at the heart of all of this and it has burrowed in deep. I sit there on the jetty, in the wreckage of our night, and I promise to myself that I will hold a pair of tweezers and I will pull and stretch that secret out into the light. No matter how long it takes me. I will watch it squirm.

Chapter 39

Bex stared at a sky that held death.

'She's a beauty, isn't she?' The man next to her shaded his eyes against the morning sun.

Bex nodded. She could have had breakfast with everyone else but the further away from the hotel she was, the less she felt as if her head was about to explode. This tent was next to the gate in a quiet spot shaded by overhanging trees. Eating another spoonful from her porridge pot, she watched the dark shape swoop in the sky.

'She's never tried to, y'know – just fly away?'

'My Artemis? Never. She's pampered she is, has a life of Riley. Knows what side her bread is buttered. If she ate bread.' Dog owners sometimes grew to look like their dogs and, Bex noted, eagle owners did the same thing. The keeper had a hook nose and eyes so fierce that Bex had almost decided not to bother him. His face had bloomed into a smile, however, at the chance to show off his friend and he had introduced himself as Gethin.

'Has she caught any?' The eagle had been employed to catch and destroy any drones sent up the hill to spy on filming beyond the gates.

'Sure has!' Gethin stooped and rummaged in a plastic box at

the edge of the enclosure, bringing out a twisted hunk of lightweight plastic. 'I think they've learnt their lesson now though – we haven't seen one for a while.'

The dark shape wheeled and effortlessly rode thermals.

'What is she?'

'A golden eagle.'

'And is she . . . is she happy?'

Gethin pierced her with a look almost as sharp as Artemis's claws. 'If I didn't think she was happy, she wouldn't be here. I raised her from an eaglet; she'd soon let me know if she was miserable. And I'd do something about it.'

Bex nodded. 'What does she do, when she's not hunting drones?'

'We're over at the nearby bird sanctuary, a few miles from here. She does the odd show, display work – that kind of thing. Here – you want to try?' Gethin handed her a huge, padded leather glove and laid a chunk of pink meat on it.

'Oh, I don't know, I—'

'Nonsense, Artemis loves meeting new folk.' He gave a piercing whistle and Bex saw the dark shape loop again in the sky, soaring to the side as if she hadn't heard but there was hardly any time between that moment and the next when a rush of air swept her hair into her face and a heavy weight thudded onto her outstretched arm.

Artemis tilted her head and gave her a long, hard stare; Bex wasn't sure if she was going to pass muster until the bird ruffled her feathers and then tore into her snack.

'She's beautiful.' Bex watched the powerful beak rip into her meal, taking in the talons and the gloss of her brown and white feathers on gigantic wings that allowed her to simply flap away into freedom, any time she chose. The bird was so much bigger than Bex had expected, and she felt her arm muscle tremble under the weight. 'Hello, Artemis. My name is Bex. I know a bird back home, his name's Bob. He's a pigeon. You'd probably eat him.'

'Hey, Bex!' She heard Oscar's voice and turned her head but not her body as she didn't want to startle the trained killing machine perched on her wrist. He paused, wide-eyed. 'Jesus!'

At the sound of his voice, Artemis stopped eating and swivelled an eye to him. It was a predator's gaze, a quick assessment of size and flesh, which bits would rip the easiest. She shrugged her wings a bit wider, shuffling along the glove as if about to dive off, possibly straight into Oscar's face.

'Whoa there, girl,' Gethin said, expertly nudging the bird onto his own glove and then clipping her onto her wooden perch outside her enclosure before giving her another chunk of meat. 'She don't normally notice anything if she's eating. Sorry about that.'

Oscar gave a nervous laugh and glanced at the eagle on her perch who eyed him like a disapproving schoolteacher. 'Yeah, what can I say? I'm just not popular with the eagle community . . .'

'Two visitors and it's not even ten o'clock yet – I'm honoured,' Gethin said with a wry smile.

'Ah, no. I came to say good morning to Bex . . . if that's all right?' Because Oscar could not drag his eyes away from Artemis, it looked as if he was asking her if they could talk. She blinked.

Bex picked up her pot of porridge and walked him away from Artemis in case the bad luck of this place set the bird free to sink its talons into his eyes. She had had enough of blood. When she took another spoonful of porridge she found it had cooled to a sludge. Oscar wore a beanie hat pulled down over his unbrushed blonde hair and there were bags under his eyes. He held a Tupperware box.

'What's that?' She nodded towards the box.

'Oh, breakfast. I have to have my meals prepared separately and then sealed – y'know, for safety.'

Bex did know. She had been the one who had plunged the EpiPen into his thigh.

'You feel okay?'

'Yeah, yeah – I'm fine. Bit paranoid, obvs.'

They stopped and Bex put her hand over Oscar's; his nails looked as if they had been recently manicured. In contrast her own were badly filed with chewed skin around the quick. 'What you said yesterday about being a disappointment – I never realised you felt that way. In fact, if I'm honest, Oscar – I've not thought about you much at all over these last ten years, except to think you got off lightly . . .'

'Well, I did, I'm not going to deny it. I'm *grateful* I wasn't there that night, Bex. What you saw, what happened, I really don't think I'd have been strong enough to deal with it—'

'No, I'm sure—'

'Come on, Bex. We all know I was a bit of a twat back then.'

She couldn't help a snort of laughter. 'Weren't we all?'

At that moment Holly appeared carrying a little cardboard tray with two coffees slotted into it. 'Morning, both. Bex, here's your caffeine.' Something swooped in the air above them. 'Bloody hell! I hate that eagle!'

'I don't think she's interested in coffee though.'

Holly gave one last look behind her as if Artemis would at any moment come screeching for her. 'Quick word, Bex?'

Oscar backed away, waving his Tupperware as a goodbye. 'See you in the hotel.'

Holly grabbed Bex's arm as they walked from the gate, up the drive to where the fountain came into view and beyond that, the hotel. 'It's about Rich.' Under a canopy, Bex saw a group of people sat eating, Richard on the end, staring at his bowl, head propped against hand.

'What about him?'

'I've been thinking about him.' Bex raised her eyebrows and Holly smiled. 'Not like that! No, I was thinking how he was mighty keen to help hand out those pizzas on our first night . . .'

'So?'

'Have you ever thought he could have slipped something onto Oscar's?'

Bex thought for a moment. 'The pizza place said they might have used nut oil by mistake . . .' The idea of Rich deliberately sabotaging Oscar's meal seemed completely out of character . . . though, if she was honest, she knew nothing about his character, back then when they had been eighteen, or now.

Holly edged the top free from her coffee cup and blew into it, the steam escaping in little curving tendrils. 'And, well, he seems a bit . . . on edge, don't you think? The drinking again, I mean. I thought he was off all of that and then the fire . . . in his state last night he could have left a lit cigarette or—'

'The fire could have been caused by anything – we don't know—'

'Yeah, okay – we don't know that. But we do know that there's something . . . off with him. I think he's becoming really unstable.'

Over at the table Richard picked up his spoon, dipped it into the bowl and then put it down again without taking a bite. He rubbed at his eye. Looking at him now, a person would be unlikely to guess that his right eye was glass. The scars had faded to silvery trails, only seen in a certain light.

Bex shrugged. 'There's something off with all of us. Why else would we be here?'

'Yeah, but he smokes, right? So he could have left a cigarette burning? Carries round that lighter with your face on it—'

'What?' Bex stopped. Holly's words were an eagle hurtling towards her from a sky that only moments before had been predator-free.

'Okay, he's trying to give up—'

'No, the lighter.' Bex clutched too hard at Holly's elbow. 'When did you see him with a lighter? Describe it.'

'Umm . . . at the production meet-up we had before you signed on? Your face was printed on it and I think Leo too – plastic orange thing? Sweet that he carries it round.'

Bex stared. She had never got round to showing Holly the lighter in the end, despite telling her about the note. There was no way the girl could have known exactly what she was describing. As Holly watched her with a puzzled expression, Bex walked four steps and counted them out in her head, but she knew they would be wrong and she would have to count again, and again, and again – and still, even then they would not protect her from those words. Richard had been seen with the lighter, literally days before it was posted to her. Richard. *It's time the world knew what happened to Leo Finch.* So what did he know?

There was a lot Bex could have said then. It probably would have helped if she had begun to talk, let it all spill out. In ancient times, diviners would often try to scry the future with runes, adding their own blood to the mix and then peering at the mess, trying to work out what it meant. The lighter. The note. Oscar choking. The trapdoor in the maze. The fire. These were her runes and try as she might, no matter how hard she stared at them, she couldn't understand what they were telling her.

Holly dragged her off to set, so many steps, each group of four feeling wrong in some way. As she passed his table, Richard gave her a weak smile. She did not return it.

Chapter 40

Once more into the darkness.

'So. Jane's room.' Jasper moved one of the locks on the door, making the metal creak. They were the kind designed to swing across and be secured by a padlock. The turret room looked the same as when they found it ten years ago, the curved walls, gilt flowers on the wallpaper and the fireplace with its tiles telling stories of gods and goddesses. Even the little wooden box, carved in the shape of a heart, was still on the mantelpiece. Bex ran her fingertip over the etched word *Cariad* on it and tried to concentrate on filming but the idea of Richard having the lighter, then sending it to her for whatever sick reason – it kept playing in her head like an off-key radio jingle. 'The wronged wife. Kept locked in here until our dear Reginald could ship her off to a lunatic asylum. You seemed to feel quite an affinity with Jane, didn't you, Bex?' Bex did not answer. 'Bex?'

She swallowed and blinked a few times, trying to focus, but all she could think about was what Holly had just told her. Someone nudged her and she tried to catch what Jasper had just said. 'Jane? Yes, Jane . . .'

Jasper continued, 'But she might actually have been mad. Maybe we should think of Reginald as poor Reginald having to put up with a crazed wife whose behaviour was so out of control he had to lock her up.'

'No.' Her words were too loud. 'Absolutely nothing, apart from what Morwood wrote, suggests she was mad. She had friends, she wrote letters to them.' Many of Bex's nights alone in her half-finished house had been spent reading the copies of those old papers she and Leo had searched out in the library. In her mind she had built a woman, kind-eyed and wry, then trapped and taken advantage of by a sinister greatcoated man. 'And her family was far richer than his. I'm guessing a lot of the money he sunk into this hotel was hers. Even before the railway line was delayed, he was in debt just getting this place built, but she wouldn't ask her father for more cash. Basically, she was getting in the way and, as a woman, she could do very little to protect herself.'

Jane had become trapped here, in this room with no way to escape and no real knowledge of what was going on around her. Bex knew how that felt.

'I don't think Jasper asked for a history lesson, Bex!' Richard tried to smile for the camera. It was cramped in the room with the cables, equipment, the boom microphone and the people needed to keep all of that in order. Too many people. There was too much going on at the hotel, much like in the days when it had been built – far too much that could go wrong, far too much temptation for the malevolent spirit of the place.

Bex turned on him. 'We could all do with a bit of a history lesson though, couldn't we, Rich? Because some people, they seem to know a bit more about our *history* than they're letting on—'

'I think we should stick to what happened to Jane, yeah, Bex?' Oscar wedged himself between the two of them whilst Jasper watched with a hard stare that would have made Artemis proud. 'Do you know what she did afterwards? After he killed himself?'

Bex knew that Oscar was trying to keep her on topic, and she took a breath, eyed the camera and said, 'That's the thing. No one bothers to find out anything about her. The conventions, the fans, it's all Morwood and his bloody curse, nothing about her. Anyway, yes, I do know what happened to her. She became a nun. Went straight to the nearest convent after Morwood's suicide and stayed there until her death.'

'That's really interesting, isn't it, Richard?' Oscar elbowed him but he didn't say anything, too busy frowning at Bex.

'I don't bloody blame her,' Bex said. 'No wonder she wanted to get away from everyone and their damned lies. I'd do the same.'

'Do you feel someone's been lying to you, Bex?' Jasper cut in with the speed of a snake spotting its next meal.

Through the door a dark corridor waited and Bex couldn't help but flick her glance to it. Out there had been the scene for the footage that she, and everybody else, had found the most disturbing. She had only seen it when Oscar cut the film together because, at the time when it happened, she and Richard had been locked in this room. Leo. Alone in that corridor. Or . . . not quite alone. Next to her Richard fidgeted, scraping at the flesh of his thumb with one nail, keeping himself close to the door, to escape.

The thing was, Bex thought, when Leo disappeared from the step, Richard couldn't have been a part of it because he had been sitting in the ballroom trying to stem the bleeding from his eye. But had he said something to Leo at some point that night, something awful enough to set him running away from them all, to those steps, to the darkness? How had he got hold of the lighter and why had he sent it to her with that horrible anonymous note? *It's time the world knew what really happened to Leo Finch.*

Maybe it was time to ask that question.

'No one is lying about anything, are they, Bex? That's not what you meant – that's not what she meant.' Oscar moved her away from the door and Richard and over to the window instead.

'Bex? Is there a problem?' Richard stared at her.

She wanted to throw the lighter at his smug face with its concerned gaze. 'What? No, I meant y'know, I'd have done the same in her position.' She wouldn't. If she'd have been Jane, she would have wiped away the brain splatter on the office wall and then she would have claimed the hotel as her own, filled it with plants and stayed safe and high up on her clifftop, with no one to tell her what to do anymore.

'But Jane is only one part of this room, and though what happened to her is very sad, very sad – who . . . or *what* do you think slammed this door shut?' Jasper gestured to the door, almost like a retro *Wheel of Fortune* model showing off the game show wheel. He had the white teeth and frozen face; he just needed the tight minidress and heels.

'We'll never know that, will we?' Richard spoke in a clipped tone. 'Most likely it shut by itself. A draught or something.'

Trying to take her mind off Richard and that corridor and the darkness that lurked there, Bex wandered over to the windowsill to look once again at Jane's pathetic little carving declaring her love for Reginald. Women were stupid, she decided. *She* was stupid for letting Richard into her trailer last night.

There they were, scratched letters in the wood. JM and then that wonky heart and then the letters RM.

Bex stared at it, bent closer, looked harder, not quite understanding what she saw. Finally, she turned to the others. 'I think we missed something here.'

Chapter 41

It was hardly even a centimetre. A line. A flick.

'Someone's messed with it?'

Four heads peered at the etching on the windowsill illuminated by bright film lights.

'Unlikely,' Jasper said, more for the camera and the eventual people watching. 'The film company bought up the rights pretty swiftly after you became an internet hit and they bought this land with it, though it obviously took longer to get the film distributed because . . . well, cinemas move slowly. So they cracked down on trespassing straight away. And the bats too, remember. This is a protected site. We had to jump though loads of hoops to film here, it's why the place has never been opened to the public.'

'I'm not seeing it . . .' Oscar muttered.

'Here.' Bex pointed to that final line in the forming of the letter R. 'So you think that's an R, right? Except, look a bit closer.' Richard leant over her to shine a torch on the spot on the windowsill and she angled away from him. 'That bit, the final kick, isn't scratched on as deep . . . in fact there's a gap between it and the rest of the letter, as if it was added on afterwards.'

'So what if it was? Jane got tired of scratching and came back to it later. I mean, is this even Jane's graffiti?' Oscar tilted his head to get an even closer look.

Jasper glanced over to Marsha who was out of sight of the camera. The woman nodded and said, 'Yes, it's the right age. Production had it tested before the film came out. Didn't want anyone to crawl out of the woodwork – so to speak – and say they did it in 1984 or whatever.'

'So what would the letter be without that line?' Bex asked, more of herself than anyone else.

'A P?' Oscar offered.

'Yes. The letter P.' There were blank faces around her. She was the schoolteacher leading a particularly dense class though a problem. 'So who has the initials PM?'

'Oh . . . wait . . .' Realisation shone in Richard's eyes. 'Peter.'

'Exactly. Peter Manning. The carpenter who fell to his death when the hotel was being built.'

It was a relief, Bex had to admit, to be focused on something else for once, not them, not Leo, but the reason she had come here in the first place – the history of the place. The mystery of it. It was why they had set out in their silly boat ten years ago. These initials had never really been discussed much after the film because it turned out that Richard had only taken an out-of-focus shot of them on the night, much to his annoyance, so there had been no way for the fans to pour over the images and come to their own conclusions.

'Okay.' Richard ducked out of the way so the camera could get a clear shot of the initials this time around. 'So, let's say that this R is in fact a concealed P which . . . yeah, I get where you're coming from. It could be. Could easily not be though, too. But let's say it is. Jane was what? In love with Peter?'

Voices spoke over each other.

'Maybe they had a torrid affair.'

'What if Reginald found out?'

'Do you think that was why he locked her in? To keep her away from Peter?'

'What if Peter's accident was no accident at all?' Bex said and everyone fell silent. Her eyes fell on the heart-shaped wooden box on the mantelpiece, the kind of thing a carpenter would make for a loved one. *Cariad*.

Jane loves Peter.

A story stitched itself together in Bex's head. Plucky Jane, her money now under the control of villainous Reginald, is stuck at the hotel with the building work going on. She falls for the dashing Peter and they plan to run away but evil Reginald finds out about the affair, has her locked away and pushes Peter to his death. She could see it, Morwood, rain-lashed on a black, black night standing on the edge of the cliff watching Peter's body fall to the hungry rocks below. But that is all it was – a story. She knew all too well how stories bloated themselves out of all proportion like corpses left in water. Despite that, she itched to find out more about Peter and the construction site. It looked like the oncoming evening was going to be a busy one for her: searching through the papers she had brought with her *and* a midnight escapade to a pit in the middle of the maze. She wanted to open that up before she confronted Richard.

It wasn't her imagination, the darkness out in the corridor seemed to get inkier.

'This is going to be great for our watchers – secrets revealed kind of thing! I can see the teaser trailer right now. Brilliant work, everybody!' Marsha clapped her hands and people began to pack up equipment.

Bex frowned and moved closer to Marsha, keeping her voice quiet. 'Is this you? Did you plant this?'

'I'm rather disheartened that you would think that, Bex.' Bex raised an eyebrow and Marsha continued, 'Look at the window-sill – has it been tampered with? No. Same old piece of wood in its rotten frame, same scratchings. I'm as surprised as you are. But thank you, you've noticed something that has given us a real boost. I always thought you were the smart one.'

Bex fixed her with a stare. Flattery would not work. Flattery was for eighteen-year-old Bex who would have smiled and flicked her overly styled red hair over one shoulder in that way she thought was attractive but was, in reality, an annoying nervous tic. Present-Bex gave that girl a kick and sighed.

The room emptied whilst she stared at those letters. Voices, a clattering of equipment and then the silence claimed her. She hadn't meant to be the last one out so when she turned and there was just her and that door, a slow ooze of dread prickled the back of her neck.

The door. It had slammed shut on her once before and she would not let that happen again, so she ran the few steps to it, grabbing the cracked porcelain handle, rough under her palm. But somehow that was worse because now she faced the corridor with its shadows, the place where Leo had run away from them after the door had got locked, on his own . . . or, not on his own. Many people had studied that clip, they had lightened it, paused it, enlarged it and still no one could work out exactly what happened in it.

The darkness beyond Jane's door was a curtain and it was waiting for Bex to step into it so it could wrap around her, bind her tight and then spin her out and into . . . somewhere terrible where ghosts stalked in greatcoats and impossible candles burnt bright.

Never before had she been so pleased to hear Marsha's voice. 'Bex? You're needed in the reception hall. It's time for you to see our surprise.'

Chapter 42

The reception had been turned into a hellish cinema room, a place for ghouls to bathe in the light of the silver screen.

But there was only space in this hell for three damned souls.

'Bex, Oscar, Richard? Please sit here.' Jasper pointed to the seats placed in front of the large white projector screen. He had changed from his puffy jacket and jeans into a smart pinstriped suit with a spotted pocket handkerchief. They were old-fashioned theatre seats, brass and red velvet with arm rests that ended in lion heads, snarling at nothing. Lions for Leo, Bex thought as she sat.

'Are we going to watch *Ravencliffe* again?' Richard couldn't keep the dismay from his voice.

There was no camera team flitting around them this time, filming every facial twitch. Static cameras had been set up around their seats and they already wore their microphones. There was no one else in the room, in fact, not even Marsha. Just them, and Jasper and that white void of a screen. Their mini cinema had been set up to one side of the main staircase, just under the first-floor gallery landing.

'Not quite.' Jasper smiled, white teeth in the gloom, and Bex could imagine this was her own personal hell. Not just how it looked: the gritty, splintered floor, the dead things in the rafters, the wallpaper peeling away like wet flesh, no, this here was her hell, to sit and re-live that night ten years ago, over and over again, to watch Leo smile and laugh and run and stand and then watch the nothing he became. Blank space.

Penance.

There was a Purgatory, so Catholics believed. A place where souls deemed not quite good enough for heaven floated in a white nothingness waiting for cleansing prayers to send them on their way to the Pearly Gates. That was her. Except there would never be enough prayers.

A flicker on the screen.

'So. Let's just go back in time to summer ten years ago. A police investigation, a missing persons case. Once that had concluded the police gave back the cameras and film and you, Richard, with Oscar's help because of your eye injury, you posted an edited version of what happened at Ravencliffe online.'

'I didn't do it for it to become . . . *this*,' Richard added in a low voice. 'I thought at the time it might help us find Leo.'

'Quite. Well, it became a word-of-mouth sensation and Echelon Pictures approached you and picked up the rights, distributing the film a year later. Oscar kept all the raw footage and he has kindly rooted through the files on the original memory card for this ten-year celebration. What we're about to show now has never been seen before . . .'

The screen flickered again.

And there he was, a punch in her stomach. For so long she had got used to the same pictures of Leo, the same way he moved in each of the shots of the film, the same full smile or terror-stricken face. The dead freeze in our memories, doomed to only move when they repeat the same steps over and over in snatches of film and in brutally short videos on phones. They become our puppets and Bex had made Leo jerk and dance his familiar routines for so long that seeing him like this: a new smile, a new movement of his shoulder, a shrug she had not seen before, made her grip the edges of her armrests so hard she thought she might break the lion heads.

For those brief minutes Leo was alive again and she could not keep her eyes from him. There were only three clips and each was far too short but they were diamonds, each one carefully hewn out of the coal face.

One: from the reception at the start, Leo bending to film something the rest of them couldn't see in the dust and debris of the floor. Bex knew it would have been something simple but poignant, a mouse skeleton, the beads from a broken bracelet, or a corner of an old pamphlet. The hem of his raincoat trailed in the dirt.

Two: the fountain. Leo standing on tiptoes next to one of those strange creeping statues gripping the basin, carefully placing his woolly hat on its stone head and giving it the thumbs-up.

Three.

She knew the clip: it was Leo in the corridor after the door had locked on Richard and Bex in Jane's room. He had taken a camera with him as he ran, his face a rictus of fear, his eyes wide. But Leo's sweet, terrified face was not what people had focused on. His headtorch had been facing down so it illuminated his face but also, when he moved his head, threw enough light into the corners of the corridor he ran through.

There had been something in the shadows.

That torchlight had flashed and in each retina-blinding beam, there it was. Another flash and it had been gone.

A face.

There are creatures that live in the deepest trenches in the ocean. They never see the light and so their skin is waxy and white, their mouths unnaturally large and too full of teeth. They are not meant to have light shine on them. The face in the corridor behind Leo had been one such face. Bex had watched this part many times, had paused the video at each of those points, freezing the image, but each time it did not want to be caught. No matter what she had done, the pale, wide-mouthed face had always trembled and blurred out of view, a nightmarish deep-sea monster wriggling away from the diver's light.

Leo had been the guppy, out of his depth.

Watching it again turned Bex's hands into claws digging into the gold lion heads on her chair. Richard's elbow touched hers, the man who had probably sent her Leo's lighter with that ominous note but when she looked at his face she saw he was impassive, simply staring at the film being played for them.

The extra bit of footage came at the end. Bex caught a glimpse of Leo's feet off to one side of the frame, darkness around him, and then his spectacled-face loomed large as he reached for the camera just as Bex leapt up and rushed towards the screen.

'I'm really sorry, I—' She stood in the middle of the screen so the projected film curved over her, making her celluloid too, fusing her into the shot. She held up her hand against the light and Leo's eyes bulged over her fingers. 'I can't do this right now. Can you just turn it off please?'

Flicker. The whirring sound stopped and the screen became, not a portal into the past anymore, but once again a plain white piece of canvas.

'Hey, you all right?' Richard stood up from his chair but didn't move towards her, caught in his own awkwardness, the theatre seat half folding up behind him, making him bend uncomfortably at the knees.

'Let's just get this over with, Bex,' Oscar said.

'No, I'm done for today.' Bex spoke to the shadows and heard the click-clack of Marsha's boots coming towards them. 'Look, I don't want an argument. Could we pick this up tomorrow?'

Marsha stopped and shrugged. 'Fine. I agree, it's getting late. We can keep busy setting up the ballroom for the next shoot tomorrow.'

The three of them were left with the seats, the screen and the silence. Jasper had already sighed, dragged on his duvet coat and made a beeline for the catering truck where they kept a bottle of malt whisky exclusively for him. His nightcap, he called it, except he started drinking it in the afternoon.

'A few more minutes, Bex, and it would have been over.' Oscar stood and dusted down his trousers, then wiped his palms together.

'You weren't there, you don't understand.'

Oscar raised his eyebrows and smiled in a sad way. 'I know what you both think of me.'

They hadn't come to take the cameras away, Bex noted. The little red recording lights blinked like a landing strip for an aeroplane made only of red velvet seats edged in brass. This was simply another scene.

'That I'm a sell-out because I go to the conventions and make appearances and do adverts for high-end brands,' Oscar continued and Bex nearly laughed at the mention of 'high-end'. 'You think that means I don't care. But I do.' The final three words had a ring of truth to them and Bex watched Oscar who, for once, did not have an eye out for his best angle but instead hung his head.

'Ah mate, we don't think that.' Richard stepped closer.

'I do.' Bex spoke fast, without allowing for any pesky thoughts to get in the way. 'I've thought you were a sell-out all along, but fair enough. You made your money and none of it mattered, none of it would bring Leo back. But that you care? Come off it. You hardly knew him. Either of you.'

'That's not strictly true, Bex.'

'I knew him my whole life!' Her voice broke and she swallowed. 'Well, as long as I can remember. You two only met him because of *me*. If Rich and I hadn't got together, you'd barely have been able to recognise Leo except maybe as the kid you sometimes made fun of.'

'It's not a competition, who liked Leo most.'

'It is though. It definitely is if you want to whinge on about your feelings and how sad you are. You have to know a person to truly mourn them. You both knew nothing about Leo.'

'I'm not going to get into an argument about it, okay, Bex?' Richard held his hands up in surrender, but his eyes weren't playing along. 'Because that's all it was with you, wasn't it? Argument after argument. Rolling your eyes and snarky comments and picking holes in us. That's all you ever did.'

'Mate, let's not do this here . . .' Oscar shifted his gaze to the cameras.

'Oh, we might as well. Because we're never going to see each other again, are we . . . *mate*?' The sneer on that last word was unmistakeable. 'This show is going to wrap tomorrow and then you'll go back to selling tat to idiots and she'll disappear again. So yeah, she's right – we were never friends.'

Bex tried to get up out of her seat, but a wave of lead washed over her, making her feel like she might never manage it. It wouldn't be so bad, to sit here forever, in her lion velvet chair watching new footage of Leo on a loop. Somewhere a hangnail part of her brain snagged on something to do with that footage, something about the final shot where his face had loomed into view, eyes obscured by the reflection of his lenses.

The three of them stood. There was nothing to say. Well, there was – Bex wanted to know an awful lot about where Richard had got that lighter from, but that would have to wait. If she confronted him now, she couldn't predict what would happen and if it meant him walking out and the shoot closing down, she would never get to find out what was under the trapdoor in the maze, or any of the hotel's other secrets. After all, that night ten years ago when the ghostly figure had disappeared from the middle of the maze – they had been standing on that spot. Maybe the supernatural had had nothing to do with their vanishing: maybe they had simply hidden under her feet. Bex hauled herself up thinking how Marsha had got more than she had probably ever hoped for in those last few minutes and she could see the headlines now: 'Reunion Reveals Ravencliffe Rift' or something equally alliterative.

But before all of that there was night. And she had things to do under cover of darkness.

Chapter 43

Bex watched the last of the sun glow and then dip behind the tree line. The hotel hugged night closer.

When she wasn't filming, Bex had taken to spending as much time as she could outside in the fresh air. Morwood was in the very particles of the hotel, his dust, his atoms probably still floating around. With all the time she had spent here, she had breathed him in like a virus, a contamination she would never be able to shake.

She took a deep lungful of air. She wasn't hiding. She was waiting. Hours and hours had to slip by before she could venture out, hidden by the darkness, and find out what was in that hole in the middle of the maze. She knew, deep in her spine, that something was.

It was actually quite comfortable in the fountain with its bed of dry leaves, and the smooth inside of the bowl obscured almost everything around her apart from the sky and the tips of the trees. A stone woman reached over her, her face sad rather than frightening: no grimace, or snarl, just wide eyes and an open mouth as if she were about to impart a secret.

'Hey.'

Bex froze. If the statues started speaking to her then she was going to get out of the fountain and begin the walk downhill right now, keep walking until she was as far away from this hotel as she could get.

'Bex?' Another face peeped over the rim of the fountain bowl and Bex let her fists uncurl. Holly gave a little wave. 'Are you hiding?'

'No.'

'Want some company?'

'No.'

'Great.' Holly got a leg over the side with some effort and slithered into the bowl next to her. 'This is cool. You can see their faces from here.' She gave one of the statues a boop on the nose.

'You really have no concept of personal boundaries, do you?'

'Nope.' Holly smiled and pulled up her black-and-red-striped knee socks which she wore over tights and a very ripped skirt. 'And *you* really have no concept of being nice to people.'

Bex returned her smile but it had a bitter after-taste. 'People are overrated.' She flicked at a dry leaf and it disintegrated under her touch.

'Isn't this Peter Manning?' Holly picked out a copy of a very old photograph in amongst the paper Bex had brought to the fountain with her, intent on using what was left of her time before going into the maze as usefully as she could.

'Yes. I thought I'd read up on him a bit more, y'know, after we found those initials that Jane carved.'

JM loves PM. The photograph was of a group of the Welsh men who built the hotel, standing proudly outside their temporary tented campsite in the hotel's grounds, their names printed underneath. Peter had his arm slung around another man's neck and though his face was a little hazy Bex could see the confidence in him. He would be the type to lead others, to refuse to speak only English and get under Morwood's skin. After the photo had been taken he had probably walked away with his hands in his pockets, possibly risking a glance at the top-floor window of the nearly finished building, where a woman's face peered from behind a curtain. Jane. Maybe she had not always been locked away. Maybe the Welsh servants sided with their mistress rather than their master and so perhaps on the days or weeks when Morwood went off to attend to other business, she had more freedom – to walk the corridors, or the maze with its hidden corners away from prying eyes.

Holly got out a chocolate bar from the top pocket of her leather jacket and split it in half, offering part of it to Bex. 'I should probably tell you something.'

'What?' Bex was only half-listening, lost in her Peter and Jane romance.

'Richard and I. We slept together on that first meet-up we did, the one before you got involved.'

That got Bex's attention. 'Holly!'

'Wait, no – it's not how it sounds. It was a whole production meet to work out if we could actually do this thing and Richard and Oscar had been the ones who got the ball rolling so they came along except Richard got pretty drunk pretty fast and Marsha told me to take him back to his hotel room.' Bex groaned. 'Hold on, you haven't heard the whole story! And anyway, you can't judge – he was your boyfriend, after all. And he's fit.'

'You don't need someone like Richard in your life – he's a mess.'

'Yeah, well . . . that became obvious. I got him up to his room, he smiled at me and so I thought, what the hell, I might as well snog his face off, but it felt a bit like I was taking advantage, yeah? Though the snog was good, the guy still has it, even when he's drunk. Anyway, he crashed on the bed and his room was way better than mine so I raided his mini fridge for snacks and watched cable television whilst he snored. Nothing happened. I napped.'

Bex couldn't help herself, she had to laugh – at the thought of Richard asleep whilst this girl ate peanuts, propped up against the pillows. But also just at the self-assurance of her, a joyful kind of composure that Bex had never had. At eighteen she had been so busy wondering what everyone else was thinking, she had never stopped to do much thinking of her own.

'You're cleverer than you look.'

'I know.' Holly nodded and stuffed the rest of the chocolate bar in her mouth. Bex marvelled at how her black lipstick didn't smudge. 'Actually I—'

'Ssh.'

Outside their fountain bowl came Oscar's voice. 'We need to talk.'

Instinctively the two of them ducked down deeper in the fountain, even though they knew they couldn't be seen from anyone outside. Bex gestured at Holly to stay quiet and she stopped chewing and swallowed the rest of her chocolate bar in one big gulp that made her eyes water.

'I know you've got it.' Oscar's voice again. Holly tried to swallow and blinked, putting a hand to her throat as she attempted not to splutter. Bex rammed her water bottle at her and motioned to her again to keep quiet. Had Oscar worked out too that Richard had been keeping Leo's lighter all these years?

'I don't know what you're talking about,' Richard said.

Taking a sip, Holly stared at Bex as she sank back against the cool stone of the fountain.

'It's all going to come out, don't worry. No more hiding.' Oscar's voice became fainter as if he had begun to walk away.

'Huh? I'm not hiding any—'

'Gentlemen!' Marsha's voice interrupted. 'We need you for your set-up shots, thank you!'

Footsteps crunched on gravel and Bex put her hand over Holly's mouth because she knew she was going to say something, probably in that whisper of hers that could be heard from space. In her head she counted.

One.

Two.

Three.

Four.

Once Bex's hand was removed from her mouth, Holly's words tumbled free. 'What's going to come out?'

Despite telling Holly about the note when she had dragged her into the maze yesterday, Bex had not found a suitable moment to show her the other part of that package that had been posted to her. Now was the time. From her pocket Bex brought out the lighter and held it up in front of Holly's face. Then, sat in the fountain and speaking in hushed tones, Bex told Holly what she thought Richard might have done, the sad stone face of the statue peering down at them the whole time. By the time she had finished, Holly's expression was as sombre as the figure above them and the sky had taken on a silvery edge.

Good, thought Bex. Night could not come fast enough.

Chapter 44

Something in the bag clanked. As they scurried out from Bex's trailer, shadows sharpened their edges and corners became wells of darkness. The place drew night into it, a terrible magnet for things that should never see the light and a time for small, weak creatures to think they were safe in the gloom, when actually they had never been more at risk.

'Did you have to bring the rucksack?' Bex whispered to Holly. They crept across from the trailers and headed towards the driveway, trying to keep their footsteps from crunching too loudly on the freshly laid gravel.

'Hmm? I thought we might need supplies.' The bag clanked again.

'We're only crossing the drive, not the bloody desert! What's in there?'

Holly looked sheepish. 'Well, just the basics. A torch, a few fruit bars, a water bottle, a foil blanket and—'

'A foil blanket?'

'One of us might go into shock . . .'

'I'm going to go into shock if we make it to the maze without that bloody water bottle giving us away. Here!' She yanked on the straps of the rucksack, pulling it off Holly's shoulders. 'Leave it there. We don't need it.'

'Can I take a fruit bar?'

'Oh my God – yes. Quick!' Bex held the bag open for her and Holly stuffed two bars into the top pocket of her leather jacket as nutritious pocket squares. Bex gripped her torch. It was very late and the trailers and production campsite stood silent and sleeping, the perfect time for the two women to find out what really lay at the heart of the maze. Only the hotel watched them.

'What do you think we'll find?' Despite it being past midnight, Holly had not yet removed her make-up and Bex wondered if she ever took it off or whether her eyelids were now more ink than skin. They reached the fountain and paused.

'Nothing probably. Some weird ice storage like we were told but . . .'

'Exactly. But . . .'

Ahead of them was a circuit-board sky lit up with stars, the trees and road beyond and the entrance to the maze.

'Shit.' Bex stopped.

The entrance was not empty. To one side they could see a chair had been set up with a clip-on sunshade and a small folding table next to it upon which was a book, a hurricane lamp and a mug. A man sat with his arms crossed, hugging the edge of a sleeping bag tightly around his chest.

'They've set up a guard to stop anyone snooping around.'

'Oh wait . . . that's Luke!' Holly smiled at Bex and then noted her frown. 'Luke, remember? From our escape to the pub? I can deal with Luke. I'll distract him, you creep on in.'

'Offer him a fruit bar.'

'Very funny.'

Bex felt as if she had wandered into a schoolgirl mystery book with midnight feasts and escapades, the kind of adventure that ended with jam sandwiches and lashings of ginger beer, not missing friends and an eye socket running with blood. She watched Holly lollop towards Luke, her slightly awkward gait, a mix of enthusiasm and clumsiness, wearing her clumpy boots and Goth Barbie clothes. He sat up straighter as she neared him. Bex had more in common with the stone fountain statues than these two young people in the distance. Her future had turned to granite the moment that glass shattered ten years ago when the three of them had climbed inside the hotel. She leant against one of the figures, using the fountain to hide her from Luke's viewpoint, watching as Bex flapped her hands about in the glow from the lamp, then she took a wide step to her side and sent the table flying. Bex heard her giggle and the two of them busied themselves picking up the scattered mug, lamp and book, their backs to the maze entrance.

Bex moved. The happy chaos of a table being righted covered any noise of her approach and she darted through the entrance just as Holly caught her eye. She thought she saw her wink.

Ariadne in the Minotaur's maze had unspooled thread to mark her passage and help her return. Bex didn't need thread now. This was her third time in these scratchy, leafy corridors of unkempt hedge and she walked quickly, able to guess the next grinning, snarling, shouting or crying stone face that greeted her upon each turn.

Soon enough she found her Minotaur: the round wooden bull's-eye with its brass handle.

Before she began to haul the trapdoor open, Bex paused. She had thought about what she might see, a curved skeleton, hugging its own bony knees like pictures she had seen of Stone Age burials. Once she saw something like that, what would she do then? Because if Leo's final resting place was in this pit, then how had he got there – and who had known?

She had never been one for edging a plaster off millimetre by painful millimetre, seeing the skin stretch with it, no – in one quick heave she pulled on the handle and the door began to lift. Then she had to use two hands, getting her weight under it so it rose higher until she wasn't sure if she could bear the heaviness and it became a widening mouth whose jaw cracked. The problem was that it was too heavy to hold up with one hand whilst she shone her light inside. It would need propping. But somebody had already thought of that before her because there on the inside of the lid was a length of wood that hinged out, much like a person would prop open a car bonnet.

Hands shaking, she aimed her torch beam at the hole.

There was nothing there.

On her knees, she took deep breaths and closed her eyes for a second, counting to four. Then four again. The fifth attempt at getting it right allowed her to open her eyes.

It was a shallow pit. The walls were stone, rough to the touch, not deep enough for a good store of ice, not deep enough for anything, really. There was no point to this thing at all, or if there was one, she was too stupid to work it out. Though when her light hit another patch of wall, what she saw made her pause.

That bit was different. It wasn't stone and, from where she knelt, she couldn't see what it was.

There was nothing for it, she would have to clamber in. She didn't really feel any danger doing so. Leaving the torch on the edge of the hole, angled so it shined into the pit, she stepped down, the top of the wall coming to her shoulder making it easy to climb out. Closer up, she could now see that the patch of wall was a mess of bare earth and smaller rocks, piled together and fixed with what looked like a mix of dried mud acting as a poor cement. She scraped at it with a fingernail. Why line the thing with stone and then bodge a part of it like this? Why leave a gap?

Unless it wasn't a gap.

Unless it was an entrance.

She was committed now. She had crept into the maze under cover of night without telling anyone and now she stood in the middle of the pit itself. Things were already incriminating. A few kicks would hardly make any difference.

So she did.

Hard swift kicks. Old mud crumbled. Rocks tumbled. Bare

earth fell away as dust. More kicks and a hole emerged, not a gap, not a mistake, not a bodged job because, as she leant down, she saw what seemed to be a very tight, very rough tunnel . . . and steps.

Then, with a sharp popping sound, the wooden support propping open the cover buckled and cracked. She ducked just in time as the lid clanged shut.

Chapter 45

Breathe.

Bex slammed her hands against the wooden lid until her palms stung. 'HELP!'

Breathe.

She pressed against the lid, trying to make the thing lift. It did not budge.

Breathe.

When she had first clambered in, the fact that it had been a shallow pit was a bonus, because it would have been easy to climb out, but now, as she crouched in the darkness with the trapdoor closed it was not a bonus at all. It was a grave. That curled skeleton she had imagined seeing when she lifted the lid was not Leo – it was her, if she couldn't get out.

Thumping her hands against the trapdoor again, she yelled and screamed and clawed at the old wood, hoping it would break softly, damp and rotten. But the bit where her foot had gone through had already been roughly patched, a square of MDF nailed over it, and the rest only drove hard little splinters under her fingernails.

Breathe.

Unlike Richard, she was not scared of enclosed spaces . . . except that wasn't really true, was it? Anyone would be scared of this, a pitch-black pit that could not be escaped – a person would have to be a fool not to be. Her torch was now useless, on the grass above her, out of reach.

How stupid had she been to trust anything, even a bit of wood, in this bad luck place?

She began clawing and screaming, bashing on the wooden trapdoor with her fists and elbows, trying to heave it open with every bit of strength in her muscles until she saw red blotches in the darkness that swallowed her. She couldn't see her hand when she moved it in front of her face and for a second it felt like she had lost it, so much so that she fumbled and grasped it in her other hand. It wanted in, this black, it wanted to press and press against her until it seeped in through her eyes and stuffed itself down her throat so she choked.

Breathe.

She remembered, then, the talisman she carried in her jeans pocket and, hands shaking so badly she was sure she would drop it, or burn herself, she spun the wheel on Leo's lighter and heard it whirr.

The soft golden flame sent the darkness snarling back, if only for a few seconds, her thumb too close to the light to keep it there for long as she felt her skin tingle with heat. But it was enough.

The support snapping had been an accident. But Bex couldn't help thinking of that figure she had seen striding into the maze ten years ago, with the hem of a greatcoat flapping out behind it. The blurred, distorted face in the corridor behind Leo. The eye pressed up against the intercom of her house. Did some demonic spirit of Reginald Morwood stalk her still, luring her back so it could be done with her once and for all? She did not believe that, she told herself, letting the little flame flare again. She had spent ten years fervently not believing that.

Monsters came in all shapes and sizes. They could pose as friends.

Richard. What was he trying to hide here that she did not know?

Because she was not trapped. Not at all. The lid was closed but before that happened she had kicked a hole out of the pit's wall, a space stuffed with rocks and old mud as if someone had tried to block the entrance.

As if someone had something to hide.

Through that gap were steps and a tunnel and a tunnel led somewhere.

Under her thumb the lighter flared once more.

She shuffled to the top of the steps. The air that came up to her was musty and old and Bex remembered stories of canaries in mines, held out first to breathe or die in the unknown air ahead of them. She would have to wave the lighter in front of her and keep an eye on its flame to check the oxygen levels. She had not checked how much fuel was left in it but she knew that the liquid must be going down so she wouldn't be able to use it continuously. For a while she did not move. Something about the tunnel stretching away below her made her want to stay on the top step.

Escape was down there . . . probably.

But other things could be down there too.

Breathe.

Holly knew where she was. All she had to do was wait for rescue. And so, for a while, she did, crouched and cold and still, but Holly did not come. That was okay though, she told herself as something light scurried over the back of her hand and she flicked it away; all she had to do was wait some more. So she did. But this hotel had taught her that you do not wait for anything, certainly not rescue. And Holly was just a kid. She was probably still flirting with Luke, batting her kohl-lined eyes.

The entrance to those steps drew Bex's gaze. There were answers down there, she was sure of it.

Move.

Into the darkness she went, shuffling down the steps,

toddler-style, on her bottom, too scared to stand in case she lost her footing, or tripped and fell. It became a rhythm of its own. Slide feet down, push with her hands. Thump. Slide feet down, push with her hands. Thump. She counted the steps in groups of four and that did not help at all, but it kept her mind occupied. She stopped on every other step to flick the lighter wheel and set the scene around her alight. It was always the same. Close stone walls, rough steps, low ceiling. Walking the other way, climbing these stairs, a person would have to stoop so low their back would ache.

Sometimes when she flicked the lighter she expected to see another face, inches from hers, a smudged one with a gaping mouth like the one that had chased Leo in a corridor high above her.

The steps went on forever. Slide, shuffle, thump. Webs clung to her, little darting things dropped into her hair and onto her neck and she jerked and batted at them until she hoped they had gone.

Had this tunnel been built by Morwood himself as part of the hotel for some reason no one would ever know, or was this much older than that? Bex had heard of smugglers' runs, secret byways and caves with tunnels connecting them, ready for when a ship went down and needed looting, or if contraband goods had to be shifted. None of the hotel's plans had mentioned a tunnel like this so close to the building, however.

Keeping her mind busy on the origins of the tunnel distracted it from the never-ending steps. Deeper and deeper she went. Down and down and down and down. Four steps, then another four, then another. The webs stuck themselves to her lips and she spat them out, things crawled around her wrists, they squirmed in her hair and her heart thumped out a warning that she should stop, or go back because this path would never end. She had to be nearly at the bottom of the cliff now, she tried to reassure herself but she had lost all track of time and she kept thinking of those myths of underworld gods in caverns under the human world and the unlucky humans who stumbled into them.

The steps ended. Bex stretched out her foot as far as it would go and it only met ground. Instinctively, she tried to stand and pain slapped her head. Ducking back down again she rubbed at the sore spot in her hair. Crawl it would have to be.

Whirr and flame.

Something wasn't quite right up ahead.

Whirr and flame.

She continued to crawl, edging her hands out on rough, bumpy rock, trying to place her palms where uneven edges wouldn't dig into her flesh and make her wince. The ends of her scarf threatened to get caught under her knees so she tucked them into her jumper. Thick wooden supports appeared every so often, like this was a mine, each one holding back the weight of the earth and rock above her head.

Whirr and flame.

The lighter's spark trembled more and more. As she got nearer she could see with every burst of light that the way ahead was partly blocked by a cave-in on one side, the wooden support here as cracked and bent as the one that had failed to hold the lid open far above her head. A tumble of rocks and earth narrowed what was already only a strip of a path under her hands and knees. It felt like she was wedging herself into the very heart of the cliff-side like one of those pieces of wood a lumberjack hammers into a tree stump to make it split, except she was the one who would split if the ceiling got any lower or the walls closed in anymore.

But none of that made her scream.

No, what made her scream was edging out her hand and feeling her fingers touch neither rock nor earth but something else entirely. Something rounded on one end.

Whirr. Flame.

Bone.

Chapter 46

Bex froze in the darkness.

Whatever she had seen, whatever she had touched – she had been wrong. She had to be wrong. A sick chill slithered into her stomach. When she flicked the lighter again, it would show her that what she had seen had simply been an odd-shaped rock.

Not a human knee bone.

Her thumb hovered over the lighter wheel. Though she couldn't see it she knew that on that lighter's plastic coating, laminated in a tacky souvenir shop that had smelled of grease from the next-door chippie with seagulls screeching outside, was Leo's face, bright and smiling next to hers. Alive.

Whirr. Flame.

This time Bex held the wheel down and let the flame burn into her thumb. A skeleton half covered by the cave-in with a tear in the knee of its jeans. It had been partly dug out so she could see ribs and wrist-bone, neck, the tattered shreds of clothing, something that looked like a pile of rope . . . she did not want to look any higher than that but look she had to. Jaw, blank eye sockets, broken glasses, a cracked skull.

It could have been anyone, from any time. This tunnel was probably much older than the hotel so the bones in front of her could have been a smuggler, or a homeless person, an unfortunate rambler – anyone, anyone at all.

But she knew who it was.

The darkness when she let it back in was welcome. However, imprinted onto it was now the whited-out negative of what she had just seen. A jaw gaping wide, the skull facing her from where it lay on the floor, empty eye sockets watching her through fractured lenses, waiting for the realisation to sink in.

She did not scream again. She did not cry. Instead she sat in the blackness next to a skeleton and time passed. Years back, when they had both been eleven or twelve, she and Leo had gone on one of those Outward Bound school trips where, one night, the entire group had camped outside in a field. They had shared a tent, watching the condensation drips race down the plastic sheeting, making Quality Street bets on which one would get to the bottom first. He had sat on his glasses and, as she had wound a plaster around the arm, he had confided in her that he couldn't sleep without a light on. When they had finally settled, Bex had kept her torch lit, subdued under her scarf, so there would be a dim glow in which he could drift off.

This time when she made the lighter wheel spin, she kept her thumb pressed on it until her skin began to tingle and then burn so that, if only for a short while, he would not be alone in the dark. The burning on the pad of her thumb became a sharp bright pain and still she did not let go. The flame wavered, making shadows jump around them.

She could not stand the pain any longer and she dropped the lighter, the tunnel fizzling back to black. It should stay there, she decided. The lighter was his. He should have it, but she scrabbled in the dirt for it anyway because she knew she couldn't keep kneeling here in this place, that she had to get up and get out and tell people about Leo. About what she had found here.

There were no tears. All the times she had cried watching

the video on her own in her empty house and now, there was nothing. Nothing. That is what he had become. Where he had been, the space he had taken up in the world, it was all gone and she thought, after ten years, that she had got used to that idea, but she hadn't. Not at all. She couldn't even see herself in the darkness: when she raised her hand, she saw no outline of her own fingers. She was as much of a ghost as Leo. Always had been. From the moment he had disappeared from those steps, she had disappeared with him.

But she couldn't disappear anymore. She had to get out and, more importantly, she had to get him out. It didn't matter what it took, but she would have his bones carried from this tomb and buried under the headstone his father had bought for him, the one with the missing date of death.

That meant moving, so she did. It meant flicking the lighter again so she could see the path past the cave-in, so she did that too. She crawled each step, trying to only think of the placement of her knees and palms but other thoughts flashed into her brain like emergency flares.

How had Leo died? Had a rock mercifully cracked his skull before the earth covered him, or was he still breathing as the soil and gravel poured into his mouth and clogged his nose? How had he ended up in the tunnel anyway? Who had found him, half dug him out and then taken the lighter? Bex had always believed that discovering Leo's body would answer all the questions about his disappearance but all it did was add more.

She kept crawling, the tunnel ceiling tight above her head, its stony hand pressing down upon her skull, and she felt her breathing become ragged. She had been dragging herself through this tunnel for what seemed like hours, only her and the black and the rock walls that got closer and closer. She used the lighter sparingly, knowing that there was only so much fuel left in it. Her crawling became quicker as she scraped her hands on rough stone and felt jagged points press into the soft parts of her knees.

She would be stuck in here until she too lay down and let the soil pile on top of her, the darkness sucking her last breath away. She should never have climbed down here, she should—

Her fingers met earth. Patting her hands over the blockage in front of her, she found that she could now stand. Another cave-in. In front of her was probably the mouth of the tunnel, she realised, which must be near the hotel jetty or in some other cove nearby. The flicker flame of the lighter showed her that there was no way through and she would not allow herself to sink to the floor and shake because that was not going to get her out.

Instead she moved again, back the way she had come. If she had to, she would haul herself all the way, return to the trapdoor and punch at it, over and over and over even if the wood never gave in, and the only result was broken and bloody knuckles.

The adrenaline rushed through her blood, numbing her knees and palms to the pain as she crawled so quickly that she nearly missed it.

A whisper of air. Colder. Bex stopped and turned her head. The breath of air sighed across her left cheek.

Edging over, she reached out her hand, expecting to find more wall but her fingers only touched that small cold breeze. Whirring the lighter wheel, its flame showed her that another path branched away, one she had missed in her rush to get past Leo's body.

If she could feel that air then there must be some way for it to get in and for her to get out.

Palm over palm, knee by knee she crawled through this new offshoot, the tunnel remaining flat, no steps cut into the rock. Perhaps the whole cliff was pockmarked with these tunnels, the old smugglers years ago within them like woodworm, beetling their way around with their contraband booty. She would get out, she would get out, she would get out.

Ahead of her the darkness became a grey, a tattered cloth that parted as she neared it. The light came from straight ahead and she kept her eyes fixed on it, afraid it would blink out if she let her gaze falter. A smudged, early dawn sky could be seen through a gap in what Bex could see was another pile of smaller rocks blocking the very narrow entrance. She shoved at the top ones.

They toppled.

Chapter 47

With the first kick, Bex felt something loosen within herself.

Sitting on the tunnel floor she raised her legs again to give the rocks another kick, putting all of her force behind each slam of the soles of her shoes. Two. It made her smile at first, the violence of it, at least she thought it was a smile but it could have been more of a snarl. She was not stuck in the bowels of this horrible place, right in its belly; she would kick and claw her way out of its very guts until she was free and . . .

. . . what would she do then?

Another kick made three and more rocks tumbled, enough for her to squeeze through but she kept on kicking anyway, unable to stop herself. It definitely wasn't a smile on her face then. In fact she could hear herself sobbing, strange, wracked, guttural sounds that were almost inhuman. She went way past four, or multiples of it; she lost count. Eventually, she stopped, her leg muscles weak. The hole through which she would have to crawl looked painfully small. Bex thought of cats, their creepy way of flattening out their skeletons so they could slide under gaps. But she was not a cat.

She had done this before back in Jane's room ten years ago. Then she had used a poker, hammering at the flimsy patch of wood in the door until she could lever it off, desperate to get out and find Leo. Now, here she was, fighting to get free once more, Leo already found, a lonely skeleton in old clothes.

Head-first like a baby being born to a mother made from rock, Bex hauled and dragged herself through. Sharp scraping edges dug into the soft parts of her flesh as she tried to wrench her shoulders free, hands clutching on gritty surfaces as she turned her face to a sky where the moon had not quite left and the sun had not yet risen. A between time. For a few awful moments she thought her shoulders would be stuck tight forever and she would be trapped, not able even to get back into the tunnel. No one would know where she was and she would die like Leo, in the clutches of this place, flesh falling from bone in the years to come.

No. The word in her mind was a power all of its own, she might even have been yelling it as she gave another almighty heave and felt one shoulder give, making rocks shift and tumble around her. One arm came free and then she could push until she was out to her waist and it was only a quick wriggle until she flopped onto the big rocks waiting for her, those ones that blocked most of the entrance.

There was no time to lie there and contemplate a sky the colour of old armour. She had to move. Looking around her she saw that this tunnel had spat her out in a different cove to the one that held the hotel's old jetty, though presumably not too far along the coast. The tunnel entrance had huge boulders blocking most of it and wide, flat rocks that led to a sliver of pebbly shore. Above her was not a wall of cliff but a staggered bank with a rough path cut into it.

She was going to have to climb.

Her leg muscles had melted away. The steps were rough and uneven, some of them carved with a giant in mind but at least there was a pre-dawn light of sorts in which to see her way. Bex kept her head down and concentrated on her footing, grabbing on to the patches of scrub and wild grass growing in between the rocks to keep her balance as the wind buffeted her. She didn't mind the slap of hair into her cheek, stinging strands flicking into her eyes or the way that the gusts punched into her. She deserved it. Leo had been under her feet the whole time, he had been left to moulder in a tunnel for too many years and she had done nothing to find him.

Instead she had hidden in her house, talking to her plants.

She hoped it had been quick, however he had died. Whether that had been by someone's hand or by the tunnel roof caving in on him, she hoped he had had no time to be scared, to cry out, to scrabble fingertips in the darkness. Why hadn't anyone found him? In those days after they had left the hotel the first time, there had been police and investigations and divers dropping themselves into the shallower water near the coast. However, there would have been no reason to search this particular cove because Leo had disappeared over at the hotel and, even if they had, the entrance was well hidden by the rocks she had just hauled herself through. She guessed that the blocked mouth of the tunnel over in the hotel's stretch of cliff was just as hard to spot.

But someone had to have known he was in there because someone had taken that lighter from him.

Not someone – Richard.

Bex continued to climb but took the familiar shape of her talisman out of her pocket as she did so. When she got to the top of the cliff she could see the trees that hid the hotel on one side and, though her view was blocked, she knew that past those trees was the wide curve of Poppit Sands with Mrs Bloom's B&B perched on top. Time had slid away from her whilst she had been stuck in the darkness. It had been past midnight when she had scurried into the maze but now there was a glow to the edge of the sky, not dawn itself, but its promise.

It was a relief to sit down on the grassy edge and feel air move around her, without the weight of earth and rock above her head. She stared out to sea and smoothed Leo's lighter in her hand, her thumb stroking his cheek, the two of them together in sunshine, if only as plastic laminate. If she wanted to, she could walk to Mrs Bloom's, knock on her door, ask to use the phone and then take tea in a pot shaped as a Dalek or a dead singer.

There was no reason she couldn't simply walk away.

It would be easy. Give the lighter to the police, make her statement, let them search, open up the other tunnel entrance that must be near the hotel steps, the one she had not been able to get out of, find the body and then all that would be left would be to wear black to Leo's second funeral. She could let them find out the details.

Under each of her fingernails was a rim of earth and grit, where she had crawled in the darkness, and her thumb left a smudge on the picture of Leo's face. She could go back home, close the door and shut out the world once more. The problem was, she had done far too much hiding over the last ten years.

Placing the lighter down she touched the glittery Ouija board planchette necklace that Diane in wardrobe had given her on the day they had filmed the trailer. The board was a way to send messages to the dead, the little pointer under her hand a conduit. But it wasn't the dead who had the answers. No. It was the living, and she wanted those answers now. She wanted to stare at Richard as he confessed to what he had done and she wanted to hear it face to face, not from some police report a month afterwards. More importantly, she wanted undeniable proof that could never be shaken, that was certain beyond all doubt.

She had to go back to that hotel she could not even see beyond the trees. Standing, she put the lighter in her jeans pocket and turned towards the building that was always waiting for her.

It would be a long, uphill climb. She began to walk.

Chapter 48

Bex knew something was wrong the moment she could see the gates.

When she had been driven up to them a few days ago, an empty champagne bottle in her hand and Holly sitting by her side, there had been guards and the bustle of a production crew moving boxes and unpacking trucks.

Now there was silence.

Guards? Gone. Bustle? Stilled. There were no people around at all.

'Hello?'

The only answer was a sigh from the trees, which began in the branches of one and then spread through to the others. Trees communicated to each other through intricate mould systems, linking trunk to trunk, Bex remembered from a nature programme. She wondered what they said about the hotel and the little humans scurrying about in it. Were those sighs in fact a warning, telling her to run while she still had the chance?

Her feet ached. The road up to the front of the hotel had been cleared by the production company before filming but that hadn't fixed its gradient so when she had got to the top she was sure an hour had passed at least, her hair stuck to the back of her neck with sweat. She could have taken the Coast Path around the rear of the building, but she had needed the longer walk and the extra time that gave her to calm her spinning mind. There had been no waiting media or photographers at the bottom of the hill, but then it was either far too early in the morning, or far too late at night, for them to have taken up their positions.

The gates were modern, the ones originally installed here broken and taken away, or stolen years back. They had probably been intricate wrought iron, but this replacement was merely a slab of plywood. Bex slammed her hand against it and then tried to pull it across, not expecting it to open but it did, sliding on its rail and stopping with enough room so she could squeeze through.

There was the fountain, the drive, the maze and trailers to her right. Tents and equipment had been left abandoned. The only people were those set in stone, clawing for water. Everyone couldn't have just left, Bex thought as her boots crunched on the newly laid gravel. She had only been gone one night and they had filming left to do. What could possibly have happened? For a few seconds, as she stood before the pillared porch, it felt like the hotel had done this all for her; it had swallowed up all the people so there could be this moment – her standing in front of it, alone. Except for the ghosts.

Of course, the front door was open. The haunted house always wants you to enter, Bex thought, otherwise what is the point of it being haunted? There has to be someone to hear you scream. But she faltered before she could step inside.

A light shone from it.

Except for the faint glimmer of dawn in a paper-thin morning sky, Bex could have been swept back ten years, to a night and the glow of an impossible candle in the window. There was a sense of inevitability about it all. Ten years had brought her back here, ten years had re-kindled that flame again and all she to do was follow it. So she did.

She heard Leo laugh.

In the reception hall, next to the main staircase, there was the screen set up from the night before with the velvet cinema seats and though daylight would soon be dawning outside, in here drapes had been fixed to the windows to keep out any glare. Bex had plunged into night once more.

There were two people sitting in the cinema seats.

'Bex! Thank God – you've come back!' Marsha sprang up and moved towards her. 'We were all so worried!' Behind the screen some boxes filled with bottles of rum and spirits, left over from their meal on the first night, had been dragged out and opened.

The colours slipped over them both as Richard pointed a remote control at the screen, the new footage of Leo playing. He paused on a frame as Leo turned, making the figure a blur of green, muddied pixels.

'Where did you go?' Richard wore a crumpled shirt and the same jeans from last night. As he got up and walked towards her, she backed away.

'Where is everyone?'

Marsha smoothed her drooping quiff from her forehead. She too wore the same clothes as last night, now actually, not artfully, creased. 'No one could find you. We've been up all night, worried sick. I just cancelled today's filming and sent the crew off-site so we could work out what to do if you didn't come back. We – Oscar, Richard and I – have had a rather important meeting but – heavens! You look like hell.'

Bex looked down at herself. There was slime on her knees and her hands were smudged with earth and grit, her hair hung in her face, the ends of it matted and muddy. But if she looked like hell then some of that hellfire was coming Richard's way.

'Leo is dead.' Her voice shook.

Richard frowned. 'We've always suspected that, Bex.'

'No, stop playing games. That's where I've been all night. I found his body in the tunnel next to the hotel.'

'You . . . found – what?'

It was the fake confusion in his voice that did it, that powered Bex's legs over to where he stood and that curled her hands into fists which she used to pound at whatever bit of him she could reach. But he was taller and stronger than her and he easily grabbed her elbows, even though she kicked at him as he wrapped his arms around her, pinning her hands to her side, his embrace a trap.

Her words were part sobs. 'Oh my God, you can stop! You can just stop. I know! I know, Rich, what you did, how you got *this*!' Here she managed to get a hand into her jeans pocket and threw the lighter onto the floor at his feet. 'You probably killed him and left him there to rot in that tunnel. It's over. I know.'

'What's that? A lighter?' His words were breath in her hair. 'I've never seen that thing before . . .' Gripping on to her with one arm he freed the other to grab the remote control. 'Look, whilst you've been gone, things have . . . Well, Marsha, Oscar and I have watched this footage all the way through and we've got to tell you something, but first . . . you need to see the last shot.'

Bex strained and struggled. 'I don't need to do anything you tell me.'

'You need to see the end.'

'No!'

But Richard held her and she couldn't move away, 'Please, Bex – just watch.'

There Leo was, that fourth shot taken from the corridor outside Jane's room when the door had slammed shut and he had been left on the other side. The infamous scene where he ran and a smudged ghostly face could be seen in the background. Except this was right at the end, his face filling the shot as he dropped and then picked up the camera and there, Bex could see, in the reflection of his glasses . . .

'Me.' Oscar's voice floated down to them from the second-floor gallery landing where he stood. 'You can see me.'

Chapter 49

Oscar, ten years ago

In the darkness, waves slapping the side of the boat like hands trying to get his attention, Oscar sat in the cove just over from the hotel.

All he had to do was wait for the crackle of his walkie-talkie. Either Bex or Richard would call, demand he come back, that things had gone terribly wrong and they were frightened – for real.

His plan had worked like a dream. No, not like a dream . . . a nightmare. Richard always thought he was so clever, with his camera angles and zoom shots, his lists of obscure films unknown to Oscar. Ever since he'd got together with Bex, he'd been insufferable; the two of them always competing, who was cleverer, who was cooler, who knew more than the other.

Neither of them had worked out his plan.

Convincing Leo hadn't been hard. Despite even his closest friends thinking he was a bit stupid, Oscar knew more about what was going on than Richard did. He'd seen the way Leo had looked when Bex had told them about their precious trip that day in the library. It had only been quick but in that moment, Oscar knew that someone else felt the same way he did. It had been a real horror show since Bex and Richard had started . . . whatever it was they were doing. They were completely mismatched and worse, they were forcing together a group of four that just did not gel. Bex and Leo. Oscar and Rich. Oscar wanted things to go back to the way they had been, him and Rich mucking about in lessons and ruling the corridors and sports pitches of their school.

Snooty Bex Harrison thought he was a fool. It had been high time to make a fool of her.

The rhythmic bobbing of the boat made his eyelids droop. It had been a long night. His first priority had been to get everyone to agree to leave their phones at home because there was no way he wanted either Bex or Rich to get so spooked they ended up calling the police. Then, after pleading his vertigo (which was true) he had set about making a 'sleeping' Oscar in the boat: a blonde wig and a blanket pulled up to it with his rucksack underneath. Not perfect but from a distance, it did the job. He had then got dressed in his 'Morwood' clothes and clambered up the rocks to squeeze himself into the very small tunnel entrance hidden by moss and hanging plants. It was just above a ledge that he used to haul himself up.

His dashing about the place began in the study to light the candle. After that he had gone down in the maze to draw Bex into its leafy madness, hiding in the pit under the trapdoor whilst Leo talked to her. From there he had run up again to close and lock the door on them in Jane's room and then follow Leo in the corridor, wearing a cheap joke-shop mask. The greatcoat, found in one of those army surplus stores a week or so back, had been a total pain in the neck and he had kept tripping over the hem. Finally he had left Leo to do his bit on the steps and used the tunnel from the maze to return to the jetty, making sure to block up the entrance under the trapdoor lid a bit with some rocks and mud just in case anyone looked. 'Fail to prepare; prepare to fail', as his chemistry teacher had often said, possibly the only thing that had stuck in his mind from those lessons.

In the end though, he had gone a little off-script – he hadn't been able to help himself. Why not add that final touch of horror for Bex and Rich? And what could be worse than seeing the boat, their only hope of a quick escape, sailing away without them? He already had an excuse prepared: he would say he had had to go back and get his EpiPen, having only at that moment realised he had forgotten it and thinking they were going to still be hours exploring the hotel.

Without the tunnels, he wouldn't have been able to do any of it. That had been a piece of luck, catching sight of the old drawing of the smugglers' underground routes in amongst all those papers Bex had spread on the table that day in the library. She had thought he was just messing with them to annoy her, and he had been at first, but then one of the original plans had sketched out where the old smugglers' burrows were around the hotel and his idea had begun to form. Swiping the original copy, he had slipped it into his pocket before Bex could see it. Those tunnels were tempting, providing as they did a much quicker, secret and more direct route to the jetty than climbing the winding steps.

A lot had depended on Leo playing his part and, to be fair, he had.

Oscar was proud of the moment of Leo's disappearance. The curve of the first step up from the jetty could be seen without having to climb them. He and Leo had spent an afternoon working out how it could all happen, hiring their own boat and leaving Rich and Bex for some quality alone time. The tunnel also gave Oscar the perfect way to get up to the hotel without his vertigo kicking in. They had come prepared – kind of. Leo had liberated the rope ladder from his old climbing frame in the back garden and Oscar knew where the entrance to the tunnel was from the plans. It had worked out even better than he had imagined. All Leo had to do was hook the ladder over one of the stone spindles on the edge of the steps, the ones that had been planned to hold up the handrail, climb down to the ledge that was under the entrance, sneak in through a small gap in the rocks and then pile them behind him to hide the hole. When they had rehearsed, it had taken only a few minutes. Leo had always been a good climber. The sticky bit was the rope ladder, sometimes it took a few jerks to get it free from the spindle but, even with that, Leo was fast. They had left the ladder ready under a bush in one of the old flowerbeds. Traumatised at seeing someone disappear, Bex and Rich would radio for Oscar to come back in the boat – the walkie-talkies had a range of around five miles – and he would let it play out a bit before shouting for Leo. Ta-dah! Big surprise and two bruised egos. Perfect.

He couldn't wait to see their faces and their shock as they realised that he'd out-smarted them and all their precious footage was a waste – especially Bex with her straight As and her books and her sneering tone.

The cold was beginning to make Oscar's fingers numb but if he put the blanket over himself and got warm, there was a real danger he would just fall asleep and miss the call. He clapped his hands together a few times and opened his eyes a bit wider. Around him was a soft darkness, light from a sliver of moon glimmering on the water as it moved and his tired eyes became hypnotised by that, another gentle lullaby rhythm to soothe him to sleep . . .

A blaring sound and harsh light jolted Oscar before he could close his eyes. Reds and blues stained the water and the siren sent pulses of adrenaline rushing through his body making him stand too quickly as the boat rocked beneath him. The jutting wall of rock between this cove and the next blocked his view but he knew what the red and blue meant.

It meant they had been caught.

Trespass. Someone must have seen the lights in the hotel from some distant shore and contacted the authorities, or there had been some kind of security system they hadn't even noticed. Trespass was an offence.

Or, even worse, somehow, despite his best planning, Bex and Rich had seen Leo disappear and called the police and they could only have done that if, despite their agreement, one of them had brought their phone anyway. Bloody Bex. He would have put money on it being her.

Oscar sat down. His father would kill him. It was bad enough that he was not Mike the Perfect Brother: perfect smile, perfect scores, perfect sportsmanship. Oscar was imperfect enough; he could not add a criminal record to the mix.

He needed to know what was going on but obviously sailing up to the jetty and hailing the nearest police officer was not the way to go about it.

There was a tunnel leading from the cove in which Oscar sat that linked to the one at the hotel – he knew this from that original plan he had stolen. The inky shadows of the tunnel mouth beckoned. He could use it and creep up to the hotel's jetty, or no, he might be seen if there was a police boat moored. Better to go to the maze and from there to the hotel, see what was happening and, if it was as bad as he thought it was, make a run for it.

As he crawled, his torch bounced light from the rock walls carved out by long-dead smuggler hands. Wooden supports jutted out at intervals. Oscar knew the tunnel was taking him upwards but there was no dizzying swoop of sickness from his vertigo because he was safe and snug, tucked tight within rock – no fear of falling. Pausing, he put a palm to the wall, feeling its rough surface under his hand, tracing the shape of the tunnel above his head, holding him firm.

'Leo!' He realised that Leo might be hiding in here still; the sirens could have sounded after he had scrambled to hide and so he could be crouched somewhere, like Oscar, too scared to come out. Their plan had well and truly fallen apart.

Silence was his only reply. The head torches had been his idea – he had known he'd need one with all the sneaking around under the earth this evening had held for him. He gave a little thank you for its steady, hands-free light.

Oscar continued to crawl in the tunnel.

Something blocked his path. The torchlight showed rubble and earth, some sort of cave-in which was annoying because he'd have to turn back if he couldn't squeeze past. The wooden support in this part was cracked and twisted, not doing much supporting anymore. There was space to force himself through, if he half-shuffled, half-dragged himself along and that was what he started to do before common sense kicked in.

When he had been in this tunnel the day before, there had been no tunnel collapse, so it was recent and if it was recent then whatever caused it might not be done. He did not want to be trapped in there, as much as he liked the comforting walls around him.

However, he had now got himself into quite an awkward position. The best idea was to turn back as he didn't know if other cave-ins waited for him up ahead, but in order to do that he had to almost dislocate his shoulder and break a knee cap, grunting with the effort. Flailing one leg out as he got it free, it hit something in the rubble.

Something softer than rock.

But denser than earth.

Oscar froze. Wriggling, he yanked the torch from his head, aiming it at the pile but what he saw made him drop the light and he heard a crack as it hit something sharp. Before the light went out though, he had seen it.

Eyes.

A face in the dirt staring back at him.

Leo's face.

Darkness settled in around him and in it his mind conjured the sound of shuffling as a body dragged itself across the earth towards him. He whimpered as he scrabbled for the torch, hoping to only touch smooth plastic and as his fingers closed on it he heard his breath hitch as if he was about to scream or cry. The torch button no longer worked and Oscar could feel a crack in the glass lens but he couldn't stand the darkness a second longer so he shook the thing and thumped it against the wall until a weak light flickered into life once more.

To reflect from dead eyes.

Oscar couldn't move back because there was wall behind him so he stared, his brain trying to make sense of the scene before him.

'Leo?' he whispered. Not that Leo was going to answer, most of his body was under the rubble with only a knee, a hand and his head mostly free. His face was dirt-smudged and those terrible eyes were open and staring at Oscar. The rope ladder was in a pile next to him. Oscar moved the quivering torch beam with care, praying that it wouldn't go out, tracking light across Leo until he saw the bloody wound on the side of his head, hair matted red.

He was dead.

Suddenly those walls that had seemed so snug and safe began to choke Oscar. The word looped in his head: dead, dead, dead, dead. Leo had done what he had asked. He had crawled into this tunnel, waiting to jump back out: 'Surprise!' Except surprise had come rushing at him, no warning, sending something sharp into the side of his skull. Oscar had sent him to his death.

Beyond him and nearer the tunnel entrance, the weighty sound of earth and rocks tumbling made Oscar's heart thump. The whole tunnel was unstable and, if he didn't move fast, he could become the next dead body crushed in this narrow tomb. A fizzing sound and the torchlight died. Oscar whimpered. There were no thoughts, only an urge to run, which was impossible, so he decided to crawl with such speed that he was certain he left bits of skin behind from his palms and knees. There had been something clutched in Leo's fist and Oscar knew he needed it so he pressed his lips together and edged his hand out in the dark until he touched cold flesh. The rubbery shock of lifeless fingers made him grit his teeth as he prised out the thing held in their grasp.

A lighter.

By its flame, he made his way back to the hidden cove.

Chapter 50

Oscar, ten years ago.

The rest of the night was a broken-legged bird, limping and slow.

Oscar sat in the boat in the cove, too scared to leave, too scared to stay. He didn't know how much time had gone by when the lights on the water disappeared and a quiet fell once more. Those words kept looping in his head, a piece of string that tied itself around his brain and pulled tight.

Dead, dead, dead, dead.

The slapping waves smacked against the side of the boat, each one a slow hand-clap, a sarcastic round of applause for what he had just done.

His fault.

He had sent Leo into that tunnel. He had sent him in and then Leo had died and it was his fault.

There were things he should have been doing. Right now. He should have been sailing back to the bunkhouse and informing authorities and making statements and other very official things that involved paperwork and police stations and records.

His father would never forgive him.

His perfect brother would shake his perfect head, his perfect hair shining, disappointment dulling his perfect eyes.

Oscar could not move. Every so often he would think, *I will start the motor*, and he looked over at it in the gloom and not one part of his body did anything. So he would then try something smaller. *I will stand*, he would think, hoping that was simple enough but he would look down at himself and find himself sitting still.

Forever passed and the sky lightened at the edge where it met the sea, like a photograph badly developed. Oscar thought, *Twitch that finger*, and this time his hand obliged. He could not sit in this boat forever. What he did now, in these next hours, would determine his entire life, not those stupid exams he had most probably failed a few months ago. He could either be the person who sent Leo Finch to his death . . .

. . . or he could not.

Whatever he did would not bring Leo back to life.

He sat with that thought for a while. It became a friend. He was the only person who knew about the tunnels. He had the only original copy of the plans that sketched them out. He knew they weren't on some internet archive somewhere because he had checked, knowing how much Bex the swot loved to research. What he also knew was that the entrance of the tunnel that came out on the hotel's jetty was now firmly blocked by that second cave-in that had sent him scurrying away.

He could not resurrect the dead.

Those underground burrows were too unstable for him to go back into them anyway, he told himself. The sound of that earth falling in a weighty thud would stick with him for the rest of his life. And he still *had* a life, one that did not have to stop here in this black night. Soon enough he found he could stand and then there was the cough of the motor. Another boat ride, the wind making his eyes sting, another jetty and then there was the hostel, a police car parked outside. And in the days that came afterwards, Oscar understood that lies were no harder, nor easier, to tell than truth. They were just more words.

'Where have you been? Why did you leave us?' Bex's blood-stained face peered at him in a hospital corridor, hollow-eyed, her hair a straggled mess, still in her purple boots and leather jacket.

'I had to go back and get my EpiPen and then the police were at the bunkhouse . . . I'm so sorry . . . but, what the hell happened?' A small part of him marvelled at how well he could say those sentences.

Other questions came from police officers, faces he did not know and would hopefully never see again. He never wavered from his story: he had stayed at the hotel jetty, warm under the blanket until he had realised he needed to go back to the opposite shore for his EpiPen, thinking he would have lots of time before they needed him. He kept things simple.

Something else he also discovered about lies – if you say them enough, they start to become the truth. There were parallel worlds, right? Richard had tried to explain it once, something to do with physics. Oscar had come away with an image of the universe as a slinky toy, a small squat tube that you stretched and then suddenly all these rings appeared from nowhere and it was really long. So, in one of those rings, in some parallel world somewhere, what he was saying was true: he had never found Leo's body. For that matter, in some parallel world, he'd never thought of his stupid prank at all and Leo was still alive, wearing terrible raincoats and eating chocolate mice.

They all went back to their lives, as much as they could. He moved and frowned and spoke and ate but it all seemed like smoke, he was smoke, the fumes of that Oscar who had run about the hotel so pleased with his plotting and planning. Bex went to her parents where she holed herself up, not answering calls or texts. She visited Richard in hospital a few times when Oscar had been there and he wondered if she felt like smoke too, because she certainly looked like it: grey and thin, even her hair a faded version of its former colour. Richard's wounds became angry red scars, his empty eye socket filled with a new prosthetic eye.

And if Leo's body was found? Well, he would be as shocked as everyone else. Heart-broken, all the rest of it. He *was* heart-broken after all, or he would be if his whole body wasn't just a lump of numb nothingness.

Leo wasn't found. Every day was a held breath of waiting for it to happen and every day it did not. Oscar never exhaled. The tunnel was as secure as it could be. Those days turned to weeks then months as they brought other problems: Richard trying to make the film but his eye hurting too much to do it so he asked Oscar to take over, which he did – gratefully – cutting out and keeping any bit of footage where he might have been spotted. He had never thought anyone would watch the thing, it was just a video on a website that they could take down any time they wanted. Then it became the film.

He had *expected* to be caught.

In the time afterwards, the only way for him to feel less like smoke and more like flesh was to move, talk, see and be seen by as many people as possible, to tell his story – again and again and again so that it was the only story he ever imagined. He knew the others thought him an attention-seeker and he agreed with them. He was. He wanted as much attention as he could get, as many eyes on him as possible because if they could see him, if they could believe his story, then maybe . . . just maybe, he could believe it too.

Chapter 51

That night, the one Bex had replayed in her head thousands of times, the one she had watched on her television for ten whole years was as pockmarked with holes as the diseased box hedge around the maze.

Oscar had lied to them all.

'So you planned the whole thing out? You and Leo?' She grabbed the lighter from where she had thrown it and raced up the staircase to the top-floor landing, Richard and Marsha at her heels. The story that Oscar had just told her had been told first to them, before she had walked in.

'Kind of – yes . . . but we were eighteen-year-olds, Bex, I didn't really think any of it through, I just wanted to make you both look stupid.' Oscar stepped away from them. He looked as if he had not yet been to bed, his T-shirt creased and his face sallow from lack of sleep. There was a bunch of tightly wound material in his hand and a half-empty bottle of Bacardi at his feet. Trust Oscar to drink something ridiculous, Bex thought.

'You wanted to . . . I don't understand, all the stuff that happened and Leo, that was all . . . what? Smoke and mirrors? It was all you?' Bex marched towards Oscar and he retreated a little, tripping over a patch of frayed carpet. When he had told them his story he had spoken in a low, hurried tone as if he had been reciting something he had learnt for a test, sounding out the details like they were newly memorised. 'And Leo was in on all of this?' She felt like she had fallen to the ground because her view of the world, of what had happened that night had suddenly tipped at an odd angle. It made her dizzy.

'It was just meant to be a silly joke!'

Bex remembered Leo's face in the library as she had once again chosen Richard over him: the frustration, the betrayal . . . she knew she had upset him, but she would never have imagined he would have joined forces with Oscar.

But then Richard moved fast, grabbing Oscar by the collar and pushing him against the landing window, one arm pressing against his throat. 'The chandelier. Did you loosen the damn chandelier?'

'What? No!' Oscar half-gurgled, half-coughed as Richard shook him. 'No! I wouldn't have done something like that!'

'So who did?'

'I don't know. Maybe it was just old and rusted and us galloping around the place set it off, maybe it was the . . . place itself . . . y'know. The bad luck of it.'

Richard let him go and slumped against the wall next to him. 'I always felt . . . that – that it was my punishment, losing my eye. The price for messing about there—'

Bex cut in. 'Leo was the price we paid – not your bloody eye.' She went to the window to look out at the jetty. They had shone a light onto the vengeful ghost of Reginald Morwood and it had turned out to be nothing more than a pile of crumpled clothes. It was the same with Oscar: each time she had looked out of this window and saw what she had thought was him in the boat, the reality had been a blanket and a wig. 'This doesn't make sense. Why didn't Leo just come out from the tunnel when he heard the sirens?'

There was silence and then Oscar cleared his throat. 'He might not have heard them, the tunnel is pretty quiet or . . . that part of the tunnel might have caved-in by that time and he might already have been injured or . . .'

Or. That small word held a whole life. Once more Bex pictured a cracked skull in the darkness. It had all been so pointless, so utterly stupid. A prank. The figure that she had thought had stalked her ever since the events at this hotel had never been Morwood, she could see that now. It had been Oscar in a second-hand coat. Leo had lost his life because of it . . . or actually, that wasn't strictly true. He had lost his life because of their childish argument in the library and the rift that had opened between them afterwards. Standing there, on the gallery landing, covered in dirt and slime from the tunnel, Bex wasn't sure who she was angriest at – herself, Oscar . . . or Leo.

'You just left him there.' The disbelief in her voice edged out the anger. Under her hand the glass of the windowpane was cold. She wanted to smash it, or smash Oscar's head into it.

'I know.' Oscar's voice, when it came, was quiet. He edged nearer to her and gently took the lighter from her grasp. She did not resist. The lighter was just an object, there was no link to Leo through it, it was not a magic talisman. Oscar studied it, turning it over in his hand.

'You found him, and you told no one where his dead body was.'

'Yes.'

'And then I roped you into cutting the film together,' Richard said. 'I thought I was helping. The police even gave me permission, keep the case in people's minds, jog someone's memory, that kind of thing. But you only helped so you could take control of the footage.'

Oscar nodded.

'You could have just told the truth then.' Bex turned. 'You could have told Leo's father . . . *his father*, Oscar – you left that man in agony.'

'I know.' Oscar was very still, his face bent to the lighter in his hand. 'Don't you think I know? There's no excuse. There's nothing I can say.'

'You let a film company buy it!' Richard strode over to Bex and stood by her side, two against one. 'Despite what you knew, you made money off it and let it become this . . . this circus!'

Here Marsha cleared her throat. Bex had forgotten she was even with them. 'Whilst you were gone, Bex, Mr Haines here got Richard and I to watch that new bit of footage, in fact only a few minutes before you came in. It seems he has decided now, ten years later, to confess to it all. I . . .' She lost her words momentarily as she gazed around her in a vague way. 'I have no idea what to do right now . . .' With no schedule and no call-sheet, Marsha looked bereft.

Above them on the ceiling shone a peeling, painted moon and some equally tattered stars, no match for the originals glittering beyond the roof.

'I think it's time for it all to end,' Oscar said in that same quiet, strangely flat voice as he picked up the bottle of rum and poured it over the wadded material he still held. 'To be honest, I thought it would happen sooner. I thought Leo's body would be discovered within weeks but it wasn't and I've done what I've done. I can't change any of it. There were so many times when I wanted to be found out, but I never was and I'm so tired of hiding it all . . . so, so very tired. There's no going back for me.'

Oscar. No longer a bit player, the one who stayed with the boat, but now revealed to be the mastermind, the one who had been telling the story all along. Finally, Bex thought, Oscar Haines had got what he always wanted – the spotlight.

'We will have to call the police now—' Marsha began.

'No.' Oscar moved cautiously to the edge of the gallery landing where there was no handrail, still clutching the lighter.

'Oz—'

'I don't know what you think you're doing—'

Oscar didn't listen to them, instead he calmly flicked the wheel of Leo's lighter and let the flame burn for a few seconds whilst the rest of them caught up with what he planned to do. Before anyone could stop him, he lit the rum-soaked wadded-up material he had been holding and watched as it grabbed the flame hungrily, burning fast and bright.

Then he dropped it onto the reception floor below.

Chapter 52

Directly below them, two floors down, the fire sprang to life in a way that suggested Oscar had not just been drinking the alcohol Bex had smelled on him earlier but had thrown it over the downstairs drapes. Flames clung to the curtains and made the screen below shrivel into black dangling shreds that fell and curled to the floor amid the growing blaze.

'What have you done?' Marsha tried to grab Oscar's arm, but he shook her off and moved closer to the edge of the gallery, gazing down at the fire, each step looking as if it took a huge effort. Bex remembered his vertigo, how he had cowered at the back of the group on that school trip ten years ago. But there was now a strange calm to him, a calculation.

'You can get out through the ballroom if you move fast,' he called behind him but didn't turn to look at them.

Smoke killed, Bex remembered. But then so did tunnels and steps cut high into clifftops, so did guns in mouths and people – people most of all. Unwinding her thin scarf, she wrapped it so the material covered the lower half of her face and wondered why her hands weren't shaking.

'Fuck! We need to get out of here!' Richard yelled.

'No, no, no!' Marsha stabbed at her phone. Bex expected there to be limited signal but she had forgotten the might of the production company. 'Hello? Hello! Oh my God! Hello. Yes, we have an emergency. No, I mean . . . fire service, fire service please. Yes, the old Ravencliffe Hotel . . . Marsha Setton. Yes, yes, I will . . . Yes, thank you, thank you . . .' She clutched her phone to her chest and leant heavily against the back wall. 'They're on their way. Thank God. We just have to wait.'

'Isn't there anyone else around you could call – some of the production crew?' Bex asked, watching as Oscar simply stood, mesmerised by the fire below.

'We're two floors up, Bex,' Marsha snapped. 'Even if there was anyone nearby – what do you expect them to do?'

Bex looked around at the hotel which was a bonfire waiting to happen. There was so much wood: panelling, handrails, bookcases and not only that, but also curtains, velvets and old silks; the whole lot was ready to shrivel, curl up and then burst into a bright orange glow. Ravencliffe was a horrible, terrible phoenix about to spring into a super-heated new life, ready to cause havoc.

'We need to get out now. I'm not waiting.' Richard headed to the stairs.

Bex watched them all through the smoke that was beginning to billow upwards, three bad singers in an Eighties pop video; their mouths moved, but they were terrible at lip-syncing and their words slipped past her. If she stood there long enough, she thought, the smoke would wrap itself around her and turn her into a ghost-girl to join Morwood in his personal hell.

She should have known what to do. After all, she was the horror film heroine, the one talked about at every fan convention, her face on posters and pin badges and keyrings. She should have been leading the way, rescuing them all, bloodied and traumatised but unbeaten. Instead she could only stare.

Oscar took another shuffling step to the edge and swayed. There was something about the way he stood, about the hunch in his shoulders and how he kept his back to them. It was a waiting focus that she had never seen in him before. Cold fear tapped her spine.

He gazed down. 'You know, you haven't asked me.'

'Asked you what?' she managed to splutter.

'Why I waited until we'd filmed the whole reunion show to tell you the truth.' Bex took a step nearer to him and, as if they were choreographed, he moved even closer to the edge. 'Ask me.' There was an intensity in his tone.

If this had been a film, Oscar was feeding her the lines and she felt a prickle of unease, unsure where this tale was heading. 'Why did you wait, Oscar?' Bex eyed the distance between them.

'Because I wanted all of this. I wanted to come back, I wanted the cameras and the crews of people all here because of us. I wanted the hype and the publicity . . . one last time. Because I'm a terrible person. I always have been and . . .' Here his voice broke and he swiped at tears on his face before squaring his shoulders and standing taller. 'And that's never going to change.'

There was a bleak desolation in his voice. The hotel had lured them in with its stories and rumours, its silly ghost scares, and they had thought they had escaped it ten years ago, but this had always been waiting for them. Oscar had left a young man dead, alone and cold, and now he would join him, not in damp stone, but in a white heat. More bones for the bad luck place. She had been wrong about him, Bex thought as she noted Oscar's dead-eyed stare. Confessing to them maybe had not been Oscar's moment in the spotlight. In fact, perhaps this was not about stepping *into* the spotlight at all but . . . stepping *out* of it.

'Oscar, come over here,' Bex said, holding out her hand, despite the fact a part of her didn't want to. He didn't deserve her help after keeping Leo's body a secret for as long as he had. What she tried to remember though was him at eighteen, all of them at that age, their unsuspecting baby faces, the faces of young people who had never yet had to make any hard choices. Silly, impetuous, foolhardy teenagers, the lot of them.

Oscar did not turn to her. Below them Bex thought she heard someone else shout her name – or maybe it was the screech of something tearing in two, she couldn't tell. Before she could reach him, Oscar let himself lean forward, too far, until his balance tipped and his body went with it, arms stretched out on either side in a pose that looked like surrender.

He let himself fall.

Chapter 53

Bex got there in time.

Lurching forward she grabbed Oscar's arm as he fell, falling to her knees at the sudden weight of his body swinging out below her. He ended up dangling from the edge of the landing by one elbow, his other arm in Bex's grip. Two floors down burnt the heart of the fire. If he slipped out of her grasp and the fall didn't kill him, the flames definitely would.

There was no way she could drag him up. She gripped Oscar's forearm with two hands, reaching down as far as she dared whilst Richard knelt alongside.

'Give me your other hand, Oz!' Richard yelled.

Oscar stretched his arm up to reach Richard but it only succeeded in dragging Bex closer to the edge. She heard the same gasp come from both her and Oscar as his elbow slipped and suddenly she took almost all of his weight.

'No,' she heard him say.

'I can hold you!' Bex yelled to a grim-faced Oscar as she hung on to him, but she could already feel the sweat making her palms slip.

It was hard to take a breath. The air was now a dry rag that wanted to shove itself down her throat and her chest was beginning to burn. Below them the flames tried to leap, writhing upwards to cling to the curtains and panelling and to the underside of the first-floor landing. Somewhere down there was the luggage trolley, its bars hot enough to sear a hand, a flaming chariot only demons would be able to use.

'No,' Oscar said again and she saw the fear in his eyes but she also caught something else. It was an emotion that flickered between them. 'You should have let me fall.'

'It's okay. I've got you!' But she didn't. Her hands ached and her wrists felt as if the tendons were pulling free. He was too heavy for her; there was no way she could haul him up so her only option was to grip on.

'Let me help,' she heard Richard say but he couldn't reach over her and she choked, her throat filling with smoke.

Everything stilled around Oscar's next words. 'Let me go.' He stared straight into her eyes.

'What?' She thought that perhaps she had misheard but when she gazed at him, she knew that what she had recognised was fear was actually mixed with something else. Resignation. Sadness.

'You can't hold on to me, you'll drag yourself over. Let me go.' Tears streaked the soot and grime on his skin, a weird stage make-up that made a mask of his face. Of course, he had been wearing a mask this whole time: Oscar bloody Haines, the one who stayed with the boat, who had spent the years hawking tat and books and waving to fans, busying himself with anything and everything so he wouldn't have to confront what he had done.

'No.' She kept gripping on, tilting her centre of gravity so she leant over far too much into a dizzying view of flames and wreckage.

'Please,' Oscar said to her, but the smoke was doing funny things to her eyes; it blurred and twisted the person below her into someone else, a young man in a green raincoat and glasses who looked at her with such faith that she would save him, that she would come for him.

Sweat made her hands slip and she slid a little towards the edge, letting out a gargled scream until she felt something clamp onto her ankle. A hand. Richard. And then, on her other ankle – Marsha.

'Please. Bex. Let me go.' Oscar had stopped trying to get his other arm up so he could hold on. Instead he hung there and did not look down. His eyes fixed on hers. It was just the two of them in this smoke-swirled, flame-roaring world and Bex realised that never, in all of the time they had spent together, had it ever been this – only the two of them, concentrating on each other.

'No! Are you mad?' She was certain her own shoulder would pop out any second. Oscar was so heavy and his arm slid out of her sweaty grip a fraction more, just as her knees were starting to drag over the rough carpeted floor.

'You'll pull yourself over. Let go.' He did swing his other hand around then but not to grab on to the landing, no, instead he slammed his hand over hers.

'What are you doing?'

'I'm not . . . taking you . . . with me . . .' He began to prise her fingers away.

'No!'

But everything quietened around her as he spoke next. 'Everyone will hate me . . . I deserve it . . . but I don't want to . . . live like that . . .'

'No, no, no, no – no, please! I can't lose someone else. Oscar, please!'

The smoke made her eyes sting and she tried, she tried so hard to keep her grip on him, but he pushed at her fingers and she felt his arm slither from her grasp. She flailed to catch the material of his jacket but the thin sleeve ripped under her hand and then her slippery grip failed her and she lurched, thrown forward into a space where there was suddenly nothing counterbalancing her weight. Richard pulled her back and she could only watch in horror as Oscar's face dropped away from her.

He fell into the flames.

'Oscar!' Richard untangled himself and crawled closer to the edge of the landing as Bex crouched and took shallow, burning breaths, pressing herself against the far wall. He didn't have to say anything when he turned back to her; she knew there was no more Oscar to save.

'Oh my God, oh my God, oh my God!' Marsha clung to the wall, her voice husky and full of panic.

There was no time to understand what had just happened. The fire did not conveniently freeze and the smoke did not handily hang in the air like a cloud. Stuck in Bex's mind was the image of Oscar's face as he fell, his eyes not shocked or wide, but closed as if in prayer. During their meal on the first night, she had looked at the people in their candle-glow and thought of amber, how the hotel had trapped all of its unquiet souls just like an insect got caught in a golden prison. Now Oscar's soul would join them. She couldn't even work out what to feel first because her body was struggling to breathe and her wrists ached and there was no room for anything other than the instinct to get away.

'There must be another way down – not through reception!' Richard put the crook of his elbow over his mouth in a poor attempt to breathe easier.

'Shadow stairs.' Bex blessed the nights spent poring over old Ravencliffe documents and the architect's plans. 'Back stairs. For the servants . . . we can use them to get to the ballroom and then get out to the lawn.'

The two of them stared at her in the smoky, swirling gloom, mouths hidden, eyes wide and red-rimmed. Sweat stuck Richard's shirt to him in dark patches and Marsha's silver-white hair was sooty and lank. It was a reflex almost, for Bex to bend and pick up the lighter once again, little faces encased in plastic smiling up at her from a different time, one where the heat came from a summer sun, not the writhing death throes of an old hotel.

They stumbled across the landing and headed to the other

side of the building where Bex might have been imagining it but it felt a little cooler.

'Stairs!' Marsha yelled, sticking her head through a dark doorway.

It wouldn't be long, Bex told herself as she ran down the steps. They would come out in the ballroom and from there freedom, air and water were within easy reach. Not long at all. The fire would not have started to lap at the ballroom drapes and they would escape.

They would.

When all three of them staggered into the wrecked shell of what had once been the glorious centrepiece of the hotel, they encountered yet more smoke and a searing heat but no flames. However, the reception was directly above their heads and soon that ceiling would come crashing down in a fiery hailstorm as the hotel collapsed in on itself.

The room was echoing and empty.

Apart from a hunched figure slumped in one corner.

Chapter 54

Black hair hung over knees drawn up tight to the person's chest, their small shoulders rounded over, white fingers clutching the ankles of black boots. Bex almost expected the head to lift and there would be Leo's face, his eager smile as the flesh slipped off his bones and revealed the skull underneath.

The boots. Bex recognised the boots.

'Holly?'

The figure did not move. The last time she had seen Holly it had been night and she had been flirting with Luke to distract him so Bex could get into the maze.

'Holly? I thought everyone had been sent off-site? Young lady? Why are you still here?' Marsha sounded puzzled, but it was hard to judge anyone's tone through a makeshift bandana. The figure coughed and Bex ran to her.

Around them the ballroom was empty. The picture windows framed a view of the sea and the recently cut-back lawn where, ten years ago on the top step, Leo had stood. At some point someone must have cleared the broken glass and crystal from the chandelier that had fallen all those years ago, though some of the darker patches on the scuffed parquet floor could well have been Richard's blood. The chandelier itself had been shoved to one corner, a battered shipwreck of its former glory. There was a ragged hole in the ceiling where it had once hung.

Something slammed into the floor above their heads and they all ducked. Above them the fire raged in the reception hall.

'Jesus! We have to go – now!' Richard ran to the nearest window.

'Holly?' Bex crouched over the girl huddled in the corner, hair hanging over shins covered by ripped tights and Bex wasn't sure if that was fashion or distress. 'It's me, Bex. What're you doing here? We need to get you out.'

Another sob and some muffled words that Bex could not catch so she bent closer. The head did not raise but the hoarse voice was clearer this time. 'I heard you all.'

Bex could see that the one window they had originally broken to get into the hotel on their first trip had been boarded over and she watched as Richard raised his elbow ready to jab at the windowpane next to it. She remembered the sound of glass shattering and how that had seemed to be an omen of some sort when she had been eighteen; now the sound was a relief.

'I heard you all talking – what he did to Leo.' Holly's voice came from behind her curtain of hair.

Marsha drew closer to them, a frown creasing her forehead. 'She shouldn't be here. She was meant to have left hours ago.'

'I didn't. I stayed behind to look for you, Bex.' Holly did not raise her head, so her words were stifled. 'I waited for you to come out of the maze – I waited so long and then we were all told to go but I didn't. I couldn't. I knew where you'd gone.' Bex had a wild instinct to tell the girl to hush about their secret midnight plan but then she remembered that it didn't matter anymore. A sob caught in Holly's throat. 'I was about to follow you through that trapdoor when I saw you walk up to the hotel. I was so pleased you were okay! But then, inside, I heard you all talking up on the gallery, I heard what Oscar said, horrible, horrible things . . . and I ran but . . . I didn't know what to do and then there was all this smoke . . .' She coughed again, deep ratcheting sounds that made her hunch over the phone she had clutched in her hand. She grabbed on to Bex's arm and raised her head enough so that Bex could see a sliver of face between the messy hair hanging down.

'Bex!' Richard shouted from the window where he had thrown a bit of old curtain over the jagged edge of the broken pane. 'Come on! Get her moving. Let's go!'

Another crash from the floor above their heads where the reception was being consumed by the blaze. Bex cringed again as part of the ceiling became weirdly soft, melting in on itself until it collapsed sending a fiery sludge of wood and plaster thumping to the floor whilst other flames eagerly raced across the ceiling. What Bex had thought was heat before suddenly roared into air that was no longer air but something that wished to suck her eyeballs out from her head and blister her skin. Both she and Holly threw themselves back from the burning debris.

They were cut off from the others – and worse, they were cut off from the window, their only means of escape.

'Holly, you've got to get up!' Bex dragged at her arm, trying to haul her to her feet but the girl was dead weight.

'No. I can't!'

If they ran now, Bex could see a small gap in the writhing mess on the floor, but soon more burning chunks of floorboard and lathe would fall and that gap would be swallowed. She knew that if she didn't get the girl moving, they would both be trapped and the best they could hope for would be smoke asphyxiation before the flames got to their flesh.

'For fuck's sake, Holly. Move!' This time she wedged her shoulder under Holly's armpit and heaved them both up. Smoothing the hair from her face she found a different girl gazing at her with tear-filled eyes. It was the make-up. The eyeliner and pale foundation had been sweated and cried away and the result was someone even younger looking, despite the tears, someone baby-faced . . . someone familiar.

'I'm not,' Holly said, placing her hand over Bex's.

'Huh?'

'My name's not Holly . . . it's . . .'

And Bex suddenly knew what she was going to say. She finished the sentence for her. 'Sophie. You're Leo's little sister.'

Chapter 55

Leo's sister. The last time Bex had seen Sophie she had been an awkward twelve-year-old with a blonde fringe that hid most of her eyes, a girl who had scooted straight to her room as soon as anyone visited. In the years since, Bex hadn't seen her when she had called by, possibly as part of Mr Finch's plan to make sure the two of them never got close.

'Look what happened to Leo when he made friends with you,' Mr Finch had pointed out.

'I don't understand.' Bex gripped Sophie's shoulders. But there was no time for explaining. Whatever the girl had done getting herself the role of assistant, this was not the moment for tearful explanations.

There was a drawn-out cracking sound which turned into a groan as a strangely liquid fire dripped down into the ballroom. The gap that Bex had spotted before was already fast vanishing, but she couldn't trust her eyes anymore because the smoke had laid a filmy gauze over everything she could see.

'We have to—' Her words ended in coughing and each new breath scratched her throat.

In the corner flames crept around the wreckage of the chandelier, giving it one final glory moment. It had never lit up a glamorous scene below it, had never glittered and glimmered whilst people danced to soft music in a mirror-gleaming ball. Even now it remained a dark lump as fire raged around it. There was so much noise, a roaring that sounded almost animal-like and Bex knew she had to move, she had to get through the gap in the flames but all she really wanted to do was cower and hope someone would rescue her.

Sophie sobbed.

Leo's sister. She had been eight when Leo had disappeared. There had been a time when Bex had plaited the girl's hair and played dolls with her, rolled her eyes because Leo had to babysit and helped with homework but that was all so long ago. She had missed going to get the younger girl's ears pierced, trying on outfits together in stuffy changing rooms, watching *Dirty Dancing* with popcorn and being a shoulder to cry on when she got her heart broken as a teenager.

But Sophie's heart had been broken a long time before that.

Bex gripped the girl closer. Those years spent grieving in her house, she had only ever thought of herself, of how Leo's disappearance had devastated her, all those nights watching him on her television, or days spent sitting on her roof with her coffee and her binoculars. It didn't matter if she had to manhandle his sister across the burning mess in front of them, she promised to herself that she would get Sophie out. The girl should never have been here in the first place. The hotel would not have her.

'Right – Soph . . . Soph, are you listening to me?' She smoothed the hair out of her face and held her chin in her hand so the girl had to look at her. 'All we have to do is get to the window. We have to move fast and we don't stop, no matter what. Do not let go of me.'

'I can't!' Sophie stared at the fire. 'I can't.'

'But I can, and all you have to do is follow.'

'No, we should wait—'

But Bex yanked her forward by the hand. A flat palm of heat

pushed at her, air that was a malignant force all of its own, determined to hold her back. But that slim gap remained and Sophie had a future, Bex kept thinking to herself, one that did not involve becoming kindling on this ballroom floor. She had failed Leo. She would not fail his sister.

She didn't close her eyes, even though it felt as if her eyeballs were about to melt from her head and she was sure she could catch the acrid scent of burning hair. She would keep moving forward, dragging Sophie behind her and that gap would keep getting closer.

Sophie's future was just beyond the person-sized hole in the flames.

It was over almost too soon. The heat washed over her, the smoke clogged her throat and the light was intense but she was through and it had taken only a few steps – just two or three strides and there she was with cool air at her back from a broken window.

But she was no longer holding Sophie's hand.

'I can't!' Sophie's shout was shrill with fear, but all Bex could see was a dark shape beyond the flames.

Richard pulled at her. 'We have to go!'

'No!' Bex whirled to him. 'That's Soph – Leo's sister! I can't leave her.'

'Leo's sis—?'

'I can't leave her in there!' She knew she was shouting, her voice cracked and wild, but she wanted to scream even louder. Despite the heat and the roar of the fire, Bex thought of snow. This was a snowglobe moment. One shake and Leo had disappeared for good ten years ago and here she was again, except this time she wasn't going to stand around and wait for her world to be upended once more.

The gap in the blaze was not even a gap at all when she pulled free from Richard's grasp and hurled herself through it. She kept her gaze on the smoke-blurred outline of Sophie and there, for a second, the outline wavered and split into two – two people standing behind the fire but that could only have been a mirage as a searing pain on her right side made her stumble and cry out.

It would take only four steps to reach her.

One.

Two.

Three.

Four.

For once it felt right, as if those numbers had been said in the exact way she needed, as if their magic spell could now work. There Sophie was, crouched with wide eyes looking at her, and Bex found the strength to grab and give her a shove that propelled her through the now tiny gap, hoping Richard was on the other side to help her through the window. She leapt to follow her, despite the pain and the roar and the smoke that made every breath a wheeze and she staggered out, dazed and shaking, falling to her knees only yards away from the window where safety waited, cool and bright.

Bex smiled.

And then a great rending sound came from above and there was only darkness.

Chapter 56

Flashes of consciousness amid the black.

A flutter of eyelids.

Bex saw a face above her, but it swayed and so did she, a soothing rhythm. It took her a while to realise that she was being carried. A grey sky swung over her and there was a face in shadow which spoke, but the words were muffled to a lullaby under the shifting sky. For a second she knew the face to be Leo's, that he was smiling the grin that lit him up and, as the blackness closed over her once more, she smiled too.

A flutter of eyelids.

Waves slapping rocks. This time she was cold, a cold that seemed to come from a tight knot at her core, even though there was also heat down her left side, a sickening, throbbing thing that made her whimper. She lifted her head and the world spun around her in daubs of colour: there was a sea spitting waves against the shore and steps below her but no figure on them, no reason for her to call out or try to reach them. She could sleep. So she did.

A flutter of eyelids.

White. Solid blank white. She was blind. But blindness was black, wasn't it? There was a beeping sound and she began to see cracks in the white in front of her. Tiles. A ceiling. She tried to say something but only a gurgle came out and then there was a warm hand on hers. Her mother's face loomed over her, hair unbrushed and limp, and she couldn't hold on to the scene because the blackness washed over her once more.

A flutter of eyelids.

'Shit!' Bex recognised Sophie's voice and she turned her head, finding herself propped up in a hospital bed. Leo's sister lurched out of the chair next to her. 'Shit, you're awake. Your mum's going to be so pissed . . .'

Bex tried to say something but her throat closed up so she waved her hand towards the water jug she could see on her bedside table. Sophie poured her a drink and lifted it to her lips. She swallowed a few times and tried again. 'My mum'll be pissed because . . . I'm awake?'

'No! Because she's missed it! She *just* went home. We had to literally force her out of the door, the woman was dead on her feet. I've got to go call her, she'll kill me otherwise.'

Bex gripped Sophie's hand. 'No. Wait.' Her brain hadn't done much thinking for Bex didn't know how long and it creaked into action like an old door in a horror film. 'How long have I been here?'

'Just over two weeks. Look, I've got to call a doctor and ring your mum. I . . . I'll be back – don't fall asleep again, okay?'

Two weeks. A lot could happen in two weeks. The world could change in just one night so fourteen of them could wreak untold damage. Bex looked around at a hospital room mostly hidden beneath flowers. Bunches of them in jugs and vases, in baskets, gift bags and pots, tied with ribbon and twine and silk. Plants too: tall, elegant orchids and sprawling leafy things dangling over the extra tables that had been brought in to hold them all. Nestled in between were teddies and quite a lot of toy ravens. She hadn't realised that ravens could be cuddly and they didn't look happy about it. The room smelled of growing and fresh wet earth.

'Lovely to see you awake, Ms Harrison. How do you feel?'

The doctor, a kind-eyed woman with deep frown lines on her forehead, performed her checks, reading and then scribbling on the clipboard at the end of her bed.

Bex tried to stretch a little and immediately regretted it. 'Definitely like a ceiling collapsed on me.'

She could remember that. The sight of Sophie climbing out of the window and the feel of cool air on her face just before that cracking sound above her and then, mercifully, her brain had paused for an interval in the cinema screening of her life.

She tried to listen as the doctor explained her injuries. Burns on her left side and arm, the wounds currently hidden under dressings and the pain hidden by drugs. Head trauma which caused the coma: two weeks of her life misted to nothing like static on a television screen. After strict instructions to not overexert herself, the doctor left the room, telling Sophie as she left that she had ten minutes only.

'Are you okay?' Bex asked Sophie. There was eyeliner still smudged around her eyes as if she had tried to remove it, but it wouldn't budge. Instead of the Goth Barbie uniform of striped tights and black skirt she wore a simple pair of tracksuit bottoms and a plain T-shirt that had no reference to Ravencliffe on it, not even a discreet outline of a beak.

'Yes. Bit of smoke inhalation, a few cuts and bruises but . . . you got me out.'

Bex cleared her furred throat. 'You have a lot of explaining to do.'

'Now?'

'Well, we've got time whilst I wait for my mum and dad. Ten minutes.' She coughed and it set off splinters of pain deep inside her. 'Explain.'

So Sophie did. As she listened, Bex's brain changed from a creaking door into one now propped wide open as a gale of information drove through it. Her brain cells tried to grip on to fixed surfaces and hold steady.

The gap year Sophie's father thought she was taking had turned out to be stuffed full of purpose. As soon as she had caught wind of the reunion rumour, she had made it her focus to use it to find out what had really happened to her brother. A false name and a fake student ID had got Sophie the job as a runner and from there the absolutely unpaid job of Bex's assistant on set. Studios called those roles internships like they had some kind of prestige but, in reality, they were glorified unpaid labour, exploiting the hordes of starry-eyed young people who dreamed of a career in film. The production team, along with Richard and Oscar, had had a preliminary meet-up in a fancy hotel mostly to work out how they could get Bex out of hiding. This next bit Bex knew.

'You ate mini-bar snacks whilst Richard slept.'

'Yeah . . . but I also did something else. I had a good old snoop around. I mean, it was my opportunity, right? I didn't know how much he was involved in Leo disappearing and I *had* to find out. It was in his jacket pocket.'

'It?'

'Leo's lighter. Recognised it straight away.'

'Oh my God – it was you! *You* sent it to me?'

'Yes. I needed you. You were Leo's best friend. I knew that if I could just get you out of that house, you would do anything to find out what happened to him. I stood outside for ages hoping you would appear, in fact I'd been visiting your house for years, ringing the doorbell and everything. You never answered.' The figure Bex's blurred door camera had shown her had not been a demonic entity come to drag her to hell, but a grief-stricken teenager.

'You could have just told me who you were – I'd have helped. We were on the same side.' Bex's voice cracked on those last words and it wasn't completely down to her parched throat.

'I didn't know that,' Sophie said in a quiet tone, smoothing the furry wing of a cuddly raven. 'I didn't know if you'd snitch me out to Marsha or someone. I didn't know *you* . . .'

And whose fault was that? Bex asked herself. She could have taken the time to become a friend to this girl; she could have pushed past Mr Finch and plonked herself in Sophie's life whether he had liked it or not . . . but she had chosen not to.

'How did Rich get Leo's lighter?' she muttered, more to herself. Sophie shrugged. 'Did you set fire to Rich's trailer?'

'What? No! What d'you take me for? Maybe his stupid vape pen exploded. I don't know.'

'Bad luck,' Bex whispered. Like the old chandelier falling on him ten years ago, weakened by time and them running about the place, the hotel itself grabbing any opportunity to maim . . . to kill, if it got the chance.

'I did move your lighter whilst you were asleep one night,' Sophie continued sheepishly but Bex's voice failed her, turning into a croak. She settled for frowning instead. 'I got a master key to the trailers. I just wanted to keep you focused, y'know – you seemed to be getting a bit close to Richard. Sorry if I scared you.'

There was quiet as thoughts reared up in Bex's head, large and unformed things like blobs in a lava lamp.

'But, wait, wait, wait – what about Oscar's allergic reaction right at the start? Who did that?' she asked.

Another shrug. 'An accident, I guess. The pizza company couldn't rule out that a nut oil might have been used by mistake or . . . some people think that Oscar, umm . . . that he did it to himself . . . for sympathy . . .'

'What? I can't believe that. You'd have to be crazy to do something like that to yourself.'

But in her head she heard his voice. *Everyone will hate me. I don't want to live like that.* He might have been willing to do anything to bask one last time in people's concern . . . and a smaller, meaner voice in her head added: *to get more screen time.* They would never know for certain; the person who could give them answers was now bones and ash.

They sat in silence for a few minutes. Bex floated on a cushion of painkillers but she could sense the pain from her injuries swimming underneath her pool float, deep-sea creatures waiting to rear up and toss her into bloodied water.

A face rose in her imagination, fierce and hollow-eyed. 'Oh God – your dad must be devastated.'

Sophie pressed her lips together and picked at a broken fingernail. 'He is.'

They both fell silent, thinking of Mr Finch.

'What happens now?' Bex asked as her cool painkiller waters began to thrash.

'Actually, it's kind of already happened . . .'

'What has?'

Sophie bit at her tortured nail and gave Bex a long look. 'The live-stream . . .'

Chapter 57

The mourners were mould spots on the green grass of the sloping cemetery.

There were only seven of them. Every day, from school, Bex and Leo had walked past this church in her hometown with its mossy stone and jewel windows, garlanded by the dead. Sometimes they had gone into the graveyard and read the old names and dates whilst sharing sweets from the corner shop before they headed home for the evening to homework and television and all the boring glorious things that make up a life.

Bex had brought a bag of chocolate mice with her.

Ten years they had had to wait for this. A resting place. Bones had been carried from the tunnel and then it had been filled in to deter any foolish film enthusiasts or dark tourists. Those bones had then been laid here, in this Catholic graveyard with its willow tree, the gold lettering glinting on the polished black of the modern headstones whilst the older names crumbled on ancient stone nearby. Bex's father fiddled with the tight collar of his best shirt and her mother shifted her stance in the low-heeled court shoes that were already beginning to pinch. Richard stood, quiet and still, at her side.

It had been a week since Bex had woken up. If she had

been sensible, she would have still been resting, she thought. However, there had been too much to do: her signature required on paperwork, her input required into plans and documents. Her left side ached and she leant heavily on her walking stick around which her mother had tied a black velvet ribbon that morning.

Marsha stood a little way off from the family, dressed in her customary oddly shaped black clothes and leather boots, her usual red glasses frames swapped for a more conservative grey.

'It's kind of you to come,' Bex had said to her as they had walked to the grave.

'I had to.' Marsha had gripped her tightly before drawing her into a fierce hug. 'That poor boy.'

Bex hadn't known which poor boy she had meant and had begun to ask her but then pressed her lips together. It didn't matter. Oscar or Leo.

Because of the live-stream, in the last week Bex had seen quite a lot of Marsha. She had come to the hospital and Bex had been expecting anger, to hear that pleasant sing-song tone in her voice which masked the steel underneath. Bex had expected to have to protect Sophie. But that wasn't how it played out.

'At first, I couldn't believe what I was hearing.' Sophie had explained it to her that day in the hospital. 'I was in the hotel reception and I could see the four of you up on the landing. I heard Oscar begin to explain and then I just felt angry. I didn't want him to get away with it, y'know? I had my phone with me and it was easy to point and shoot, to live-stream it to the Ravens. I wanted them to know in case . . . in case something happened to us and the truth never got out.'

In Greek myth ravens were the gods' messengers and these Ravens, the ones watching on the fan sites, they made Sophie's video fly. Before Bex and the rest of them even reached the hospital after the fire, Oscar's confession had been spread as a much faster flame. Sophie had expected Marsha to be angry, for the whole film company to bring the weight of its wealth and power crushing down on her – but that hadn't happened.

Mr Finch and Sophie stood on the opposite side of the grave. His old suit looked dusty and creased but he had shaved and combed what was left of his hair and had tucked a silk handkerchief into his top pocket. The priest did what priests do – tried to soften it all with melodic words in a rhythm meant to lull, the breeze pressing his robes tight against his ankles. Green material discreetly covered the mound of earth that had been dug out for the grave as if it was the soil that was distressing, not the coffin next to it. Soon, when the mourners had left, the earth would be shovelled back in and the surplus wheelbarrowed away.

There were no more words. The priest stood back and the mourners edged forward, casting glances at one another. Their grief was no longer raw, it was a deeper thing than that, nestled tight within and sometimes hardly felt until a sudden twist brought jarring pain. Sophie held her father's arm as they stood at the lip of the grave and he clasped her hand in his, the two of them staring at the polished wood of the coffin.

Seven become five as Bex's mum and dad gave her a hug, patted Mr Finch on his shoulder and left, her mother picking her way around each grave as she made her way back to the path, her father striding straight across them.

The wind set the trees shushing each other as if they too knew they had to be silent in the presence of grief.

'You brought my boy back.' Mr Finch didn't turn his head to look at Bex but kept gazing at the hole at their feet. 'I won't forget that. I won't forgive either, mind—'

'Dad!' Sophie interrupted. She wore a black blazer and a pair of trousers that seemed borrowed and a little too big for her, her hair now back to blonde and swept up in a ponytail.

But Bex didn't want to be forgiven. She may not have known where Leo's body had been all of those years, unlike Oscar, but that hadn't made her blameless. She should have tried harder, she should have kept searching for him, she should have done so many things. There was a part of her that was angry with Leo, for going along with Oscar in the first place, but it was a part that was going to have to join up with all the others, making her a poorly patched doll. Ten years had been wasted. She would not waste any more.

'Yes, yes – I know – she's your friend now. But you remember, my girl, she was Leo's friend too and look where he's ended up.'

'She saved my life.'

'Hmm,' Mr Finch continued, this time fixing Bex with a look. 'Mark this, Rebecca Harrison. If anything were to happen to my daughter when she is with you, it would break my heart. And I would then rip yours out.'

Bex nodded and glanced at Sophie. The Goth Barbie look was hard to shake, Bex could see elements of it creeping back into the purple tips of her blonde hair, the huge black boots and the plum tinge to her lip balm. She had moved into Bex's London house a few days after Bex left hospital. Already the girl had opened up some of the half-finished rooms, painting them in strange colours that nobody would think worked together but somehow did, cooking large batches of soups and curries, freezing the leftovers and making sure the fridge was stocked. It was at first a shock that there were ornaments on side tables, in fact it was a shock there were side tables, but Bex was getting used to the rooms looking like someone was proud of them, instead of being dumping grounds for the limited detritus of a broken life. Maybe, in a misty future Bex could not quite imagine right now, she would even move them both back to Wales.

Five became one as Richard walked off a little way and Sophie and Marsha guided Mr Finch back to the black car that waited for them, his hands already shaking in anticipation of his next drink. 'I'll see you later, at home, yeah?' Sophie whispered to her before she left and Bex had smiled at her. They had a busy couple of days coming up.

On her own, standing next to Leo's grave she could have done with a bit of Marsha's direction, or Richard's – a script, maybe. Someone to tell her how to look and what her thoughts should be. If she had been given the choice, she would have done one of those firework send-offs, packed Leo's ashes into a Roman candle and sent it into the sky in a burst of colour – not this. This was putting him back into the darkness again.

'I'm sorry I couldn't save you from the monsters,' she whispered.

In the end there was nothing else to say. It had all been said before, in articles and fanzines, in internet videos and on social media, hours and hours of other people's voices, thousands of other people's words all describing a Leo that was theirs, not hers.

Before she left, she placed a chocolate mouse on his gravestone.

* * *

In the vestry a weak sun gave a spotlight in which the dust motes could dance. Bex leant against a chair, crossed her arms, decided that was too aggressive a stance and so fiddled with one of her rings.

'I just wanted to say . . .' Richard's sentence trailed off into nothing. After the funeral, he had tapped her on the arm and beckoned her into the cool quiet of this room. 'Well, I don't know what to say, really. I just didn't want to leave without talking to you first.'

Bex nodded and twisted the ring round and round. It was a gold buckle-shaped thing her parents had given her as a child which now only fit her little finger. Richard was thinner than the last time she had seen him, hair brushed back, wearing black. If she poked him in his middle he would simply fold over like paper.

'I wanted to—'

'—Are you—?'

They both smiled.

'You first,' Richard said.

'I wanted to say thank you. For getting me out of the hotel, out of the fire.'

He nodded. Time had passed so quickly since they had stumbled out of the burning hotel and been swept away to their different lives. 'Well, you got me out all those years ago. Thought I should return the favour.'

A wooden Jesus on his cross looked down on her in this room with its stock cupboard of altar wine and Tupperware boxes of communion wafers. The holy miracle of Christ becoming flesh had been boiled down to two shelves above the sink, near the drain unblocker and bleach.

'I'm not going to Oscar's funeral,' Bex said.

Richard nodded again and pushed himself up to sit on the counter next to the sink. 'I still can't believe it all – all those years of lying . . .' Believing it was not a problem for Bex; understanding was the part that was going to take time. 'I can't even imagine how horrible it was to find Leo—'

'Don't. Don't imagine it.' The lighter was in the pocket of her coat. She took it out and showed it to Richard. 'Soph stole this from you, the night of the production party. But what I don't understand is how you got it.'

'Ah.' Richard turned the tap on and then off again at the sink next to him. 'Thing is, I didn't even know I had it. I picked up a jacket to go back to my room, thinking it was mine, but it wasn't, it was Oscar's. I didn't know, I mean, I was a bit of a mess that night.'

'Yeah. I've heard.'

'I didn't even check the pockets myself. Passed out on my hotel bed and Holly, sorry . . . Sophie . . . found the thing. She must have thought it was me keeping that damn bit of plastic – she must have thought I knew more about her brother's disappearance than I was letting on. And if so, she knew you'd be able to get the truth out of me.'

The chunk of plastic in Bex's hand had had quite a journey

to end up here in this vestry amongst the saints and sinners, she thought, turning it over in her palm. Each of them had taken possession of it at some point in its travels. Leo first, dying with it in his hand in the tunnel. Then Oscar, taking it from his dead body to help light his way out, keeping it close out of recklessness perhaps, or out of a feeling that he wanted to be caught. Richard had come next, picking up a jacket he had thought was his and unwittingly allowing Sophie to find the lighter in his hotel room . . . who in turn had packaged it up and sent it to Bex, with that note. It truly was a talisman, but she wasn't sure whether it was one of good or bad luck.

Sat on the kitchen counter, Richard rubbed his forehead as if he had a headache coming. 'It was my fault though, wasn't it? Oscar was my friend – I brought him along to the hotel. None of this would have happened if . . . well, if we'd never got together.' Taking his hand from his forehead, she held it in hers, her thumb stroking his fingers like she used to do back when they had strolled the corridor of their old school, the reigning monarchs of such a narrow kingdom. He sighed. 'I wish things had been different.'

'So do I,' she whispered and she leant her head against his chest, standing between his legs. It would have been easy to lift her head, to tilt it to his, to let whatever might happen from there. Instead she pushed herself away from him, the pain in her side flaring from the sudden movement. 'But it's not. What's done is done.'

Wishing that something could be different was pointless; Bex had no time for it. That was how a person got stuck in the past and the past had held onto her for far too long.

'We won't see each other again, will we?' Richard said as she neared the door.

Bex didn't need to answer.

* * *

Beyond the wall of the graveyard though was another wall, a human one.

People had come from across the country and the globe. They had set up little tents outside the church wall and brought flowers and handwritten posters laminated to protect them against the rain. They had unfolded camping chairs and unpacked snacks, lighting fake candles they could leave on the pavement along with pictures and paintings, notes and teddy bears.

Bex could have tried to avoid them. There were side gates and a narrow lane at the back of the church that could have been cordoned off. But she was done hiding. Instead she walked along the path away from the graves and pulled on the old wooden gate that let her into the small dim porch with its little roof. For a second all was dark and quiet – her shoes scuffing the dusty stone floor. But she was done with dark and quiet too.

She stepped into the crowd.

Chapter 58

The crowd waited patiently.

It had been a few whirlwind weeks after the funeral but now all that was left for Bex to do was stand and say her words. In her hand was a copy of an old letter. She had spent many nights practising what she was about to say in front of her plants and Bob the pigeon, who nodded in a way that Bex took to be approving, though in reality she knew he was probably looking for an errant seed to peck.

In this moment Bex was alone. Sophie stood at the side of the stage, but Bex hadn't wanted anyone to wait with her. She knew what the fans had nicknamed this event: RavenCon . . . Clusion. There had been a lot of speculation over whether she would appear and what she would say – she could almost hear that expectation like a high-pitched tinnitus whine coming from the crowd. They had had to hire a bigger venue to accommodate the numbers.

She heard her name and stepped on stage.

The counting had begun before she could stop herself. One, two, three, four. But those numbers no longer had much power; she knew there was no safety in them, it was just a magic spell she had conjured to get through the days. It would take many more of those days, however, to stop reciting them and that was a process only just begun.

Lights. A mass of people. Applause that vibrated through her but no cheering. Nobody felt like cheering this story anymore. The crowd was a wave only beginning to swell and there was no clue as to how big it would grow – one wrong word and it would crest and crash right over her. She raised a hand and silence fell.

'Hello.' Her voice seemed so loud that she flinched. 'Hello and thank you for coming.' It felt wrong to be the one on a stage instead of Oscar. Everyone had an opinion on him, social media was ablaze with righteous anger, disappointment, disgust, eager to pile all of their words on top of a dead man until the grave buckled under the weight. Liar, cheat – he had made a fool of the *Ravencliffe* fandom with his trickery and dragged Leo with him. She was yet to work out her own opinion of either of them. That would take time.

There was one item on a table in front of her. She picked it up.

'Do you know what the most popular bit of *Ravencliffe* merchandise is? It's this.' She held up the snowglobe, gave it a shake and watched the tiny figure within disappear into the storm. 'Leo. Before we begin, can I introduce you to the Leo I knew? Not the tragic figure who died and was abandoned in that tunnel but my friend, the one I loved very much.'

The lights dimmed and she stepped to the side, turning to watch the images that came up on the screen behind her. Mr Finch and Sophie had helped her choose them, had even allowed her to take some family photos and videos. There was nothing from *Ravencliffe*. Instead there was Leo at four, ten, sixteen, each goofy smile, each shy ducking-away from the camera, each gawky run, wind-blown, sun-tanned, laughing, eating, pointing, all the life he had, all the life he was allowed packed into a three-minute running time. The tears, when they stung her eyes, were welcome because they were only love – for him, the boy he had been and for the man he had never been allowed to become. The montage ended.

In the darkness before the stage lights came back on Bex could feel the crowd-wave that she was standing in front of pause above her head, ready to sweep her away or pound her against the rocks. She was the only one left to stand and bear it. Richard had taken his daughter on holiday, left on a plane a week ago, his destination unknown to her. Her next words were chosen with care. 'Stories. A story brought us to Ravencliffe in the first place, a silly ghost tale of a spectral Morwood striding around the hotel, seeking vengeance on those who would dare to step on his land. And then we – Leo, Richard, Oscar and I – we became the story, many stories in fact . . . theories and rumours. But I want us to begin to forge a new story that we can share together: me, Leo's family and you, the fans. Leo's story will not end with *Ravencliffe*. There will be a charity set up in his name, the Leo Finch Foundation, which will fund all sorts of deserving projects aimed to help young people in whichever way they need. Echelon has pledged a very generous amount of money to fund the project. I hope it is a fitting memorial for Leo.'

There was cheering from the audience. Bex felt the thrill of a soldier leading troops into battle, the electricity of knowing that these people were with her, were listening to her, were waiting for her command. She was a warrior cry.

'I'm not quite finished with this story of ours, however. There is another person in all of this who has been forgotten, who should have played a leading role and, instead, was sidelined. Jane Morwood. I'd like to tell you her story, if I may. Recently, I went to the convent where she spent the rest of the days after Morwood's death, the place where she wrote a last confession on her deathbed. It's never been heard before . . .'

Whilst she spoke, Bex saw it all unfold in her imagination:

Candlelight. A woman with bright eyes, in a high-necked Victorian dress, her hair neatly pinned in a bun. A room with locks on the outside but on this night the locks have been opened by one of the few servants remaining. A friend. Not of hers but of Peter's.

Her beloved Peter. Cariad. The man she had grown to love in the sunlight at the edges of the shadow her husband threw over her. The stolen moments had been snatched when Reginald had left for business in the city. She remembered Peter in that sunshine – his deft hands, the way he could see the beautiful shapes in blocks of wood, the beautiful shape within her – and she tried not to think of his broken body as they found him on the rocks below.

She cannot prove it, but she knows her husband is behind Peter's death and the servants that are left seem to agree with her. Her husband has not been a well-liked master.

Leaving her room, she walks without making a sound. He does not allow her shoes anymore, so she cannot run away. It is for her own good, he says. Madness. She has caught it like a fever, apparently, though she feels fine – cool, in control. Madness is just a word he needs to use to get what he wants.

She knows that she only has days, weeks maybe if she is lucky, before a doctor somewhere signs a form and she is carried away to another four walls, insanity stamped on her head in an ink that will never scrub away.

Her footsteps take her to Reginald's study. He spends each night in there, surrounded by paper, trying to save this place, his dream, and each night he fails, the brandy in the decanter going down, down, down until he sleeps in his chair. The railway line will not run here. The people will not come. He will have to let this wretched hotel go. Good. She hates every brick of this building.

But she hates him more. She pushes the door of his study and there he is, head thrown back, snoring. The brandy has done its job, but she has had help in this regard too – a little powder slipped by a servant hand into the decanter, something to make sure he stays asleep.

He is not wary of her. He thinks he has won. He will wave his hand and away she will go, into an asylum and he will be left with what he loved her for in the first place: her money. It is a pity for him that he never got to know her, because if he had, he would not have left himself so vulnerable here asleep in his chair. She crosses the room to a cabinet.

The handgun is heavy. It is an ornamental thing, the metalwork engraved with flourishes and scrolls, brass not gold, but shining as if it is treasure. He does not use it; it is simply another thing he owns, like her. The bullets are in a box next to it. She loads it. Just one because that is all she will need. Her hand does not tremble, she does not hesitate. She crosses back to his chair and stands to one side, holding the weapon awkwardly so that it is in the correct position, how he would hold it in his hand.

Pushing the metal barrel into his mouth, she feels it scrape against his teeth and before she squeezes the trigger, she looks at him. Up until this point she has had very little control over what direction her life would take. Her father first had taken the reins and then this man's hands had closed over them. Those hands are lying limp in his lap, thick, meaty fingers that had prodded her flesh, pushed her this way and that and then written deceitful letters to doctors.

When the gun fires, it is a starting pistol for her. She will need to run, to be away from here as soon as she can, because, with her husband's blood freshly splattered on the study wall behind his chair, she is now free. She could stay and wait to regain control over her money, her estate, but she is not sure much is left and she does not trust that some other sneaking man won't crawl out of the woodwork ready to grasp at her once again. Anyway, she knows where she wants to go, to be free of it all.

She places the gun under one of his hands and surveys the scene. Perfect. The tormented man facing bankruptcy cannot see a future for himself and so ends his life. There is no time for gloating – she has to move and so she does, through the corridor and down the stairs, ignoring the reception hall and heading straight for the small back lawn and the steps.

Where Peter lost his life, she will begin her new one. There is a boat waiting for her at the jetty. It has a pair of boots in it. Both boat and boots are another gift from servant friends of Peter's, those people who share her anguish and have helped her bring justice. She will row the boat herself, sticking to the coastline until she comes to another cove further on, one where she can get out and walk, all the way to the convent. Sisters. She's never had those.

Through the paths lined with flowerbeds she runs, past the empty pools that no one will ever lounge in. Before she darts down the final few stone stairs to the boat she pauses on the last step where Peter's body was found. Looking back up at the hotel as it looms over her, she stands in the wind and balls her hands into fists, cursing the place that had become her prison, wishing no good to anyone foolish enough to step on this land in the future.

Then she disappears into darkness.

Bex stopped speaking. The crowd remained silent. Even though she saw it all unfold in her imagination, this story she had given Jane – it was just that. Another tale, this time told in a confession letter.

'So you see – we got it wrong. When I visited the convent and read Jane's papers, her last confession, I realised that this idea we've had of Morwood's ghost striding about the place, trying to wreak revenge on anyone who trespassed on his land is only seeing half the story. Morwood didn't curse the hotel; Jane did. People have always thought I am the heroine of *Ravencliffe* but, in truth, it's never been me. It's always been Jane.'

Among the mass of people, she could see the outlines of ravens and candles on their T-shirts, the hotel as a white silhouette, a sketch of a figure in a greatcoat. Bex hoped that, after today, some new prints would emerge: Jane in a long skirt holding a gun maybe, or standing on her own, windswept on the final step.

Bex cleared her throat. She knew her next words might not be popular. 'Ravencliffe will be destroyed.' She paused, let the idea sink in, like a shipwreck to the seabed. The crowd stayed quiet, listening. 'That place should never have been. There are buildings like that; they are diseased trees, leeching only the worst from the earth, sucking it up through their roots. There is no way of saving them. A person could scrub at the blood splatter and bleach the mould, but the stains will always seep back through. So, we have decided that the hotel will be knocked down and the land left to turn into a nature reserve, a space for life – not death. We have had enough of that.' She let the silence fall, the hush of expectation for her final words. 'I think it is time, to finally say it . . . Ravencliffe, the dream, the nightmare, the legend, the lies, whatever it is and was . . .' She paused and gazed out over the heads of all the people waiting for what she was about to say. '*It no longer awaits.*'

And at those words the crowd-wave above her head finally crashed, not as destruction, not shock and disgust for what she had suggested doing to the hotel – but as approval, as hands clapping and feet stamping, a rush of movement and sound that washed over her.

Bex remained on the stage, turning slightly to nod to Sophie who came and stood with her, slipping her hand into hers. The stage lights were fierce in their eyes. Of course, the darkness was always waiting. You couldn't fight that. But you could make the best of the light when you saw it. In Bex's mind the story of the hotel was as layered as the cliff it perched upon: story upon story upon story, Jane's and Peter's and Morwood's and Leo's, all pressed together like layers of silt and chalk and limestone. Her story nestled amongst them.

It was time to find a new tale.

Sleepless

Don't close your eyes. Don't fall asleep. Don't let them in.

Thea is an insomniac; she hasn't slept more than three hours a night for years.

So when an ad for a sleep trial that promises to change her life pops up on her phone, Thea knows this is her last chance at finding any kind of normal life.

Soon Thea's sleeping for longer than she has in a decade, and awakes feeling transformed. So much so that at first she's willing to overlook the oddities of the trial – the lack of any phone signal; the way she can't leave her bedroom without permission; the fact that all her personal possessions are locked away, even her shoes.

But it soon becomes clear that the trial doesn't just want to help Thea sleep. It wants to *control* her sleep . . .

An unputdownable, gripping psychological thriller for fans of *The One*, *Behind Her Eyes* and *Girl A*!

The Safe House

She told you the house would keep you safe. She lied.

Esther is safe in the house. For sixteen years, she and her mother have lived off the grid, protected from the dangers of the outside world. For sixteen years, Esther has never seen another single soul.

Until today.

Today there's a man outside the house. A man who knows Esther's name, and who proves that her mother's claims about the outside world are false. A man who is telling Esther that she's been living a lie.

Is her mother keeping Esther safe – or keeping her prisoner?

Acknowledgements

Well, I will never *not* find it weird to have the story that for so long has only been in my head exist as an actual book that people can read.

Weird. Lovely, exciting, exhilarating, nerve-wracking weird, but weird all the same.

It is not just me who checked into *The Hotel* though; there are many people who kept the lights on, kept the place running and me on my feet. Here they are, those people that the hotel guests don't get to see.

The team at HQ – design (eternally grateful for that amazing cover), sales, marketing, copy-editing, and proofreading. All are stars. But the brightest is my editor Abi Fenton. I don't really plan my novels much beforehand (though I do a lot of structural work afterwards) so Abi works tirelessly to shape and polish the drafts and bring out the things that need to shine. In this book she was Chief Wrangler for the lighter – an object that often had a mind of its own! I will also never stop thanking Lisa Milton, my literary fairy godmother. She gave me my chance and I will never stop trying to make her proud.

Hugest of thanks to my brilliantly supportive agent, Kate Shaw.

There is no one else I would rather have in my corner, and she deals with my crazy story ideas with tact and aplomb (seriously, you should see some of the stuff I've come up with and shelved . . .).

Quick note about the gorgeous setting I chose for Ravencliffe – the West Wales coast and particularly Cardigan Bay. There is a well-known hotel on the cliff called The Cliff Hotel and Spa and back in 1889 the hotel was put up for sale with a plan for 'The New Brighton' on this stretch of coast. For the purposes of my story, I've played a bit fast and loose with dates and added in some inspiration from the hotel in Ravenscar, near Whitby, and Reid's Palace in Madeira. As for trying to establish a Cardigan train station – that struggle was all too real in the 1800s. In fact, Cardigan train station opened in 1886 as part of the Whitland and Cardigan Railway, too late for my debt-ridden fictional hotel owner . . .

To my Crime Cymru and Gŵyl Crime Cymru Festival friends, my Twitter/Insta/Facebook chums, all the amazing bloggers and the ever-supportive D20 authors, you make writing a less lonely place.

To my friends and family (and friends who really are family . . .) The Coven: Em, Fi and Liz – you're all as bonkers as me, you just don't write it down for people to see . . . Knibbsy, Chris and the Lynch tribe: Dan, Will, Dennis. Who thought I'd become Inappropriate Auntie? Not me! My Village Gym Combat Crew who give me a reason to leave the house at least twice a week. To Mart, Cath, Gwen, Aidan and Ffion, my lovely family.

To my mum and my sister. My mum worked so hard to give my sister and me a start in life and has always been a brilliant example of determination, tenacity and self-sacrifice. My sister made up characters and worlds with me when I was younger and, crucially, always dressed my Barbies first – a sister couldn't ask for anything more.

Finally, to my husband, Jason. It is your fault this whole author lark started. I remember us sitting in a pub when you asked me what I would do if I had the chance to do anything. I replied, 'I would like to get a book published.' All the books I create are part yours because I couldn't write them without you. I promise I'll stop writing short stories about women killing their husbands . . .

Most importantly though? Thanks to you for reading this book. I hope you've enjoyed your stay at *The Hotel*. Please do find me at my website www.louisemumfordauthor.com and sign up to my newsletter for freebies and fun or say hello on Twitter @ louise_mumford and on Facebook/Insta @louisemumfordauthor.

VOX
DIVERSIFY
THE HONEY BUS
BISH BASH BOSH!